BAD HOUSEKEEPING

Also by this author:

No News Is Good
(Novel. North Point Press, 1986)

Bad Housekeeping

A Novel
by
JULIE EDELSON

BASKERVILLE
PUBLISHERS, INC.
DALLAS • NEW YORK • DUBLIN

BASKERVILLE Publishers, Inc.
7616 LBJ Freeway, Suite 220, Dallas, TX 75251-1008

Library of Congress Cataloging-in-Publication Data

Edelson, Julie.
Bad housekeeping : a novel / Julie Edelson.
p. cm.
ISBN No. 1-880909-31-6 : $21.00 ($28.00 Can.)
I. Title.
PS3555.D44B3   1995
813'.54--dc20   94-49210
                                                       CIP

Manufactured in the United States of America
First Printing, 1995

To Roy, Abbie, and Aaron Hantgan,
Susan Baum, Bill Meyers,
Jay Jerome, and Julie Huff Jerome
for seeing me
through this.

1 Easy Street

I don't know how long I've been sitting here. I remember pulling up in front of the sty, the heap—a twenty-year-old Citroën nobody in this tobaccospit lintlung inbreeding ground for bigots and thrillkillers knows how to fix and that was always called Ze Lemon, that my ex wooed and won me with, God help me, before I learned those smears on the glovebox betrayed a daily habit of Yoohoos and Moonpies, and stuck me with when we split up as though it was costing *him*—shuddering to a stop, and I didn't unbuckle and bolt toward my badgering chore list but sat, staring: at November, leaden, wet; at the silver maple lurching over me, half of it hacked out by the power company so it looks like a beehive taking a hairpin curve; at my daughter's truck, its one red, one cracked white taillight dimming like too many for the road; at the mud lawn; at the skate ramp in the middle of the walk, the painstakingly bent plywood 4x8 warping away from the base and spewing nails, a Venus fly-trap; at the eighteen-year-old, blind, fat, white cat, Victor, asleep (or dead) on the dead petunias in the wonky flowerbox; and at the roof, splotched like the soles of a dairy farmer's boots with Black Cat. No smoke from the chimney, but all the lights are on, except the porch light, which either burned out in 1986 or is hidden under the bushel of insects.

Anyway, not long enough to figure out how the hell I wound up here.

What gets me going again is the thought of asking the neanderthal next door to jump my daughter's battery. This guy keeps his barbecue grill five feet from my bedroom window, and I have tried everything, from asking politely to blasting the opening bars of Beethoven's Fifth—it worked on the Nazis!—but I'm still on exhaust March to December. I have my son watch "America's Most Wanted" in hopes of fingering him for some felony that carries a mandatory life sentence. And here he is, sure enough, beer welded in fist, poking up the brim of his "if it smells like fish, eat it" baseball cap with the bottle in greeting. "Evenin' ma'am. Slipp'ry when it's wet, ain't it?" He squeezes charcoal lighter directly from his crotch onto the coals for Hamburgers Hiroshima; where he sees his irresistible splurge of fiery jism, I see My Lai. He grins at my flinch. His truck tells me it's protected by pit bulls with AIDS, that if I don't like his driving I can dial 1-800-Eat-Shit. He is an argument against literacy. Do I want his truck coupled to my daughter's? I would rather drive her and all her ditzy friends from the Pizza Hut to the mall and back again every Friday and Saturday night for the rest of my life, with the radio on.

He has his radio on, redneck warbling, in retaliation for the speed metal almost visibly disintegrating the sty. I reach in Ariel's cab to push off her lights. It stinks of cigarettes. I dump the ashtray slap on the seat. Composing a tirade: "Years off your miserable life! Too short of breath to scream at your deformed kids! Foul yellow teeth crumbling out of your painwracked cancerriddled body!" There's something wrong with this approach. I puncture across the mud in the stupid heels I wore to impress the clients, a pair of yup tobacco execs wanting to know the "historic value" of their 1926 bungalow and how much it will run for our company,

Retro Revert, to strip the thirty coats of paint off their insignificant woodwork, to peel the linoleum off floors patched with tin can lids, to convert the chicken coop that is their second story to a "master suite" with skylights and Exercycles, to rewire for air conditioning, Jacuzzi, and security system, to knock out the kitchen walls so they'll need shuttle service from freezer to microwave, but then again they eat out, and next year they'll move to Atlanta. The really disgusting part is we're going to do it. As I rip open the door, mouth open and ready to rip, I hear, through the Concrete Migraine, the phone.

It's my mother. "Where have you been?"

Up the Nile. Down the tubes. On the rag. In the mood. My mind riffles like a Rolodex. I sit on the bed and slough my purse. The orange cat, Nancy, claws onto my lap and featherdusts my nose with her tail; Sluggo, the tabby, rubs the ankles. My house smells like the tobacco lobby. Furtive hurry-scurry in the kitchen.

My parents moved down here from Brooklyn when the cold and the crime got too much for them, to be near the infinite solace of me. They live in a full-service retirement residence called Heartwood Acres, where, in exchange for everything they did without, they get room, board, bridge, and ballroom dancing lessons. My father owned a liquor store; my mother was a secretary for the AFL-CIO. She wants to know if I can go with her tonight to visit my father in the rehabilitation hospital. It's six weeks since his second stroke flung him from the camp chair where he was an impassioned observer of the decline of the empire to a slump in a wheelchair. My mother thinks I'll cheer him up. I think he's fixing to die.

"Six, six-thirty. As usual. Like we said." I toss Nancy, and she's back, purring like a motorboat.

"Carol, I can hardly hear you. What is going on over there?"

3

Sexual ecstasy, Ma; the Indy time-trials. It's like wearing conch shells over your ears, like standing on the local platform while two express trains crash up and downtown. "One of the kids has the music on loud."

"That reminds me. Don't bring the kids."

Why ever not? Dash could practice his ollies. Ariel could smoke and grunt. As if I would. As if I could. What's in it for them?

"—it's nothing against them, you know he adores the children, he just can't face nobody right now. To tell you the honest truth, he don't want to see you, he tells me, 'stop dragging her—'" She twists off the tap. "It's not easy."

They must be playing chainsaws, weed whackers. The Suburban Blight. Oh, in fact, the old lady across the street is having her leaves blown with what looks like a Stinger. The house reeks like a smoldering ashpit. Since Ariel is not allowed to smoke in here, the cats must be earning a merit badge. I drop Nancy on Sluggo, like dropping sodium on water.

"Ma, it takes time. This is something that happens with a stroke, they get depressed. It's something to be depressed about." Synopsis of *Reader's Digest* article. "His doctor is aware, I assume."

"How should I know? Does he speak to me? Do I see him? The *nurse* calls me." She makes nurse sound like tadpole.

I wire into my circuitry: hassle doctor tomorrow. Nobody has to feel depressed anymore, not even those who have been so selfish as to get old and sick.

"So I'll see you later?"

I have to confirm my reservations. "Why are you going?" I ask her. Is this what she wants me to do? "Take the night off. You gotta take care of yourself, or you're no good to anyone." I feel like a simultaneous translator: who's doing the talking?

"Carol, I can't. Anyways, I got to help him with his dinner."

"I can do that. I've fed two kids."

"I still think of you as my little girl." The wistful lilt abruptly stiffens. "Look, you don't mind my saying, you know shit from marriage. Today the mouth looked a little better. Not so droopy."

Bean soup and cornbread again. Once I would have told myself simple, wholesome, peasant fare. Now I think slop, grub, fodder. I've got about an hour. The heels are off. I pluck overalls from the chair. Digging up a shirt, I realize it was warmer outside; the air in here is like a cold compress. Before I can move on dinner I've got to get a fire going. Socks and boots so I don't notice sticking to the floor. I'm calculating what to do in what order so that every second will be pulped of its utility, which is tough with the climax of a Tarzan movie issuing from the stereo. I scoop up the mail and park in front of the woodstove. "Would you like to see graphic evidence of what is really happening in Central America?" An announcement of my twentieth college reunion. "You may already have won TEN MILLION DOLLARS!" A catalog that seems to specialize in duck paraphernalia. The first major electric bill. I ball up everything but the bill and light it, but it's like trying to light sponge. Of course there's no kindling in the basket, just medium-sized slats you have to cajole. Fortunately, several days of newspaper lie strewn about at my disposal, among the homework, paper airplanes, pencil shavings, Cheerios, dirty socks, and three cats are going up in smoke if they don't stop bullying me. In an industrial-strength bray I make out the lyrics: "My mother was a witch, she was burning like hell, Satan's little bitch—" And that's it. I'm on my feet, knees cracking like old treads, cats weaving a deliberate trip; I pull the plug on Nausea and the Nightmares.

"Hey!"

I turn toward the kitchen exactly like Dracula when he's ready to sink fang. Now I can *really* hear the leaf blower, the gasping furnace, the twang of the Ramblin' Crackers next door.

My daughter and a companion swigging Junk Colas and cramming Eatos, smelling like slag. The blue-brown haze nips my eyes. Ariel's look brined. Is she coming down with something? I take in the open window over the sink where it's raining in, the gummy crumbs and slops in which their textbooks and scrawled notebooks lie, the spillage from the stashed ashtray, the yellow ring around Ariel's lips when she prunes, "Do you mind, mother?" and then I catch the companion.

She. I pick that up from the makeup, perhaps because the ultimate effect is battery. White girl, some kind of Altamont mutant, hippie crossed with Hell's Angel— hippitaur? Studded leather bands and peace signs; crosses, ankhs, safety-pins, and happy faces in her ears; ring though one nostril. Her jeans are louvered. And what I think is called whitewalls: a two-inch band shaved above the ears and around the nape, the crown uneven lengths with one thin braid sprouting straight up and over to the shoulder, dyed mustard and soot black. No shoes; horned toad feet. I get it. She wants to see what you look like looking at her. She wants to see who's coming. I find myself amused. After all, I used to traipse around in bedspreads at that age. I glued carnation petals around my eyes. I haven't always been passing for dull. Ariel has burned or buried any clothes I ever bought her. She's strictly Sears, two sizes too big.

"—and some of these guys play so fast you can't see their hands," Ariel defending the music, "I'm not kidding, it's like hummingbirds."

"I didn't know they had hands!" I josh.

"You interrupted me." Coiled snake demeanor of Ming the Merciless. What gives me the right to barge in here and,

and I want to give it back to her, especially her flagrant violation of the smoking ban, but not before a witness. She so seldom brings home a friend. I bang down the window—"Why don't you just burn dollar bills?"—and pull out the soup pot.

"She said you've got a boyfriend in a rock band." The companion rumbles into her chest so you can't see who's coming and maybe you won't hear what, in which case she won't care.

I dice onions. "Did she also say he's a landscape architect?"

"Why would I care?" (Was I right?) "Landscape is for cows. Give me a parking lot or, better yet, a major airport."

Ariel looks so pleased I have her check on the fire. She lumbers as though it's a ploy to get her to crawl in the stove.

"You got some great albums. Or did they come with the boyfriend?"

"What Eric plays?" Ariel barks from the other room. "It ain't what we call rock 'n roll. More like electrocuted country. Grits and gravy in a toaster. Zttttttt."

"Were you at Woodstock?"

This girl has a future in law enforcement. "Almost."

Actually, I had a panic attack bumper to bumper on the New York State Thruway and made my friend Billy get out and direct traffic, an inch this way, a few feet that, using bullfighting techniques he developed on station wagons in front of the high school and perfected wrecked in Pamplona, so I could drive across the median and flee for the asylum of the city. After acknowledging applause, Billy got several kinds of lift in the van that took my place.

"Almost doesn't count." She's ballpointing her thigh.

"What's your name?" I ask, so later I can tell Eric this story.

"Why'd you name her Ariel?"

Tabloid television, and I'm going to have to account for

some hardcore depravity. "I thought it sounded better than Tiffany or Kimberley," even odds one's hers, "but I admit I was partially sedated—"

"Some Shakespeare thing—" Ariel hollers. "Hello, Miss Nance," she drools, "my homecat, my pie, my slice." Loud: "Hasn't anybody fed these cats?"

"Not Sylvia Plath?" Soot risks another squint into my inmost depths while I rib a green pepper. Her eyes seem charred, like my burners.

She's read Sylvia Plath? I once thought of doing a comic strip called "Lady Lazarus." Rube Goldberg suicides. Trouble was, it kept ending. "I really can't think about Sylvia Plath so near an oven."

"That gives you something in common with all the other women near an oven." She crosses her legs and dots her eyes. "You can't think."

Is her racket strung tightly enough to return serve? I don't mind being insulted if I get to volley.

"I always thought it was like the antenna on a tv." Ariel returns, bucks the chair a little deeper into the floor. Nancy boosts lightly to her knees; Sluggo and Hugo, the insatiable kitten, rummage the cupboards. "Rabbit ears, right? I thought that was something my mother would think was cool. Name a kid after a thing."

I stir and season.

"What?" she squalls, as if I said one word! "You said you wished you'd named me Grommet."

"Rhymes with vomit," Soot points out.

"Or Demerol, you said, Darvon."

"Maalox!" The match girl has a puffy, gasping laugh, as though it's something new for her, and she's working at it. Fake drawl, "'This here's our darlin' May Lox. Play a little somethin' on your organ, sugar.'"

They laugh loud to push me out. I could bring up Mea Culpa, every mother's pet, but not in this border saloon.

"I'm not kidding," Ariel pursues. "My dad had to get her to agree *in writing*," as though writing were a mystic art akin to barefooting live coals, "that he got a veto so she wouldn't sneak something like Deliria on my birth certificate." She nuzzles Nance as if they're both orphans. "That's all right. My brother has the same name as the dog in his first grade reader."

"Spot?"

"Dash."

"You must've done some serious drugs." Soot inks slashes across her left wrist. "Like what?"

I keep slicing. "Too paranoid."

"To do it or to talk about it?"

"She's just naturally weird," Ariel covers for me.

"How about you?" I counter.

A look, sharp, shiny, scissors between them. Whose secrets are we keeping?

"You did this stuff on the walls?"

She's talking about a series of imaginary botanicals, and not, I swear, the sludge and cobwebs and pops of tomato sauce.

"What's a—" she peers through the mascaraed grillwork, "a 'mompato'?"

I come around to look at it and to get a mixing bowl. "A root crop that, when eaten, makes you feel terribly full and terribly empty at the same time." This legend is scribbled in copperplate. Colored pencil on cream construction paper, shape of a breast, brownish pink, with bumpy sienna nipples, raised veins, heart-shaped leaves, and corkscrew suckers.

The snort means what?

"Too booky, you know what I mean?" Ariel observes. "You got to read it, and then you got to think about it."

"Don't strain yourself," I snip.

"Boring," Allumette pronounces flatly.

I look down, and I'll admit I'm looking for a weapon, at a looseleaf binder on which, in a Gothic lettering growing thorns and tongues from every cav and vexity, she seems to have engraved, is that her name? "Is that your name? Fauve?" I try to picture her mother. Miss Taos, 1968. Friend potential? "You must be an artist."

"What makes you say that?" She's clenched. "Do you think it's good?"

However strong our urge to eat the young, it can't beat whatever angel (Raphael!) protects fledgling art. Those fluttering encrusted lashes are his powerful wings. "It's hard to read," I say, "but it draws your eye."

"It says Fawne, like Bambi, with an e." She googles as if up the barrels of a pitiless, drunken rifle, and my immediate impulse is to poke. "Who's this Fauve?"

"F-a-u-v-e." Broth and tomato puree into the soup. I set marge to melt. "Means beast in French. A group of post—"

"Man! The Beast! This is so seriously bad." She hunches to make over her identity with the globbing Bic. (I was midwife to the Birth of the Beast!) "See, I know I'm going to be some kind of artist or poet or actress or something—"

"Whatever," Ariel tells the cat. She's overly familiar with my crusade against the vague.

"No, really, or like, you know, a performance artist— well, maybe you don't, around *here,* but I mean, what's it take? You just get out and be—you know—outrageous. I can do that." Her grin glints like sun off chrome.

"Around here it's called making a fool of yourself," Ariel says.

"So's everything else worth doing," I retort. Why can't she sit up? She just hangs, as though her outsized clothes are lined with lead.

"And it don't sound Christian," she adds.

Fawne is undaunted. "Because I'm not wasting my life holed up in some cheap office or chasing some jerk's snotfaced brats. I'd rather die."

"An artist's life for me!" That's what the Fox and the Cat sing when they're seducing little woodenhead in the Disney version. I need time with this child. "It's too much work and not enough money." I'm saving a life and beating cornbread batter: What a woman! "Nobody can afford to pay for the time it takes. There *are* alternatives. Find a profession. I know whereof I speak."

"That's for damn sure." Ariel sniffs our rancid life. "So when the jerk ditches you in the hole with the brats, you don't care." Nancy escapes; Ariel's palms are furred, and she wipes one up her nose covertly flipping me the bird. "All I want out of life is a horse."

No horsetrade for Fawne's kingdom. "Unless you're a star," she says earnestly.

"Oh right, excuse me." Ariel looks like she's been smooching a yak. "At whatever."

"Well, I can always be a high-priced hooker," Fawne smirks.

"Something to fall back on," Ariel admits, studying her cuticles.

"You're from New York." (Is she psychic?) She smiles. "I could tell there was something wrong with the way you talk." (No—sensitive.) "How can you stand it here?"

I look at my big dumb frowsy kitchen, my brooding lump of reliable, down-to-earth daughter. "I like it here," I discover. I have to think why. "It's so easy."

At once I'm reminded of a story Eric, a native, told me. He was on Main Street one sweltering afternoon when a former high school classmate, a mind-expansion casualty, crept up to him, hugging the façades, switching his gaze over his shoulder like a swimmer, to whisper, "It's too easy." Then he sunk his nails into the next doorway and wheeled off.

"—bo-ring," is what Fawne is saying, as one would speak

11

of the negligent shepherdess. "And none of the dorks around here even know it, they are so functionally braindead. When I lived in D.C. with my dad, man? it was so cool, we used to—'"

A noise like an icebreaker chewing the crust of Hudson's Bay announces that my son Dash has heeled his skateboard up the steps and let it smash into the side of the house. He wallops the door. "Airhead! Mom? Hey! I'm home!"

"My brother," Ariel explains.

"Hey! Isn't anybody home? Mom? Airhead?"

He'll keep this up until we respond, even when he's in the kitchen with us, like a voice-operated yapping robot puppy. Ariel and I bellow, "Hey!" to turn him off. He's wearing shorts and no pads or helmet, but a headrag, right? he's soaking wet, including sixty-dollar sneakers, and one knee is raw.

"S'up? I busted. I'll patch the knee. Gotta do my homework." Smoothly exiting on the wind from my sails, he ticks his head toward Fawne and asks Ari, "What's that?"

"He's a jerk," Ariel tells her.

"Coming from you, Airhead," he trails off.

"Fawne, would you like to stay for dinner?" I spoon beans from the can to the soup. "It's not much, but there's plenty of it, and you're most welcome." There's a joke about moose-turd pie that winds up something like this.

"Fauve, right? I mean I'm serious. No, listen, I gotta go. I'm on groundation." She stands in stages like a zigzag ruler, her seams are so binding. Her t-shirt is slit to expose, occasionally (so it's your fault), a black lace bra and advertises Anthrax, which I think is a disease. Can you get one for vaginitis? How about lung cancer? How does her mother let her out of the house like this? "My mom thinks I'm at the library." She tugs with gritted teeth at an invisible leash attached to the balky Ariel. Are they still going to the bathroom together? "I gotta change."

Into what?

Into a sky-blue shirtwaist, hose, and flats. Most of the earrings and the nosering are gone. Her face is scrubbed; her hands look blued as though she does laundry. Suddenly her hair seems penitent. Postulant. She rakes her books into a pack, pulling a mouth at me like I'm an accomplice. She's leaving her house dressed as the blessed Virgin and mine as the whore of Babylon? Using the sty like a gas-station toilet to cheat a woman exactly like me? Uh *uh*. "Now wait just a—"

Ariel can smell the shellac. "You want a lift?" She wants out.

"You left the lights on in your truck again." I've got to get on someone.

"Excuse me. I made a mistake. You never make a mistake, oh no, you're so perfect—"

"I didn't make this one," I smile. This is a holdover from the job where, when materials are not ordered, caustics splash, tools tumble from the roof, the New Age tells me, "Entropy. Go with it."

"Did you leave them on to teach me a lesson? Should I stick my finger in the lighter?"

"Why don't you admit your mistake and try not to repeat it?"

"I did! That's what I just did! Why don't you try to make me feel worthless about a stupid little mistake?" Her jaw sags with loathing.

"Hey, go easy. Your mom's cool." Fawne smiles like a cracked egg.

"Yeah, like I said, she's perfect."

I'm not falling for it. "Go wash your face," I tell Ariel. She bobbles on her chair. "When did you get to bed last night?"

"You want that lift or not?" Ariel sounds like she means on a stretcher.

"My mom catches me coming home with you, she'll skin me. I'll stop by tomorrow."

"Now listen," I start, but Ariel says, "I'll call you."

"I can't use the phone." Fawne throws the ten-ton pack to her shoulder. "My stepfather thinks I'll order out for banned substances. Or sex." In a nasal boom, "'I'd like a couple of boys to go, and make sure they're horny.'" Her own chitter, "Maybe he thinks I'll call for help. Ariel said you know karate? Wow! See ya, Mrs., Mizz—"

"Most people call me Cee."

"Cee! Gee!"

"Cee bee gee bee," Ariel mumps.

"You ever go there?" Fawne turns to ask.

Ariel butts her out. Why people who weigh a normal hundred twenty, thirty pounds walk like Babe the Blue Ox merits federally funded research. I go to feed the fire, and when Ariel comes back, I ask her to set the table.

"Why are we eating so early?"

"I've got to visit my dad."

"Why can't we go to McDonald's like normal people?"

She doesn't make me say I'm not normal. One minute on line and I'm choking, wet as a rice paddy. I've gotten as far as paying, but then I can't wait for them to assemble the food. "Youall want sauce with thishere? Was 'em fries a medium or reg'lar? Hey! Where they be at?" McDonald's and K Mart: Run! Instead, she asks, "You want me to go with you? I've got this English test—"

"Which is why you were sitting here schmoozing and smoking and blaring Scab and the Screamers—"

"I don't say anything about your music or Eric's, which I so totally hate—"

Who I hate. Eric is ten years younger than I and very handsome. Ariel has never had a steady guy. Nor, for that matter, a lasting friendship. "Look, this thing with what's her face coming over here to change into Rocky Whorror—"

"I know." She shies me a smile like a sardine to a seal. "She had this weird idea you'd be cool about it. She *wanted* you to see."

Why? I can't picture Ariel talking about me, except to complain, like I'm the weather. I am her weather. "How long has this been going on?"

"Coupla weeks. She only moved here a few months ago." She ducks my scrutiny. "She never asked if I minded."

"Would you make the salad so I can feed the cats?"

"That's Dash's job."

"You want him here right now?"

"You never make him do anything. Dock his allowance." She needs a gavel. "Do I have to?" Not whining—defining terms.

"No."

She moves as though hauling out of bread dough. They must have more gravity. Nevertheless, she moves. I bang the cat bowls over the trash. We do-si-do at the sink.

"She seems kind of wild. Her parents are divorced?"

"Whose aren't? Her mom remarried. They live a few streets up."

"And she hates it here."

Ariel peels a carrot before she decides to say, "It gets really old hearing how great it is somewhere we're not. How cool her friends were, how much harder her school was—"

How flattered I feel when Ariel is straight with me, especially in light of how resentful I feel when she treats me like dirt. "Where's she from anyway? Washington? A swamp with mausoleums."

"Listen, she's not really that wild. She's wild the way everybody else is, you know? Mostly she's boring."

"She looks so different—"

"Like from me. I'm so normal."

I pause over the can of seafood stench to check her expression. She's frowning down at an apple with her knife poised. "But that's good." My face shrivels into the same puzzled frown. "You're normal, but you're open to—"

"It's a compliment?" The frown draws her face shut like a tobacco pouch.

How else could it be taken? I'm in a crouch like a pre-Columbian fertility figure, breathing cod slime, savaged by starving cats, I'm about to fall on my ass in a mess worthy of a Loony Toon, and I don't have a clue what's going on.

The knife descends through the apple like the curtain on Act IV. "It's not just that."

What? I may be having missing time experiences. Am I being periodically seized by aliens? Gray hair count!

"All I know is every store we go in, it's a hassle. Everybody watches us, everybody cops an attitude."

"She's an original—"

"Yeah, but she's also a pain. She reads me her poetry—"

"You could do with some poetry—"

"All about death and stuff. It's depressing—"

"She's going through some heavy changes—the divorce. You remember—" I'm plying my eyes like Lassie; she won't look away from the cutting board.

"It's a bummer, Mom."

"Does she drink? Do drugs?"

"You're the experienced one. What do you think?"

Where is this coming from? "I never really—and besides—"

"Sure. Well, *I* don't know anything about it. I'm so *normal.*" She drains it. "And none of the other kids like her—"

"So?"

"So that should tell you something."

"Yeah, she's lonely."

Ariel is reddening, tremulous. "Maybe she's hurtin', but I don't think she's very good for me, and—"

"But you're just what the doctor ordered." I chuck the empty can, punctuating my insight with a nice ching like a cash drawer. Sold. At least I am. "You've been there and made it. You're solid, secure. You can afford to stick by her. And she might have something to offer you. Sparkle. Imagination!"

"I don't believe you." I've initiated a sulkathon. "Look, see the main thing is, she hates her stepdad."

"Oh, well—" I return to the soup. "It must be hard to get used to a new father." Mouthing the conventional wisdom. As far as I'm concerned, you only get one, that foreign correspondent who never quotes you accurately. "Telling you what to do, criticizing how you do it, making up all these rules—"

"No, he's mean. He hits her."

"Get me the phone book."

"No, no, nothing like that." She squelches me with the pinched lips of someone accustomed to a whistle. "But see, she got in trouble at school? and he grounded her like forever."

"What did she do?"

A visor drops. "That smells good."

"I'm just curious to find out what other parents think is bad. How they handle it. I'm faking this mother business, you know. You didn't come with a manual."

"Didn't you learn anything from Gramma?" This is sly. She jabs two spoons in either side of the completed salad and takes it to the table. A formally composed salad with a radish rose in the center like a nipple—it must be today's theme: "Bitter Titty"—and she hates radishes. "Well, see, she found this lighter in her desk, and she had a can of hairspray, and she—" She lifts opposing arms like Swan Lake and on the count of three drops the hammers. "You get it." The arms flop. "Armageddon it."

"Geez Louise!" Flames all around me; I'm a cow in a burning barn. How long before our pyromantic Arsonia teams up with the neanderthal? A match made in Ohio.

Strike anywhere. (Check the woodstove.)

Ariel is enjoying my reaction. "She got suspended for a week. The black kids? They call her 'Torch.'"

I have to suck in the pads of my cheeks to quash a hoot. As Betty Boop: "I would call that really bad. Do you think she's a pyromaniac? That's when—"

"I know what it means, mother, God. No, she just wants attention." She flaps on a fresh face like a clean tablecloth. "And no, I'm not going to set fire to my hairspray just because she did."

What is really on my mind is a painting: "Santa Barbie." Moonlit beach. A giant bland bikinied blonde holds the sty (it is Saint Barbara who holds the burning house? I used to know this stuff cold) atilt in three-quarters section, and we're huddled in it, like bales? or with features? No, we're blissfully unaware, tucking into a big birthday cake, with candles! and devils in baseball caps and happy-face earrings spume flame in great golden arches from cans and aerosols. On black or—what about that black velvet you see Elvis and German shepherds painted on at fireworks stands? I wonder how long it takes to get good on velvet. I haven't painted anything in years. Later. I scramble to reenter the conversation. "Anyway, I'm on the stepfather's side. What about the mother?"

"*Normal,* I guess you'd say. Hairsprayed. She's got great *hold.*" Ariel shrugs. "Nice enough when I'm around."

"Ooh, I had this friend Sharon used to ask me over her house after school." She had one of the first color tvs, and we used to do our homework and watch the kids on "American Bandstand" gyrate through the spectrum. "Her mother would hang around us and ask these sort of abstract moral questions, like should a mother have to tell her daughter to do the dishes, and everything I said was good, and Sharon should learn from it. I could never figure why Sharon wanted me around. Turned out it was so her mother wouldn't belt her."

"God, that's awful! And you couldn't tell? Too busy listening to yourself talk. Hey," she's nibbling a lettuce leaf; forbidden to pick from the trough, but she can see I'm *relating,* "if he didn't overreact so much she wouldn't be pulling these numbers. He came by the school one day, and he saw somebody, I mean *nobody,* nobody anybody knows, smoking pot? and he drags *her* off to Mandala."

They meditate? I better ask.

"It's this hospital where they put druggies, drunks, nut cases. And he made her *look* at them—" Aquarium gawp.

Bedlam. The hospital permits this, what? spite-seeing? magical misery tour? "And on your right, in a really classic example of withdrawal—" I should show parental solidarity. "Maybe he has reason to believe—"

"He's also an idiot." She flumps to the chair. "I mean, he's on his third wife, so what can you expect?"

I hope I left my memory running so I can repeat this verbatim to Eric. I get stuffy to hide my mirth. "Your own father is on his second, and he's a prince."

"Then why'd you dump him?" Her beautifully manicured talons tine a slice of apple. Smug as a hen on a nest.

I have this prepared: "We didn't see eye to eye anymore."

"Oh right. Tell it to somebody else." She's forward, taut, her bone structure clicks out like the staves of an umbrella. "I was there, in case you didn't notice. He embarrassed you. He didn't appreciate the finer things like you do, and when you got thin, he got fat, and you didn't want people to think you had such bad taste."

I spin out, blind, into this moment: We'd just moved here, into the 1890 Queen Anne that was my compensation for moving. Lacy spindlework dripped from the porch pillars and the columns supporting the bedroom balconies and, inside, between the living and dining rooms, like Cinderella's ballgown. None of the paneled doors had ever been painted nor the carved oak mantels nor the bannister. The windows were rimmed in squares of red, blue, and amber; my children traced the shafts of colored light with dreaming fingers, gleaming bare legs, twirled in them with chins lifted and smiles trickling from their lips and eyes like strands of honey. Twelve-foot ceilings and the original pendant pink glass lighting fixtures wired for electricity and a conservatory and rooms for every worthwhile human employ, except, okay, okay, cooking and shitting. I had just begun to polish this jewel, when, as a surprise, while I was in Brooklyn with my father's first stroke, my husband had burnt-orange shag wall-to-wall carpeting installed. "It's Stainmaster!" he cried. His expectancy, leading me into the hallway, already savoring my delight, my gratitude, preening in his reflection on me: How do I love her? Let her count the ways. I knew where every cent he'd spent on it was meant to go. And I thought, this is hopeless. That night I slept in the guest bed, and I left as soon as I found the sty. "But it's Stainmaster," he kept saying.

"Let's face it, Mom, you're not the thick and thin type."

The bell on the stove rings. The cornbread is done. Or I need to return to my corner. I certainly feel punchy. Dash heaves into his chair, sits in wait for his meal to be brought to him, drumming, has to get up, tipping his chair over backward, onto a cat, which wauls, and plod to the stove for his soup, which he spills, and when I tell him to clean it up, he says, "Yeah, sure, later."

"When is later?"

"Never." He smiles at Ariel as he takes his seat.

"You dweeb," she curls, dividing up the cornbread.

"Airhead."

"You want me to nag you about it?" I ask. "If I have to talk about it, I might as well do it."

"Might as well," he sighs sympathetically. "Is this a salad or a natural habitat for roaches?"

"Look, I've got to go see my father, and I'm not going to feel like cleaning when I get home. I'm relying on you to take care of things and do a good job on your homework—"

"She's riding for a fall," Dash clucks ruefully.

"Doesn't it make you sick when she appeals to our pity?" Ariel, salting before tasting. "Waving her poor father around. It's pathetic."

I can't wait for the next time she hits me up for money. "You two are just plain hateful."

"No we're not. You want to see hateful?" Ariel plonks her cornbread in her soup with the splash of a sizable meteorite. Scalding soup splatters her chest, her face, Dash's arm, everything. Dash curses and smacks her as she spurts up, pulling the steaming shirt away from her skin, and she whacks him on the backlash of her pain. I restrain him from full frontal assault. Looking not a little like Lizzie Borden at her big moment, she winces a steely glare. This is my fault.

"Cold water!" I urge.

She makes to throw her milk at me, then unwillingly, at apogee, as though brain-snatched, douses herself. She stands, blinking, drizzling. Hurls the glass against a cabinet; it smashes on the floor. Dash picks up his spoon and accelerates soup to mouth.

"Who's going to clean this up?" Someone with a gas mask and a firehose.

She turns and walks. We hear water run, she mounts the ladder to her room, her dresser drawers thunder, descent.

"What about your English test?" I call.

The front door slams. The malicious truck starts.

She is too big to hit.

My father once told me that when I was about three, I yelled at him, "I hate you," and he felt happy and proud to have reared so fearless a child. Why did he tell me this story?

I want to say it to her now. I am rotten with fear. I wish I never had to see her bovine slack, her waspish petulance,

21

again, and I can't imagine a day without her, a future she doesn't completely saturate. Something is plummeting through the hollow caves of my heart: a stone.

I have to leave.

On my way to the car, the neanderthal calls out, "Evenin', ma'am," in a voice just faint enough to make me look to where his lips are lit by his cigarette and lean slightly toward him. "Sorry night not to be stayin' in bed."

I find myself behind the wheel of Ze Lemon. I start heem up, and he rattles and stalls. I sit. I was sitting here before. What happened? Was I abducted by aliens? I look up. Please.

2 No Hard Feelings

It's my father's second stroke in seven years, fifteen since the heart attack that cured his two-pack-a-day habit, but even when I was little, when every Friday night he'd bring home cartons of Kents or Chesterfields, and I'd use the packs to build igloos, Mayan pyramids, staircases, ramps while we watched the fights, he'd ask, "Will you miss me when I'm gone?"

What does it mean, as a child of seven or eight, to snap at your father, "Act your age!"?

"Be prepared" is a motto for repeat offenders.

I wave at the receptionist, Chantal? Cerise? some extravagant French name, maybe Haitian—the undulant diction. Her hair is ironed into a mushroom cap; someone has ironed and starched those ruffles. She insists on keeping me at the desk until she phones upstairs. Slow grinding mill department. Who would break in to this rag and bone outlet? It's new, which is why my mother calls it beautiful; it looks like it's made out of cigarette packs, cellophane and all, and considering who pays the bills in this county, that's probably not far wrong. I could take it apart with a nail file and mail it anywhere in the world. It smells like Scotchgard and sickly sweet disinfectant, as though someone has re-

23

cently vomited port. The carpeting and upholstery are burnt orange. The plants look plastic, but they're real.

I'm allowed to take the elevator. I get out across from the dining room where, past carts stacked with used trays, I see my mother, the back of my father in his wheelchair. Only a few others are still eating. A woman, crumpled as the tissue stuffed in her chenille sleeve, lets her leather-tan husband push goo in her mouth. He talks for both of them: "Is it good? Oh it's so good!" I imagine their sex life; I imagine electrical storms of protest crackling the praline of her brain. A bronze nurse zooms the spoon at a young woman whose Olyve Oyl noggin wobbles like a tethered helium balloon and whose hands randomly thwack out; the nurse looks like Dash playing "Afterburner" at the pizzeria, dipping and dodging, stings of pleasure when she scores. One of my father's roommates, a blue-black man built like a defensive linebacker, maybe thirty, sits in a wheelchair, in a neckbrace, crying. Tears glaze his face, channel his nose, dance off his earlobes. His arms are bound to the chair, so if the tears tickle, that's tough. The tv is on: "Wheel of Fortune."

Ida is feeding Lou white ice cream. She brings up the spoon with her own lips parted and lapping. Suddenly he explodes, "Shit!" and shoves back.

Now I have heard some paradigmatic bad-mouthing at my parents' table. I can remember months when my father echoed every word my mother said in an adenoidal whinny. For a full year he wouldn't speak to her at all because once in company he maintained Beulah was a Communist, and she laughed for five minutes. During 1956 he called her Stalin; later, Moron, as in "Why did the Moron forget my sister's birthday card?" But I have never heard him use gutter language. He prides himself. He is practically deaf, and both of them shout.

"What?" Ida splits down the middle like a ripe peach. "What did I do?"

"Too much on the goddamn spoon. What do you think I am? A pig?" He jerks at the wheels in an agony of frustration.

"I'm doing my best." Her eyes steam.

"Goddamn it!" He wrenches the wheels, chopping his heels at the upright footrests.

"Look, you need to eat. I'll try again. He eats so little," she explains to no one, schlagging the spoonful to a dab.

Lou tries to put down a pivot foot; it stutters in midair, a stalled copter. He looks up as the spoon is bearing down on his bald spot. "Shit! What the hell is wrong with you?" He slaps at her hand, missing completely. "Why don't you ask the goddamn schwartze nurses why I'm always the last fed? The food is cold, and the ice cream is water. If you were paying the least attention to what goes on in this shithole—" He finally rams the chair backwards, and turning, he sees me. "What are you doing here? I wish to hell you'd stay home."

"He don't mean it," Ida laughs, glancing anxiously at the nurse, absorbed in food-tag, at the roommate, crying.

"Oh I don't? Why don't you stay home too, you bitch?" He tries to run through me; his right hand and knee could run a lathe. "You wanna make yourself useful? Find out why I'm the last one gets the food. Not that I want the shit they serve anyways—"

"Oh, it's good. You liked the fish, you said so."

"'It's soooo gooood.'" Lou mimics the tan man at the neighboring table, who looks up expectantly, as if we've asked his opinion.

"Hi, Dad, how you doing?" I kiss his freckled forehead. He smells like an old baby blanket.

"You, at least, I thought, was intelligent."

"You sure are getting good with that wheelchair."

"Get this moron outta here."

"You first," I say jauntily.

25

My mother glowers at me. "Don't she look marvelous?"

You'd think I just blew in from the coast. I was here Tuesday.

"She looks like she looked yestiday." He bats the broad side of my barn. "You could stand to lose ten more, kiddo."

Ida nods the spoon as if gauging its heft, as if she's preparing to hurl it at a target. "I can never get over how good she looks now."

"Compared to what a mess she was before, huh?" His eyes slide sportively between me and my mother.

"Won't you try a little more?" Ida begs. The spoon pants eagerly.

"You want I should blow up big and fat like she used to be?" He chugs his cheeks, scallops his arms around a duffel bag. Then he splats the old me out. "Now we know who to blame, huh, Carol?" He's leaving. He's in such a hurry he steps on my hand as I push down the footrests.

My mother follows with the tray. I take it from her, not without struggle, and stow it on a cart.

"What kept you?" she mutters.

I joined the circus; ran into Bigfoot; held by white slavers; the tornado set me down in Barbados. I look at my watch. I'm not late.

"Well, keep it to yourself. Try to act pleasant for once."

We trot along on either side of the chair. A flaccid man in a baggy leisure suit like institutional pajamas dodders close to the wall in what must be his exercise regimen. I remember walking the hospital halls after my kids were born; the object of the game is to convince the nurses it doesn't hurt so you can go home and suffer in peace.

"He's just not trying," the man comments in the creamy voice of a radio huckster for no-physical-required health insurance. "Why, sir, if I had these lovely ladies visiting me, I can assure you my condition would improve dramatically in no time a-tall." He seizes my mother's wrist and busses it.

She coughs up a chuckle.

The man inclines toward the wheelchair. His scalp sparkles like vellum. His cologne bottles me in wintergreen. "You aren't really trying," he's sorry to have to say.

Lou, who bowed his head and went limp when we came in range of this doberman, starts rolling again. They should post a sign, "Watch for falling rock."

"He's not really trying." The man shoulders the wall like Sisyphus and scuffles on.

"Who needs him?" Ida asks between her teeth.

Ingmar Bergman. The Shining Path. The manufacturers of Prozac.

A nurse in a pink cardigan eases out of the room of an ancient woman with surprised red hair. "Louie!" Bubbles froth from her voice to her eyes to burst in blonde curls. "This man!" She bends down into his face, then looks up at me. "Is this man your father?"

She must know he can't hear very well. She speaks distinctly—introducing the Beatles at Shea.

"Susie, this is my daughter, Carol," Ida tells her. I put out my hand; she minces her eyes. "You're here so late?"

"Doing somebody a favor," she crinkles, as though admitting to shoplifting. "This man is a real character, do you know that?"

I grin, hard as nails. I'm an armadillo.

She puts her hands on her knees like a chorine; when she stands up they hitch to her waist. She's a Little Teapot! I wonder if my folks are fondly recalling my cousin Joey's bar mitzvah, where, after consuming an unwonted amount of alcohol, my mother performed, with gestures, "Ballin' the Jack," and later, or so legend has it—I imagine Ida, rigid in rayon, Lou, ardently advancing with his polkadot boxers around his ankles—I was conceived. "Do you know what this man said to me yesterday?" She fluffs his hair. "Do you remember? What did you say?"

"What?" Ida gloats, ready for a good one.

Fuck a duck. If you don't like my driving— To be or not—

He's smiling, eyelids lowered, like an iguana. He shakes his head. It doesn't necessarily mean he doesn't remember; it could easily mean, "spare me."

"I asked if he wanted me to take him out for a nice little tour of the grounds—" (the red clay equivalent of a demilitarized zone) "You remember? It was beautiful yesterday—" (if you like auto emissions, muddy backhoe ruts, sinus headaches, and nowhere to hide from the cancer-causing rays of the sun) "And he says to me, 'I just want to wallow in self-pity.' Wadn't that it? 'Wallow in self-pity.' Can you believe it?" She whoops.

Ida and I are hanging. I can't tell if the nurse actually thinks this is funny or if she's candy-coating a professional message: the man is *down*. Put on those rubber noses and *clown*. Should I tell her he's always been like this? Asking the junior architect, "Will you miss me when I'm gone?"

"Oh, you!" Ida snaps out of it and twits his ear.

My father joggles his right hand like he's trying a doorknob, and Susie takes it. "She's a wonderful girl," he moons up at her. Instantly I feel guilty. I should be telling cute stories, fluffing his hair, pouting and winking and mewing. What can I do? I'm *his* daughter.

"These nurses are all just wonderful," Ida tells me, "a godsend. But you need a decent union!" Buddy-buddy to the nurse, "You know he snuck another shower this morning."

"You're kidding me!" Bug eyes, hiked shoulders; I swear they're going to link arms and kick.

"He got Martin to do it. He din't tell him he wasn't due till tomorrow. He conned him." Ida is as proud as if her six-year-old has sassed Art Linkletter in twenty million homes.

You expect Susie's Mr. Pointer to wag, and oh yes he does. "You so and so. You're a sight!" Next she'll be singing "Be Optimistic" in crinolines. "You know Earline? She's on the station most mornings? Well, she told me, she got so tickled, here he comes, rolling up to the desk, you know, solemn as an ol' owl, and he says to her, 'We've got a problem.' Naturally, she's upset, what is it? where? And he points down. Martin put his shoes on the wrong feet. Laced and everything. Well, did she laugh! 'Yes,' she says, 'I guess we do have a problem.' Did we howl!"

Ida and Susie laugh heartily. Lou cranks up his eyelids like the awning in front of the store. "Not much of a woman, are you, Carol? You look like you got a pin stuck in your ass." The eyes submerge into a smile as flat and dirty as the East River.

I thought I was smiling. I try to make a better job of it. My mother demonstrates. She looks demented.

"When you come Satiday, I want you to meet the little girl who helps me wit' my therapy. What's her name?"

"Who?" Susie pounces.

"Pretty girl. What? Jeannie? Joanne? She's so sweet. She helps me walk."

"You don't mean Trish?" Susie frowns.

"I don't know. I got Alzheimer's now too."

"All the nurses are just wild about your daddy," Susie tells me.

I feel as though I've got to assure her, "So am I, believe me!" I feel like Cordelia. Only Cordelia looks better because she gets the gate first. And why are they treating me like a stranger? I'm here every other evening, Saturday or Sunday afternoon. I've heard the shoelace story twice.

"Well, I've got to go see about Mrs. Woodruff." Slipping her hand very gently from Lou's absent shaking. "You enjoy your daughter's visit now, you hear? He's doing real good; he'll be out of here in no time."

"I don't see no difference, one day to the next." His hand lolls in his lap, and the shake shims up to his head. The salt is shaking out of him. He's gone pasty.

"He's doing just fine." Susie injects my pupils with a sincerity that smarts. Then she stoops to clasp his shoulders. Is the view down her blouse part of the treatment? His eyes lift, and each radiates like a child's spiky, smiling sun. The sweetness of it hurts. "You cain't stay with us forever, honey. Now you be good!"

"Can I help it?"

"Listen at him!" The flirty moue of disapproval. "This man!" She straightens, massaging the small of her back, moving down the hall. "Nice to meet you," she calls softly, and after all the shouting, I almost fall over.

Lou finds the wheels but can't budge them. "Did your mother tell you I don't want you coming no more?"

I take the handles, although Ida wants to fight me for them, and we set off.

"The broken record," Ida carps. She watches me as if we were sisters and our mother had just let me be the first to push her new baby in the buggy.

"I heard Harry called last night and really cheered you up." My brother, an auditor, who has done exactly the same thing every day for twenty-two years and earned three cars, four kids, and a tract house with a pool in Jersey for it. He is their brag, while I'm their sob story. Of course, they get more mileage off me.

"Harry cheered Harry up. After he got done talking he felt so much better."

I laugh.

"Oh Lou! You're so unfair to the boy." I think my mother wants to bite me.

"Well, now you have to let me try," I pursue. "Tell me about this walking. You've been doing some serious walking."

"Very little. A few steps. Holding on all the time."

Ida objects. "He can walk the whole length of the room, it's like a bowling alley—"

"Dad! That's terrific!"

"They tell me he'll be home in six weeks." Ida flattens his collar. "They send somebody over to show me how to get the place ready—I want you to be there—like maybe take the door off the shower—"

"Sure, no problem. Great!"

"Listen to the two morons. 'Great! Terrific!'" he pipes. "This stroke was so good, maybe I should have another. Like a couple parakeets."

"You would prefer what?" Ida bristles.

He cheeches shrill bird static until we reach his room.

When I used to ask my mother about divorce, she'd tell me women aren't meant to be happy, she'd cite Scripture, her own mythic mother intoning over the everlasting Polish stewpot; besides, he's not as bad as some; besides, she's too old. Too old since her forties. I'm forty. She obviously confused divorce with the millennium or Coney Island, September, 1945.

Now she's explaining, for the millionth time, that Lou wants to talk here rather than the lounge because his ass aches from sitting all day, and he hopes a nurse will put him to bed so he can stretch out. I hate thinking about my father's bony ass. As usual, I offer to move him, I flex my rehab biceps, but they both vociferously nix the idea; I'm a girl. Besides, it's against the rules. Instead, I rearrange the chairs for chat.

He shares the room with three other men. Mr. Hairston, *café au lait* with a big dune of thoughtful forehead revealed by a receding hairline, is probably in his sixties, but I'm only guessing from the number and ages of grandchildren who visit Sundays; his skin is as smooth as a deer's except for the spokes that radiate from his eyes. He's a double amputee. Both legs are gone from just above the knees. Yet he's cheerful, even agile. Once the nurses dropped him on the floor, and he laughed about it, he recovered before they could get over their distress, he consoled them. He's watching one of the tvs that hang from the ceiling. He waves at us, then puts his finger to his lips. He's in final "Jeopardy."

The man who was crying in the dining room is still crying, lying in bed. I've never seen him not crying. A woman who has been introduced as his fiancée stands holding his hand and murmuring quiet reproofs. His brother Tod slouches in a chair under the window. With each tear Tod fidgets one side higher, then the other, until he blurts out, "Quit that!" and collapses, like some kind of modernistic hourglass.

"Such a shame," my mother commiserates. "Any improvement?"

"He's doing fine," Tod says. "You?"

"Oh really, much better, thanks."

The fiancée ignores us. She seems to be casting a spell. I hope it's working on her.

Directly across from my father's bed Tuesday night was a gray man who looked dead. His wife sat and talked to him, he was moved to and from a wheelchair, his eyes opened sometimes, but he looked dead. Now there's a twenty-two-year-old motorcycle accident victim. He resembles Tom Hanks, or Tom Sawyer, under a hairdryer of bandages. He's asleep.

There are two empty beds between those that are occupied.

My mother asks Lou if he wants to watch tv.

"What's the use? I can't hear it anyways."

I remember when I returned to New York from a year studying restoration in Florence, I found my father watching *Gentlemen Prefer Blondes* on a screen so snowblind you couldn't make out the women, and the vertical twitched

32

like slumbrous eyelashes. "How can you watch that?" I asked him. He stared at me, and my mother came out of the kitchen to hiss, "You had to tell him!" I can tell you, I wanted to hide both of them in my capacious bosom. I thought, that's why it's so capacious—big enough to tote two cranky, Eurosized adults. What did I do? I ran.

"—I want to talk to my daughter. So, how is Little Miss Fix-It? How goes the business?"

He asks this every time. "Fine" won't cut it, but I try.

"This means what? You eat steak, you bought a decent house? You still driving that wreck?"

"Every time she goes out in it," Ida tells the fiancée, "I hold my breath."

I wish. At least her tongue. The fiancée is impenetrable. "I talked to Jim today—"

"Jim? Who's this Jim?" He consults Ida. "The boy-friend?"

"Jim! Jim is one of the original collective," and, as always, he pretends collective means someone who works for a collection agency, like detective or operative, defective, and I consider selling the idea to the OED. "An original partner. He's moving to Maine in June. His wife inherited some land. Dave wants to go back to school, and Marty's thinking about starting a cabinetry shop. Which leaves me. I either have to find another job, take on new partners, or run the whole show myself."

"You?" My father honks.

"Piss or get off the pot," Ida smirks. "You should talk to Harry. My son has a genius for business," she tells Tod. He ratchets up two notches. "What you gonna do about the kids? You spend little enough time on them as it is. It's a bad age. There's no telling what they could get into—"

This from a woman who farmed me out to aunts and art lessons so she could sustain the United Front. And I'm glad. She's gotten conventional now that she has to get right with the bridge gals. "It's not what I want. It's been so ideal. I've been able to set my hours, choose my tasks— I don't want to keep books and scrounge lumberyards. But if I don't—" What I want is to crawl in a bed and ring for medication. I've been avoiding thinking about this all day. Shouting it is like publicly upchucking.

"You got insurance coverage?"

If he didn't ask this once a week it might seem off the wall. "Sure. But that's the kind of thing—"

"So how much you make?"

"Enough." I refuse to shout my monthly income. My mother hunfs and looks significantly at Tod. He rears up and locks a leg across his knee like a barricade.

"Peanuts. What about the kids? How they doing in school?"

"Fine."

"In other words, not so hot."

"They're basically good children." Ida is now addressing a general board of appeals. "Coming from a broken home, it's hard for them to—"

"Alice, don't she go to college soon?"

"Ariel. Next year."

"So how the hell you gonna afford it? You know how much it costs to send a kid to college these days? And for what? So they can get AIDS and smoke crack. You still get money from Karl?"

"Yes." My mouth is a fist.

"You was crazy to let him divorce you. He came to visit me last week, your mother tell you? He's a mensch. He seen you since you lost all the weight?"

"Dad, it's been seven years. He's married. They have a child."

"So what do I know about your personal affairs? You still fooling around with that bum?"

"Which one?"

"Carol!" Ida claps her hand over her mouth and denies it to the others, including sleeping Tom, weeping Will. "He's a landscape something or other—"

"A gardener. I hope at least he's white. Haven't you got any morals?"

Guess not. What did he call Karl when we started dating? Marx, of course; and "that bum." As young parents, living in a cosy walk-up on Spring Street in the quaint warehouse district, near the docks—Karl was a public defender, and I was pastelling prepubescent princesses in despite of a real job or daycare—we used to imagine my father singing a little ditty we'd fake to the rhythm of the rails on the subway ride home from Sunday dinner:

> She married a bum,
> They live in a slum,
> They feed off a crumb,
> She paints with her thumb,
> Her kid is still mum.
> How could she be so dumb?

It could go on, depending on how much we'd managed to drink.

It's times like this I really miss Karl. He's such a swashbuckler. He drinks schnaps, eats with relish, smokes cigars at weddings; he's hairy, sweats, and argues—long, hard, and fair; he likes to dance and play cards, knock out a tune on the piano; he'll even take a swing if some guy rubs him the wrong way. How he can jolly my father into the bad joke life is. And I'd say or do anything to have his big, broad, easy laugh break over me like cold water on a sticky day. But look: when Karl read in his Boy Scout Handbook that the Indians walked by putting one foot directly in front of the other, he was so persuaded this was the only correct way to walk, he made himself walk like this. I loved that about him, how he would alter himself to be what he thought best. I never dreamed that truly believing he knew the best way to walk, he would try to force me into it—knowing that because I walked like a duck, they made me wear orthopedic oxfords and do exercises in legirons—that he would hector and heckle me *for my own good.*

My father is saying, "You should be teaching, not working like a glorified super. All that education and for what? Where are your great women artists? Name one!"

"Berthe Morisot, Mary Cassatt, Georgia O'Keeffe, Frida Kahlo, Helen Frankenthaler, Louise—"

"I mean what you heard of. You finally got your hooks in the poor fish, you let him go. How many times I tell you, no man in his right mind marries a fat girl? So he steps out on you, what you expect? You couldn't forgive him? You was always too good for everybody, and look what it got you. You got nothing."

But damn it all! I feel really lucky to be able to sit here in the ultimate body shop listening to my stricken father bawl out my worst fears, follies, and failures. Somebody up there is a fucking sadist, like Groucho on "You Bet Your Life." The secret word is run. "Next time maybe I could bring you a book."

"What, you leaving already?"

"No, no, I'm just—"

"There's nothing." He looks down at his knees, and his wattles weigh like beanbags.

"I could read to you. A mystery maybe—"

"Ida, press the nurse button for me."

"What's wrong? What'd she say? She din't mean it." Ida's daggers warn me: retract, whatever it was.

"I need to use the commode, if you must know. But keep your girdle on, nobody's coming for ten minutes the least. You know, Carol, I wouldn't change places with you in a million years. This world what's coming—I don't want no part of it. When the schwartzes take their revenge, it's gonna

36

make the Holocaust look like the teddy bears' picnic. And the Arabs! Animals! I just wanna die and be done with it."

Jesus! My mother is simpering at Tod and the fiancée. I'm not sure I'd mind them strangling all of us. Mr. Hairston searches the channels for a game—or signs of intelligent life. "Oh, Dad, I know things seem bad right now." How do I sound? Rickety—the earth keeps rifting under me, and the heat, the fumes— "It's awful being in the hospital. But once you're out, you won't—"

The nurse comes in, a stocky, red-brown woman with gray hair springing around her cap, wearing a buttercup sweater. I'm stifling, and most of the nurses wear sweaters. Tod and the fiancée are in sweaters; Ida's still in her coat. It makes me feel—uncool. Maybe I'm numb. Glum. Scum.

"How you doin', Mr. Lou?"

Names ending in vowels being unheard-of below the Mason-Dixon. "Here we go loop-dee—" starts cycling my brain.

"What took you so long?" Lou kvetches.

She takes the chair's handles. "You ready for bed, honey? Let's go empty the keg."

When they're in the bathroom, Ida leans over to tell me, "He had a lousy day today, and you're not helping. I'll tell you later."

"Does he have any cards?"

"He don't want them. What are you, bored?"

"Maybe I just want to take some money off a sick man."

Lou returns in a gown, and while my mother bags his dirty clothes, and I shift the chairs, the nurse puts him to bed. She does her best with the rumpled, sour sheet. Smoothing his forehead, she asks if he needs anything. His watery blues cast up like a fading drunk's. "A rope to hang myself."

"Aw, Mr. Lou. You got no call to be talkin' like that. You be skippin' rope here in no time."

She raises a helpless eyebrow at me and moves on to the crying man. I take her place. Lou finally looks comfortable. He closes his eyes, asks me to put on the tv and leave.

"You know, Dad, every time I visit, all we do is worry my financial situation. You never tell me anything about your life. I don't know where you're from, how you came over here, what you did when you were a kid. I'd love to hear." His dome is filmed with a pearly sweat, and his skin looks translucent.

The eyes rush into black like sinkholes. "What do you want? a travelogue? What's to hear? We lived off the smell of a cabbage, we got beat up good and regular, we had to eat shit for anything we wanted. A great life. Sensational. You wanna put on the tv?"

"I thought you couldn't hear it." I turn brightly to my mother. "Earphones!"

"What's to hear? Please, I'm sick of talking."

"Next time, I'm bringing a deck of cards," I threaten. "I'm going to kill you at gin."

"Do me a favor."

On the way to the parking lot, I remark to my mother that I've never heard him say "shit" before.

"Ach, lately? it's his favorite word. Something happened today, I din't wanna tell you. You know he's lost all the weight? So sometime, nobody knows exactly when, his wedding ring musta fell off his finger, and now it's gone."

I stop. I have to grip the top of my head. Why the hell didn't we look for it? I'm good at finding things—yet another unremunerative skill. I know I could have found it. I see it in my hand. I'm going back.

Ida grabs a piece of my jacket. "We turned the place upside down. It musta got vacuumed. Maybe it'll turn up tomorrow. Who knows?"

"Did you search the bed? It's got all those gizmos—"

"We looked everywhere. We stripped the bed. You know,

he never had it off since I put it on him forty-eight years ago." Her eyes flood. I make a move to hug her and sock her with my purse. "He thinks somebody took it."

I'm wrung out. "Geez, this is sad."

"It isn't worth nothing." She sighs like someone is sitting down on her. "So. I'll see you Saturday."

The night is sepia, and the mist smells like the cherry blend the second shift is packaging across town. I'm out walking for bagels with my papa after he switched to the pipe, and his overcoat pocket brushes against my face. I can't move. "I could come tomorrow."

"Saturday is good. This time bring the kids, I don't care what he says. The girl is good with him."

And the cards. Lou and Ariel quibbling about some stupid rule. She gets his goat, like Karl does. Maybe the goat is what keeps us hanging in. The horns. I see a wedding ring on a sharp, slender, twisted horn, and all of us on a carrousel, snaggling after it. "Why don't you stay home this once?"

"I don't wanna say this again. I stay home, he's gonna croak, I know it, outta spite."

What can I say? She could be right.

3 Got to Get You Into My Life

I have to sink a quart of oil in Ze Lemon on the way home. The bored attendant asks how I think I'm going to pass the new emissions inspection. (A fifth on the seat.) The neanderthal warns me it's downright reckless for a pretty woman to be out so late on her own and shows his scuzzy teeth. No sign of Ariel's truck.

The sty is still a sty. Dash watches some mindless comedy on tv, his arm greased to the elbow in a bowl of popcorn. I know what the kitchen looks like: what's under my hood. That business with the elves and shoemaker is a fairy tale. But he's kept the fire going; it's a good fire. I get a glass of scotch and sit on the springshot sofa facing the stove, taking Sluggo, once again lying so close he's singed his whiskers, into my lap. I watch the cobwebs chase the cracks across the ceiling to maniacal laughter.

"What's the matter, Mom?" Dash turns off the tube and comes around to plant his lubed pincers on my shoulders and rub, much too hard. "Grampa not doing so well?" He squeezes down on my purely physical response as if he wants to pop it. He seems to be rolling ropes. "Geometry test tomorrow, but I've got it knocked. Don't worry." He digs the balls of his fingers into my collarbone, gives me an affectionate jounce, then goes to the stereo and burrows to find an album, Woody Guthrie singing "Irene Goodnight." We used to have to play this for him every night, over and over, until he drowsed out.

"IIIII-reeeene, goodnight Irene, IIIII-reeeeeene goodnight—" Like a sine curve etched on glass; the bear grincing over the mountain on ice skates. Couldn't they take the clothespin off the guy's nose to record?

Dash smiles as though he's invented novocaine. "I remember how much you and Dad loved this one."

He's treating me like Peter Pan treats Wendy. Like a Lost Boy. I hasten to play my part. "You did a great job with the fire."

"Is it out?" he asks, on the rise.

I wave him down. I seem to have the same difficulty communicating as Cassandra. "It's a great fire."

He moves the needle back. "IIII-reeeene, goodnight Irene—" I'll hear this in my dreams. Mercifully, before "Take Me For A Ride in Your Car-Car," he kills it. "Eric coming over?"

"He's in Myrtle." Stag for shag weekend and beach blanket bingo. The fact that it's doubtless raining there too is hardly a comfort. But what's up? Dash asking so sweetly about Eric is like Sweeney Todd asking if you want a little off the top, Blanche Moore asking if you've tasted your banana pudding.

"Well, I'm going to bed." The elaborate stretch and yawn of Goldilocks. Without my saying a word? What time is it? Not nine. "Unless you need to unload?" As though taking the bricks off my chest will not only develop his pecs but build him a nice little pedestal. Are we entering some inscrutable new Oedipal phase? I decline. He smiles gently and saunters to the bathroom in this at-my-disposal mode. He's singing "Another Brick in the Wall" while he performs his ablutions. Damned mind reader. My clone.

I feel trampled. I didn't run today; that's probably all it is. Tomorrow I'll get up at five-thirty and run before work. Tomorrow I'll seize control of my life with both hands and milk it of its satisfactions. I'll *make* decisions and abide by them. I'll accomplish things. I'll make time. I'll pay strict attention to my children and spark them to be demanding, diligent, and high-minded. I will fill my father's last days with laughter and reconciliation and brighten my mother's outlook. I will ride Eric like the Pony Express and completely forget about him when he's on the road. I will paint something gr— Well. I'll paint.

Am I taller? Firmer? Am I *done?*

Dash exits for his bedroom in boxers. He's grown like the beanstalk, bruised as though he's tumbled from its top. The knee is a tarred pothole. His legs look like a relief map of the Pacific. How did he get that dink in his stomach? "What happened to you?" I ask. "Lose a fight with a bus?"

He looks down at himself as though awakening in the hospital after sitting on a grenade. "Oh. It's nothing. Mom?" Long pause. "Can I talk to you sometime?"

"Now's good." The new me. The phone rings. "Maybe it's Ariel."

"It'll keep." He makes tracks and flings his door to.

It's his guidance counselor. He got into a fight today, and tomorrow he has to stay after school, and one more fight, it's a week of in-school suspension. It goes on his record. He seems to be asking for trouble. She's very concerned. We set up a conference.

When I get off the phone, he's in a coma. I can't rouse him. Bash. I want to pummel him, shrieking about Jesus, Gandhi, and Dr. Martin Luther King, Jr. Threaten him with—but what could be worse than school? Also sob and ask how he can do this to me. Also: run! There's a potato jammed in my throat. Later. I move back to the couch to keep vigil for my wayward girl. And what do I say to her?

"Where have you been?" I know the answers to that. Do mothers only get a certain repertoire? Shit.

What a day. A regular last day of Pompeii. Looking back to assess exactly where bad turned ugly (and what *I*, as a responsible, *caring* parent, can do about it!), I find Fawne's little white, wacked-out, wise-ass innocence is its bright spot, the ghost in the machine. It's been so long since I've been intrigued by anybody. Sure, I hope she'll hotwire my sluggish, lowbrow daughter, be the shot of Camelot to lead her up and out of the manure I've planted her in. But I'm drawn to Fawne myself. I remember what it's like to look at your adults and wonder what's to become of you. And what's the point. I remember lying in bed at night listening to their drone and bicker, thinking, is this it? Bury me now.

And then I met Elspeth.

Let me explain.

I was fourteen and in the tenth grade at the largest high school in the world: three sessions, eight thousand kids in a building like a medieval fortress, all that was missing was the hot lead pouring from the turrets, in one of which I suffered remedial speech under a sawed-off screwball who told us we were verbal cripples and would never hold jobs or have sex.

But I had friends. We all contrived to be in the same Shakespeare elective that term and were cooking up a musical version of *Hamlet* using the songs on "Rubber Soul." Or we were banging together my sinister I-was-reading-Kafka sets, Dan and Billy's grandiose light-up-and-grunch machine that ground out ideal teenagers in Sharon's she-was-reading-*Frankenstein* script for the annual sing. Or we were planning the Friday night party or going to hear the Fugs at the Bridge or to stand in line for standing room at the opera or to picket segregationists and warmongers, or *Duck Soup* was playing at the Thalia. Maybe we were headed for Dan's to smoke pot and do our homework. Maybe it was the day Mad-Man Meroney had us make ammonia, and for some reason he wouldn't let us open the windows, and about two seconds after successfully producing ammonia, we were fainting, retching, and Meroney— he looked like Snuffy Smith—was screaming, "You will get back into your seats this instant! No one excused you!" Maybe it was the day Shelly Goldblatt O.D.'d in gym, and Francy pulled me out of French on a fake pass from the Philosophy Club—only, see? there was no Philosophy Club—and we convinced the teacher it was diet pills, and she didn't call the cops. It could have been the day Helen Fein committed suicide in the girls' bathroom for no one specific reason, as she said in her note. Or in Economics when the all-city chess champ soaked the desk behind me with lighter fluid and set fire to it, and Alan yanked me out and walked me under his arm through all the bureaucratic flak into daylight and bought me an ice cream cone. Butter pecan with chocolate sprinkles.

I think that was what Paul saw in me: my friends. He stood at the curb, smoking, watching, alone. He seemed to have no friends, and that was what I saw in him.

That day he was taking me to meet his sister-in-law. He was mysterious about it. He was often mysterious—go out of your way to visit a relative? don't they sponge meals?— but I knew it was a test, a blindfold taste test, and I wanted to pass.

We took the BMT to Atlantic Avenue, transferred to the IRT, got out at Prospect Park. But it wasn't the Prospect Park we were in fifteen minutes ago, the one I'd schlepped through all my life. I imagined a conspiracy with stencils and spray paint, dummy turnstiles, a body slumped in the token booth, padlocked exit, BUT WHY?, or a newspaper blows in my face, IT'S 1925!, or I was through the looking glass, finally. We emerged on a side of the park I'd never seen before and bore along First Street under a twittering canopy of trees frilled in the feathery parsley of seedheads, in a light that shimmered like the skin on a lake, and flanked by brownstones like drip castles—some brick, some rough block; on others, the stone seemed to have been floated like plaster, with garlands of flowers tied in ribbon, baskets of fruit, and sunbursts in relief. We stopped at one, of a pink sandstone so seamless and curvaceous I had to round my palm over its prickly contours up the stairs to the door, at some slight expense to the skin. Paul rang the bell.

Barking, the click and scratch of claws, quick footsteps, the crunch of the key. The door breached just enough for Paul, rail-thin and empty-handed, and not enough for me and my embrace of encumbrances. I bunked into the bent back of a tiny woman restraining a huge, shaggy, slavering lunge. She spindled her arm in the dog's neck, and it wound into the apartment as obediently as a tape. We followed. I was hardly in when the dog's snoot slotted my crotch, then it hoisted its paws to my shoulders and saluted me in the French manner. Its coat was long and silky, many colors, desert colors—what a prince might don to pass as a beggar.

"Brindle," the woman said. "Afghan. Rathbone!" The dog bounded off me and sawed into Paul, detaching his glasses and snarling at his throat. It looked like a dragon, white eye and tooth. I worried about my smell. I felt like food.

"Rathbone!" She deflected it toward the windows with the fluid assurance of a professional ballroom dancer, although it measured against her like a bike. "These dogs bring down leopards and gazelles in the wild, and I breed for size, muscle, and coat. Otherwise, they look like french fries. Bedroom!" It slunk for the rear of the house. "It's funny, he only attacks tall, dark, skinny men with glasses. Like my husband." She laughed witchily, the quickening blub of boiling water. "And his ilk. How are you, ilk?"

Paul retrieved his glasses. "I brought someone to see you. Be great." He sounded like her manager. I felt like the gofer. I wanted somebody to tell me to go.

"I use aikido to handle him. Japanese style of self-defense. You use your opponent's momentum against him. Effective for the short. You're Carrie."

Her voice had a grain, a nubble, like tweed. She was chalk-pale, stark in a tent of fine black hair that fell to her hips. She wore rose-colored plastic glasses, frames and lenses pink; they looked like something a clinic would donate to some desperate batblind foundling—stigmatic, as it were—permanent pinkeye. Behind them, her eyes were the weird red of eyes in a flash photo. I'd hardly ever seen a grown woman—other than a nun or a very orthodox wig-wearing woman, at both of whom I'd be afraid to be caught looking—without lipstick. She was not five feet tall. The hand she put out to me was an urchin's, clipped nails, maybe bitten, even dirty. Her wedding band might have been a cigar band. She was in jeans and a boy's striped, long-sleeved t-shirt, and she was busty, like me, like a ratio of me, only I was glossing over the fact in a dowdy jumper. She looked like those round-breasted bathing beauties with Krishna in Indian miniatures, their arms angled behind their aquiline profiles or around musical instruments. There was a recorder among the junk on the mantelpiece.

"Alto, pearwood, wedding present from the hubby, Joe. I'm Elspeth. A name impossible to say without spitting. My parents' first attempt on my life. What names do you like?"

Not that I hadn't thought about it. I couldn't say Ruby.

"I like Bronwen," she said. "Welsh." She took my hand and shook it. "You can tell everything about a person from the handshake. I had to shake hands with Andy Warthog once, and his hand was a dead fish, like this—"

Now I was sheathing a limp Playtex Living Glove.

"I had a job teaching in a Yeshiva, and the principal or

rabbi or King Shit wouldn't shake my hand. Might be menstrual. Unclean." She blatted her tongue. "Let me take your things." She swiped them away and threw them on the floor, cackling. I felt stripped. I expected shackles to appear next, a branding iron.

Paul pulled a chair out from under a big round black table and sat, lit up, crossed his legs. Waiting for the floor show. Elspeth tootled something monkish on the recorder. Even my friends' rooms were less messy, even the alcoholic kitchen before Sharon got home was less grubby. It smelled like the drycleaners'. The walls were painted amber; the wainscoting was red mahogany, as were the fluted columns that supported the arch that opened into the second room. A tall mirror, opaque with dust, hung over the mantel. Someone had written "CLEAN ME!" on it. Each window in the three-sided bay facing the street had a waxed paper shade pulled to the sill so they looked like sticks of margarine. Stiff sheets of white light slipped in around the edges—ransom notes.

"I like it dark," Elspeth said, wiping the tip of the recorder on her shirt and replacing it in the mantel clutter. "I like to choose my light."

A Tiffany lamp, like a rose window made into a hat— "Genu-ine!"—hung over the round black table hemmed in an intricacy of monkeys in vines—"Indian!"—and reddened Paul's Caravaggio curls. Twelve feet up, in a snowy expanse drifting spidercotton, two bare lightbulbs kinked from the ceiling rose.

"Still looking. This place was like a guano island when I got hold of it. Laissez-faire plumbing. Paneling painted turquoise. Floor dried to tinder under molding remnants." It was parquet, stained different shades of green. "Hands and knees. Sanded, stained, sanded, three times, three coats of sealer rubbed with steel wool. My hands used to be as big as yours." Ten exclamation points. "And we only rent!"

Silent scream. "Paul tells me you're an artist."

"Oh no!" As though I'd have to paint my way out. My voice startled me. "I just draw." I suddenly noticed the canvas on an easel canted between me and the windows. A gooseneck lamp goggled at it; another aimed at a small magnifying mirror on a stool beside boxes of paints and cans of brushes. Elspeth switched on the goggler. A sinuous woman, paperwhite, with a flow of black hair, on a reddish batik bedspread, legs apart and genitals rendered in fine. One arm snaked over her head; she cradled a telephone receiver to her ear. The black cord spiraled up her belly and between her round breasts. The dial read BE-4-5789, and I was singing, "'You can call me up and have a date any old time.'"

"Yes!" she delighted. "You may not be an artist, but you sure can see. Cee! That's your name! Carrie is such a burden."

My heart lifted like a barge in a surging lock.

Paul flicked his cigarette into the fireplace. "Got to go."

The "go" was a long fall down a deep hole. An emotional goiter prevented my wailing, "Go?"

"Go!" Elspeth wailed. "You never even got here!" She hung on my arm like a tantrumming two-year-old.

"Said I'd meet this guy. *You* don't have to." His eyes on some apparition between a bow-legged, shocking pink, vinyl settee and me. "I wasn't going your way anyhow." He lit a cigarette getting to his feet, exhaled whatever his expression might have divulged. "You can handle it."

I knew this was a test. Now I knew I was a walk-on Vandella replacement at the Apollo. "Think you can bring that down an octave, Martha? Anybody out there remember the words to 'Dancing in the Street'?" I was dogmeat.

"*You* can show yourself out. Of course *you'll* stay." Elspeth tillered me to the painting. "The technique on the cunt is really tricky. I'm using myself—you know those Victorian novels where the male member is called his 'self'? They must not have heard the more tasteful 'schlong'." The door closed so quietly you'd have thought we were cutting diamonds. "We sat here one night trying to pick our least favorite expressions for the male organ, and that was mine. 'Prick' is vicious; 'schmuck' is cute, like 'the family jewels'—I take it back, it's disgusting. What do we get? The cruel and the medical, well, and 'pussy,' so there's hope. 'Bush' isn't bad, as in 'My Twenty Years in the—'"

"I hate 'piece of ass'—" My tongue slugged up out of the slime.

"Oh, and 'meat,' and '*that*,' as in 'I'd like to get into *that*.' Shudder! Anyway, I sit here with one knee in Saskatchewan and the other in Tierra del Fuego in my split-crotch nasties from Frederick's of Hollywood, and I use this eyelash on a stick and twenty colors at the very least, and it's some combination of a pelvic and an appointment at Elizabeth Arden, and sometimes, I must tell you, I do get a leettle aroused, and the animals are truly baffled—" She shrieked a laugh like a skid.

Did this come under the heading "girl talk?" It was nothing like the eternal crabs of Linda Lopez or Nancy Silverberg's epic efforts to secure birth control pills, recitations that had scared the pants to me hermetically. What was I doing here? How would I get out? I tried not to give myself away.

"Come back while I change. You must be wondering where my manners are. I haven't offered you sustenance."

"That's okay," I trilled, "I can't eat with my mouth open." I heard that and wanted it sealed with hot wax.

She staggered as though enfeebled by hilarity. "Wonderful girl! The real reason is bare cupboard. I must eat nothing as I have a metabolism straight from another solar system. Some are born without senses, limbs; others struck down in their prime. It's not the worst hereditary cross. But if I don't quaff a Coke jiffy pronto, I will quake to complete prostration. Also a smoke. Secret. Forbidden. One a day only. Do not tell Paul." She probed my eyes as if I had something on her. "The candy store is practically in your subway stop."

She snapped on the light in the next room. The bed was brass, unmade, black sheets. Rathbone sat on it, gazing regally, or like a congenital idiot, into space.

"The American Kennel Club describes the Afghan 'gazing into the distance as if in memory of ages past.' Sit." She indicated a carved wooden settee upholstered in tortoiseshell vinyl, the twin of the shocking pink job—"French Improvincial," she said. A black Persian cat was sleeping on it. "Haroun el-Rashid. Rashid, for short."

"I read *The Arabian Nights* all the time!" I exclaimed, as though I'd had my hand up for hours. "The Dulac illustrations?"

"He has orange eyes. Another cham-peen. I'm not hustling you out, you understand, this will take time. Antecedent to adventure."

She delved into a black armoire, pitching out clothes and shoes, while I chafed over whether to repeat my slighted remark. I didn't want to disturb the cat—we didn't have any pets, and the only black cat in my ken was Mr. Poe's—and, peevish, I didn't want to do what I was told. I turned my back and knelt to study a big canvas propped against some stacks of books. A fat, white, middle-aged woman in a housedress at the laundry line, next to a white, two-story, wood-frame farmhouse. In each room, seen through mullioned windows, someone worked or dreamed in apricot illumination. The sky bruised to storm. Trees thrashed their silver underleaves; sheets and shirts bellied out. I felt a billowing like early spring inside me, a kind of expanding ache. I brought my face closer as though I would see more.

"Look! Courrèges boots. New! And dress. Real clothes.

Cost the earth. These short skirts look great with our sturdy gams. In colored stockings?" She displayed a white space boot and a severe space-nurse dress with red piping. I thought it would make her look like a paperdoll. I thought I'd never have the money, and I'd always be too fat. I thought you could clothe Crown Heights with what it cost and that fashion is selfish, stupid, degrading, and vain. I probably smiled.

"Of course it is bold and wondrous and makes one crave wealth like crazy. Does he always treat you like that?"

My eyes fled to the painting. Let me in.

"What I mean is, do you really like him? Is he nice to you?" She was still holding up the boot and dress, so rather than short, she looked far away—The Little Prince, semaphoring from another planet. The mess became galactic; the dust, cosmic. "Weren't you hurt he just left you like that? How do you feel about him?"

I fell back on my heels. My chin was trembling. "I don't know how I feel about anything." I was gripping the bars of a cage. "I feel *everything!*" The bars were my teeth.

Her smile draped over me softly like a silk scarf. She threw the boot back in the wardrobe, hung up the dress, kept hunting. I imagined thousands of pairs of shoes, ensembles for sports and special occasions like the doll costumes I traded on the sidewalk for hours and then forgot in a shoe box. I had the same feeling of falseness, waste, and inanition.

"Cee, listen to Mother Else. If you guys are fucking, you've got to use some kind of contraceptive. And if you can't go to a doctor and get on the pill or fitted for a diaphragm—that's like a rubber stopper, but it's not uncomfortable, maybe safer than the pill, so *ask*—then your next best bet is this stuff you can buy at the drug store, it's a big nothing, you find it on the shelf, although sometimes, to humiliate you, they hide it and make you ask for it, so then you shop somewhere else. I don't know what it's really called;

we call it Fuck-O. Look in that drawer next to the bed; go ahead. It's got a pink cap."

I moved to the bedside table like something joined with pegs. I found the can among emery boards, pennies, papers, pencils, a plastic compact, a passbook, keys, paperclips and dutifully examined it, wondering how the paperclips got there. I shut the drawer, perched on the edge of the bed, and clasped my hands on my knees. Rathbone sighed and laid his head on my thigh and made sympathetic eyes.

"Anyway, it's a spermicide, sends the little buggers about their business, you just shake it and squirt it up you, and it foams, a little sloppy but not unpleasant. And not 100 percent. But you use it, because if he's telling you he's taking care of it, not to worry, you will be knocked up in nothing flat. And I mean this only *if* you are fucking, and you fuck only *if* you really want to, *and* you really like him *and* trust him, *and* he's really, really kind to you."

My face burned like a party bulb. I couldn't think how to hide it except under the bed or my skirt. I wore a smile like a bandaid.

She swung out from the armoire. "I haven't got a thing to wear." She went to a chest that had a mirror and drawers and little balconies holding candles and perfume bottles, sat on a piano stool, and pinned up her hair. "Next week I'm having all this cut off at Sassoon."

"Oh no!" I reached out, and Rathbone started, nosed my palm. I thought she looked like a lady in a Japanese woodcut. I was Jane Eyre helplessly watching the scissors crunch off Helen's tresses. I had pretended such hair with a nylon stocking. It trailed me in all my fantasies.

"No, it's too thin, a continual grooming nightmare. I hate it. Besides, they do that W on the nape bones. Fetching. Have you met the rest of his family?"

I shook no, exhausted, as if I was on a Tilt-a-Whirl that stopped only to start again, backwards.

"Well, you know his father is dead. His mother killed him with rich stews and oily, spicy sauces and by keeping him in cigars and whiskey." She pulled a long white cotton rectangle from top right and wound it around her head in a very authentic-looking turban. "He has two brothers—"

"Two?" I spoke to the reflection.

"And two sisters. The older brother is a Marine; in other words, a hired assassin. The older sister married a guy in construction with a steel plate in his head; they live in Jersey. The younger one, as dumb as they come, is dating a bookie. Has he mentioned Tony?"

"The gangster?" Paul saw Tony as the universal solvent. Any wound, real or imagined, he silently invoked the wrath of Tony, with only a significant crook of his brow and a wrinkled smile. I didn't believe in Tony.

She traced her eyes with black pencil and began a mustache. "Tony is great, if you don't object to him packing a gat. His last name is Marcopoulos, half-Greek, half-Sicilian—talk about your ethnic time bomb—and he's convinced he's a direct descendant of the famed Oriental traveller." She tweaked a smile over half a mustache. "Patsy, aptly named, used to date a, uh, member," her brows up-and-downed, "of a rival family, and actual shots have been exchanged over this scrawny, titless, teased chewer-of-gum. It's a mad house. Watch out for their mother. She had cloves of garlic implanted in their brains at birth that can suddenly cause them to treat you like you were the commandant of their POW camp. You get up from the table shredded. A death of a thousand cuts begins with but a single quip."

She was making me feel like I'd never been born.

"There!" She made a jubilant mouth and looked like the cartoon Turk who advertised Bonomo's Turkish Taffy. Oh oh oh! I was going into the street with her dressed like this? I had no idea how late it was. I didn't know how to get home, I'd be wandering the subway alone after dark, which anybody can tell you is asking for it, and my only hope of even locating the station was the drag Gunga Din. Whatever had tightened around my stomach was moving up to my chest, my neck, my skull. "Nowhere to run to, baby—" I knotted my arms, and Rathbone snapped, and the cat momentarily roused and spat.

"So if you're invited to some intimate family bloodletting, count on me to be there. Wear full armor, and don't eat anything you don't see her swallow first. Shall we go? We want you home before dark." She came over to sit beside me and buckle on a pair of the clunky orthopedic dress shoes I had to wear until I threw a pair down the sewer. Round toes, straps, perforations, decorative stitching. They looked comfortable, eccentric with jeans. I coveted them. But now my feet were too big. Were all my mother's dire predictions coming true today? At what stage had my face frozen?

Hastily gathering my belongings, I was stopped by a small ink sketch of a naked lady with round breasts and hips and long sleek black hair, done in three or four quick, clean, exuberant black strokes. "Is your husband an artist too?" I may have sighed.

"Old b.f. from college."

And her husband let it stay up? I scanned the confusion for a photo of him. The mirror barked "CLEAN ME!" "It's great. It's like those Picassos—"

"Picasso is a slob," she said offhandedly. She was looking around the radiator for something.

"Oh no!" Only lowbrows like my parents said such things.

"Look again. He takes the easy way. Quick and dirty."

I stood up slowly. She kept cruising past the right answers. "Yours are more like Bonnard—" I was afraid she'd change the name she'd given me to my grade, but I wanted to leave some impression. "Or Rousseau—?"

"Yes!"

"I love the way he paints the moon. And the sun. And the sky—" Ever-widening gestures dangerously freighted with books.

"Yes, and those jungles of monster houseplants—I mean sansevieria, for Christ's sake. At a Matisse show, Rousseau is supposed to have said, 'I could finish these for him.' Naive, huh?" She stopped fiddling to appraise my uptake. "I call what I do abstract because I abstract form, color, and texture from reality. All that so-called abstract art you see is concrete: paintings of paint." She fished a leash from behind the radiator and picked up her keys with a jank. Rathbone paced out like a thoroughbred in a negligee. "Yes, all right. Would you mind, Cee? You'll have to hold him while I'm in the store."

"Mind?" I hoped an enemy would see me. Then I saw: the beautiful, exotic dog and the fat, splayfoot frump.

"It's your clothes," she said. "You know, one can still have physical *and* spiritual weight and look terrific. A little self-love and self-adornment can free you to pursue the truly cardinal virtues, and there is nothing wrong with attracting a decent selection of males. Consider the butterfly, the pheasant. Of course, without big bucks, nobody can look very snappy less'n they makes they own." She wiffed a green, blue, and gold fabric off what looked like the original Singer. "I found this on Canal Street. Antique brocade. Soon to be short-shorts and jacket. Set off frenzies of envy for eight simoleons." She dropped it and attached Rathbone's collar. "I'm hoping the mustache will prevent the usual to-do about whether I'm old enough to buy cigs. So, what do you want to make first?"

I'd lost the thread in my stupefaction that the twenty minute make-over into Ali Baba was to avoid showing ID.

"Threads, darling. We'll make something gorgeous and unique to match you."

"Gee, Elspeth." Her name *was* hard to say, especially for a lisp-crip. "My sewing teacher gave me a seam-ripper. We made these Jackie Kennedy sacks? and I sewed up the armholes." I didn't want her to promise me anything. I didn't want her to think burden was still my name, and I didn't want her to disappoint me. "Is he hard to handle?"

"Here, practice. He's got to let strangers handle him if he's to show well. What about a cloak? No sleeves! Like Jane Eyre on the moors. Midnight blue velvet. We can look for the goods next week."

"I'm not—you know—what you said—with Paul." It came out like I'd been holding my breath all this time and astonished me as if I'd called out in a dream and waked myself. "I'm too chicken." Tears burned. I squinched them back, dipping to rough Rathbone's neck. "He's trying to help me be braver, more independent." I looked into her dry bemusement. "Girls *should* be more independent." I was pleading.

"Sure. Makes it easy for him." She opened the door while I straightened and wiped my face. "If he wants you independent, he should leave you alone. Otherwise, he deals with you." She pointed the key at me as Rathbone hacked into the hallway. "As is." She turned it in the lock. "Now, tell me exactly where you live."

The truck's lights wash over the windows. Slam. Thumping. Slam. Commotion on the porch. Why do I always touch down in a fog bank with no landing gear and number one in flames? Fawne! She tears in, barefoot, barelegged, mudspattered, clutched in a filthy green army coat, so she smears across my visual plane like pond scum. Only after another slam do I register, "Have to use your bathroom."

What *is* the matter with her own?

Ariel crosses the threshold and whangs the front door shut. She poses for a moment—the irritation of the Little

Rascals' babysitter—then follows Fawne as if she's taking her first steps after ten years of paralysis. She bangs on the bathroom door, repeating Fawne's name. I join her, barbed with questions. Her hair fumes as though lit. She slopes against the wall and seems to coagulate. What time is it? Ten-thirty. Of course, she's up before six, frying that hair. She ought to cut it off.

We can hear Fawne vomiting. I'm reminded of Nancy, who will scratch to be let in, vomit on my one nice rug, then scratch to get out. At least she's not using the sink. With her head in the toilet, the green hump of her looks like a giant frog. I know I've seen a movie where the dread family secret is a thirty-year-old giant frog twin brother. Obviously, I'm having trouble focusing on the crisis at hand. I bend over and hold her clammy neck. Noises like dredging. I wish I didn't smell alcohol. I wish I didn't smell anything. Ariel is fixed on the mirror, combing her fingers through her limp raffia with a file of expressions from anguished solicitude to lipbiting spleen. I should be asking her to walk a straight line, but I told you about her father; she's ingrained Iroquois. I suppose I could ask her to touch the tip of her nose. But I don't want to touch off the barrage of her defenses, especially when, compared to poor sick Fawne, she seems like some hard-pressed battlefield angel.

At last Fawne lifts her head, gasping, snot stringing from her nose, croaks, "Fauve!" and drops against my chest. This means laundry. Fauve! Geez. I wish she weren't so taken with this affected moniker. I know it'll be backtracked to me someday, in print or in court. My purely vocational patting tenderizes. I kiss her damp forehead. "Does one of you want to tell me what's going on?" I look to Molly Pitcher, fading fast.

Her lids flow up slowly like coats of varnish. "Well, see, after what happened at dinner and all, I was feeling pretty bummed and pissed off, so I thought I'd go over to dad's for awhile, but it was Elly's night out, and he had to cook for the kid, and he was— Well, you know. He can't really be expected to do two things at once, and besides, I just drop in on him like—"

So sweet and understanding. "Cut to the chase." At this rate, we'd learn the lowdown on Fawne sometime after we're asleep, like waiting for the weather when the game runs over.

"Hey, I'm getting there!"

"You sound like you're playing for time. When did you and Fawne start—"

"What's the rush?" Her eyes tighten like slipknots. "You got Eric cooling around here somewhere?"

"Look—"

"It's all my fault, Cee." Fawne rolls up eyes as sincere and vacant as the dustbowl. "Ariel really bailed me out." Vindicated, Ariel leans on the sink, so tall in the saddle I want to whack her mount with the toilet brush. I'll leave Fawne's hawking, snivelling, heaving delivery to you. "See, my mom—I know he put her up to this—she went through my desk."

They go through her desk. Our eyes narrow on each other like tubes fitting together to pump our common out-rage. I hope Ariel appreciates how much worse things could be. She's mapping the mildew.

"I know—it's a trip—and I mean, I went *off* something bad. But she found these poems I wrote, and she read them, and she showed them to *him*, and they take everything so literally, you know, and they *were* pretty explicit, so then we had to 'talk about it.'" She uses the orotund tones of Nixon when she quotes them. "But first, since I'm 'out of control'—I mean I was mad! who wouldn't be?—she made me take this tranquilizer. The shrink she hired in case she ever wants me certified says I gotta take them four times a day, but I don't." Defiant chin, real ride-into-the-stampede stuff.

"Well, good for you." I bring my cheek to her temple. Her little paws clip my shoulders. Doctors! Passionate? Medicate! Christ, it's all just one big rehab hospital. Take the key and lock her up, so we can confer in Aruba.

Not to mention the parents.

"And, get this, Forrest isn't supposed to know because he's down on pill-pushers. Well, so then we all had to go in the living room and 'discuss it.' I think it's about my privacy, you know, but my mom just wants to rag on my dad, like how he's so irresponsible and an alcoholic, which is such a crock, they just can't stand that he gets some fun out of life, that he *has* a life. *You'd* love him. He's—"

"Yes, yes, but—"

"Anyway, I say fine, you know, send me back. Which gets Forrest going, about how his parents were alcoholics, and he's an alcoholic, and if he wasn't 'honest' about it and didn't go to meetings and all this, 'he'd be dead right now'— and like *I'M NEXT!*" The imperiled Pauline. "And I'm going, like, what's this got to do with me? The Thought Police are bugging my lunchbox, and he's— So he pulls out my poems and starts reading them. Man, it was so embarrassing. He doesn't understand any of it, he can barely read, and the way he talks! Festus! So finally they've 'shared' all their shit, excuse me, they send me to bed, but I can't sleep, so—and this is where you're gonna get kinda annoyed with me—" her eyes actually widen, "I had this bottle of Thunderbird? I just wanted to try it, you know, but then I got the whirlies real bad, I was sweating— It was the pits. So I climbed out the window and crawled to the Hop In and called around until I found Ariel. And she picked me up and drove me here." She smiles weakly, hopefully. "You don't think I could die, do you?"

There's silence while I summon the furies, fear on my right hand, loathing on my left. The whole thing seems like

Dumbo's drunk. One viewing of "Pink Elephants on Parade" ought to cure her. Maybe we do need a VCR.

"Pretty fucking-A stupid, Fawne, start to finish," says Ariel. Buttressed by the sink, with her arms tied over her chest and head cocked, she's the spit of her father, lowering the boom on some deadbeat client trying not only to walk the charge but, more importantly, Karl's fee. Right as always, I think. Always first on the moral highground, these scouts. No ambivalence, no baggage. They live above the treeline, and they travel light. I should make her troop leader. Award her the keys to the sty and Ze Lemon. "And now you've landed *me* in deep shit," Ariel accuses. "Thanks a lot."

There's nothing I can add except it's time to take Fawne home, and I'll deal with Ariel later. "English test," I remind her. She screws up her schnoz like a rat's.

Of course Fawne doesn't come quietly. I've got her strapped in the front seat, and Ze Lemon is showing who's boss before I can get through the waterworks and the hare-brained cons she wants me to help her run. "Look, Fawne—"

"Fauve!" She stamps. "Fauve! Fauve! F—"

"Fauve. Look, you know you took a tranquilizer. You've been warned about drinking. What do you do? You down a bottle of cheap wine. You have no way to predict what it will do to you. To avoid the inevitable confrontation, you go out the window almost naked in the middle of the night—that's Russian roulette. What are you trying to accomplish?"

She sobs. The engine is flooded. I shut it off. I listen to distant traffic on the interstate. I wish I were driving on the Bonneville saltflats. No—running. At noon. It begins to rain.

"Anyway, who cares?"

"You do!" I almost pound her with the zest of a Rotarian for giving me an opening. "Never mind that your parents, whatever their hangups, are telling you in every possible way, loud and clear, that they care. You only get one life.

This is it. You trash yourself, you never get to find out what happens next. You never get to the good part. The part where you get what you want. What *do* you want?"

She turns up eyes like clearies. "I don't know." Then she screams, "Everything!" Then she hardens. "What have you got?"

I sink the key, squeeze Ze Lemon. Juice. "Plenty."

4 Easy Out

I nto the spotlight. Fawne looks like a refugee from the *Circus of Horrors*. What do I look like? Whoever cleans up after the elephants. We're standing on a 1970s front porch tricked out like a Mississippi steamboat; it's got one of those painted statuettes of a black boy holding what? a bullwhip? Christ, a noose? I can't bear to look. I wish I'd let Fawne climb back in her window. The door opens on a tall, rumpled, puffy man in pajamas and bathrobe. Two hairy yipping pekes yoyo at either hand. With the sound of a ball bouncing, a woman, pulling on a long, navy blue bathrobe, steps into the doorframe, puckered, but her hair is great—frosted, sculpted. I've always wondered about people who have their bathrobes at the ready. I feel like Emma Goldman doing a guest shot on "Ozzie and Harriet."

"I'm Ariel's mother, Carrie Krasnow?" I venture, hand extended, rather bravely, I think, since they're both grimly launching their investigation, albeit in measured tones, at the same time. Added to the dogs' hysteria, it sounds like immigration at the final frontier. Nobody shakes with me. I plunge on, making a gesture out of it, conveying only jitters or fresh off the boat. "Fawne drank some wine, and it made her sick, and she called Ariel, and Ariel brought her to our house." Keep it simple. I should have written a note, pinned it to her, knocked, and scrammed. The left dog boldly advances to champ the hem of Fawne's coat like Toto unveiling the humbug wizard. They can see she's starkers under it.

She's glooming at the doormat (whimsical geese, "Welcome Friends"), a flagellant in *The Seventh Seal*.

Clearly, I'm at the movies. *All* the movies.

"You get into the house this minute, girl." The mother seizes Fawne by the shoulders and abruptly jerks her to face me. "Thanks for bringing me home." She rattles her. "Say it!" *Attack of the Puppet People!* Fawne's face is china. The mother swivels her around and marches her in. I'm left with the dad, roughly rubbing his eyes.

"They do their drinking at your place or were they driving?" He's not accusing, just bone tired.

"Fawne said she had a bottle of Thunderbird in her room. I don't know how much she drank." Do I mention the tranquilizer? Friend or foe? Let me out of here. "She was pretty sick, vomiting, you know, but nothing worse. It's amazing how fast they recover at that—"

"Well, there's your first lie. We have got ourselves one heck of a problem here, Mizz— Why don't you come on in?"

"Oh, look, it's awfully late, and—"

"I know it." He ladles on the significance.

Run!

Cloying scent of dried roses. The walls are white, the decor, sky blue and gold. It's the lap of Holy Mary, Star of the Sea. I want to put up two fingers and gaze heavenward. Maybe I do. Cee of the Sick. An Audubon print of a pair of wild ducks hangs behind the couch. Sitting, I make three. The dogs circle my feet, spiral into cushions on the carpet, sigh wetly, and snooze. I can't begin to fathom the silence upstairs.

The stepfather tilts back in a blue recliner so I'm looking at the thick yellow calluses on his feet. He seems to be trying to rub out his eyes with his fists. "How much do you know?"

Loaded question. I offer palms up. "Your daughter wants to be Marilyn Monroe. She's infatuated with the glamor of suffering and death. Fairly frequent teen phenomenon. I was a little like that myself. She needs an outlet. Maybe her poetry?" Just to see what he says.

"Well, that's simple enough." Not a ripple of remorse. "You know a lot about psychology, don't you?" His smile pities me. "You a nurse?"

Or a teacher or a housewife, I always forget which. "I fix up old houses."

"Z'at a fact?" Skeptical. He peers at my hands. He must think it's my second lie. (What did he mean by that?) "And what about your own daughter?"

"What about her?" I bridle. There's a pendular movement to his approach, and I'm tied prone, starting to flinch in rhythm.

"She's the one told Fawne she could get high burnin' money—"

I have to rewind and play that back. "She what?"

"I can see you don't know a blessed thing." Lighting a cigarette and sinking into folksy shtick. "Sometime after supper, we smelled somethin' funny, so Lacey went to check on Fawne, and she had this Dr. Pepper bottle up to her nose? and she was sniffin' the smoke off some burnin' dollar bills, and when we got through all the ruckus, she told us your daughter said it would get her high."

"That's impossible." I exhale into a laugh. Miss Penny Pinch? I often suspect her of padding her expenses, I don't know where a dime of her part-time salary goes (but she eats out a lot, and gas, and you know what movies cost), she's pulled some fast ones on her brother, and she's been that way since she was five and tried selling him the Necco

Wafers and raisins out of her Halloween haul, but if there's one thing I'm sure of, she's not burning it. So how do I call this guy off without convincing him Fawne is either a liar or delusional and unleashing the forces of shrinkery, the almighty therapeutic, and possibly getting her put away for good? How did I get in so deep so fast? Let's play the joker: the Two Little Idiots. "Honestly, Mr.—"

"Taylor. But call me Forrest—" He's got big yellow teeth. They look a lot like his toes.

"I don't think Ariel has the imagination for a stunt like that. Could Fawne have been burning some of her poems?" This just comes out of my mouth, but instantly I believe it. "What she told us was—"

"Mizz— What was that name again?"

"Carrie, please."

"No, your last name. What kind of name is that? Jewish?"

He says "gee-you-ish." I hear those wheezing Gestapo sirens. "What kind of question is that?"

"It's unusual is all. Don't need to get—"

"Krasnow. Polish. My ex's." Name, rank, serial number. Waiting for my chance to go over the wall.

"—riled. No wonder you can't believe she'd burn money." He yuks. "Hey, I'm joking. You all have such chips on your shoulders."

As opposed to between our ears. I'm thinking cow. Buffalo! "Carrie, please."

"Well, Carrie, I don't know what Fawne told you about what went on over here tonight, but the book on her is if she's talkin', she's lyin'. I can say for a fact that she didn't have no bottle of Thunderbird up in her room when Lacey searched it after supper. Which means she got hold of it after she hitched up with your daughter. Hold on a minute." He bangs the recliner down. I can see the skimpy floor structure from the resonance. In a few seconds he's handing me a dirty, pleated piece of notebook paper, emanating a kind of pep, as though we're going into business together. He returns to the recliner and rumps it back. "I found that in Fawne's purse."

He goes through her purse. Each detail drubs me, like I'm being reeducated by the Cultural Revolution. It's definitely Ariel's angular scritch.

> Hey Girl!
> S'up? I'm in english dieing for a smoke. About Friday— I'm spending the nite at Jennifer T.s while her fokes are A WAY. David L. and Mikel with the HOT BOD is coming over and maybe we'll get toasted and then WHO KNOWS? I'm so stoked! Tell the a-hs something and drop over if you want to but BYOB for BOY. Gotta go. Later—

I can only stand to read it once, but I sit staring at it as though it's damning results from the lab. Not so much the content—deceit, intoxicants, sex: the pillars of the age— but that "is." That "is" is a life sentence. I see the slippery switch who sat across the kitchen table from me the night we moved into the sty, and I finally realized where all this frantic running had left me: on empty. She looked at me, her lips ruched in a rueful smile under her angry knuckles, and she said, "Are we there yet?"

And I have never felt closer to, nor more in love with, anyone. Was she really that good, or do I flatter myself? Who failed who? And how? And when? Each breath balloons my heart thin to bursting. My sweater, my body, trap me like a steam cabinet.

And the only way out is past dad. He squints through his smoke, patiently drawing a bead on me from his blind.

Oddly, Ariel pulls me through. Once Karl said something was a paradox, and Ariel, four or five at the time, asked, "What is that? Like two ducks?" From then on, Karl and I saw those two ducks flying over us at every impasse.

We'd stop fighting and watch them flap slowly out of sight. We pointed them out to the judge. I glance over my shoulder. Now I'm nesting with them. I only pine for Karl's particular witness. Why isn't he here? (My fault.)

"Of course I have to hear Ariel's side of it." I start to get up.

"But you got the evidence right there in front of you." He lunges forward to whap the note, and I fall back. "Where do you think she picks up that language?"

I want to say her teachers. "What do you mean? The kids—"

"Not all the kids," he smiles. The smile is the upper hand. "She didn't learn that in her church youth group. It's the blacks, the drug dealers, the—"

"Oh now wait a minute. Of course she has black friends—"

"Oh of course!" He bats his lashes like a Hasty Pudding queen. "Let's be realistic. If she hangs out with them, she's—"

I hate to be presumed innocent because I'm female, and I hate when decency is despised as innocent. "Ariel is an athlete. She works at a stable three times a week, training horses. She would never—" Except for the little matter of the cigarettes, which is pure spite, and I'm certainly not explaining it to this bigot.

"The facts speak for themselves." He lofts his cigarette.

"Not to me." Ariel looks at photos of her parents in paisley with pinwheel pupils like the twin looks at the frog. "You don't know my daughter."

"No, you don't know your daughter." He's burning up what oxygen hasn't been absorbed by those musty roses. There aren't any green plants. Drapes smother the windows. "You're divorced, aren't you?"

"What's that got—"

"Discipline, Carrie!" He's been to management training seminars. "I understand why you're so defensive, believe me. I've seen it a thousand times. But denial never works. You got to face it squarely. I know from experience. My parents were alcoholics, and so am I, and I've had to learn the hard way. I've paid more dues than the members of the most exclusive country club, I can tell you."

I almost want to agree with him, but then I see Ariel's euphoric posthorse energy, I hear her straightarrow some bullshit to the marrow, and it bumps my return: uh uh.

"—and I know how hard it is for a single parent. I saw it with Lacey. You got your job, the housework, and when your kid throws you a curve, you just can't cope." He contorts to jab his cigarette out in one of the twenty cute ceramic receptacles littering a table so shiny the wood looks like glass. "But you have to!" His vehemence clouts me. "Your child needs a strong hand. Control. What do you know about tough love, Carrie?"

He's using my name like a crowbar to jimmy me open. I'm pissed at the suggestion, from a man sprawled out in Ozzie Nelson's pajamas with his fly separating, that a man is the solution to my problems. The ridiculous thing is I wish Karl were here to tell him. "Yeah, man," Karl is up, bearish, pacing, examining their knickknacks with radical disdain, "Cee can handle it. I'm *no* help. Sound and fury, signifying bupkis. *She's* the fixer. And Ariel, well hell! She's fine!" "Yeah," I say, "I've heard of that, on radio call-in shows." I've even slacked into Karl's mocking posture. "That's when you can't be bothered and cut the kid loose. Sounds dead *easy* to me."

Reproving, "It's a lot more than—"

"Yeah, well, maybe, but—"

"Will you let me finish?"

"Why?"

He's not used to backtalk but prides himself on keeping his temper. Humpty Dumpty! He has to light up. Studies the smoke. "Let me share some—"

"Look, I'm tired. And I'm not the one with the problem. The one with the problem is Fawne." Saying this is like coming to. Where have I been? Somewhere noisy and hot.

He starts again as if I hadn't so rudely interrupted. "Let me share some background with you." Board meeting. Where's the overhead, transparencies? "Lacey and I got married and moved here for business reasons about six months ago. Up till then, whatever issues Fawne had at home, she didn't take them to school. She was in all honors classes, As and Bs, excellent SAT scores, model behavior, nice friends. Soon after meeting your daughter—"

I have no evidence of my daughter's qualities. That at one she stacked cereal boxes and cried, "I make an acrobat!" That in preschool she depicted the life of Prometheus in crayon. That she has a way with animals. That within one minute she can tell who's screwing whom in any situation and backs the screwee to the hilt. That she does justice and loves mercy and walks humbly—well, with everybody but me. No honors, no As. "Yeah, yeah, but you're forgetting the move, leaving her friends, her father—"

He lowers his eyes and takes a long drag. "Fawne's father gave Lacey complete custody, no contest. He wasn't cut out for fatherhood. A child just doesn't fit in with his lifestyle."

I see the slick bastard weaseling out of his child support in an impeccable suit. I don't know whether Forrest's reticence is a stepfather's tact or male bonding or if he won't betray a fellow alcoholic, but I respect it.

"Soon after meeting your daughter, however, her grades began to slip, she was suspended for—"

"I heard about that. But nothing is happening to Ariel—"

"That you know of—"

"Come on, I see her every day. I sign her report cards." At least they're not getting any worse. "Don't you think this could be Fawne's way of—"

"—she says she just wants to be high all the time, she hates us, she doesn't care about nothin'— You've seen what she looks like—" Real aversion. How does he look at Fawne? "She talks about killin' herself—" His voice catches.

"Couldn't it be drama? I'm not trying to play it down, but I remember my own youth, I remember Ariel right after the divorce. She's lonely and hurt and resentful and—"

"You people and your psychobabble." He drags his hands down his face. "Where does it get you? You don't know what it's like."

"Maybe not." His obvious misery stirs me from freezing over. "But life with any teen is hard. Look, I like Fawne, and I'd like to help. I'll get to the bottom of whatever's going on with Ari, and—"

"There was no bottle in this house, and Ariel was the one told her—"

"According to Fawne." I don't trust myself to bring up the tranquilizer or their reading her poems. "I've never seen the behavior you describe. Ariel and I have a deal. If she needs me to pick her up, I do it, no questions asked. She's never called. There's never been the need."

"Yet. That you know of. Maybe we should keep them from seeing each other—"

"That would be the worst possible thing to do." Fortunately, I don't say "dumbest." I can't believe he hasn't heard the news about forbidden fruit. "Fawne needs her friends right now; she should be going out more, having fun. I think she's very unhappy, and I can't see *punishing* her for it—"

"What's your idea?" He's challenging, but he also wants to know.

"I want to find out what she's interested in, what she wants to do, and help her do it. I only met her this afternoon, but she was talking art and music and—"

"This afternoon? When?" From above, in the calm timbre of an airport page, "Forrest, honey, do you know what time it is?"

Where was she ages ago?

"Well, Carrie—" He clunks forward and sprads from the chair. My overalls are pasted to the backs of my knees with sweat so I can hardly stand. "I think you better look to your daughter, cause where there's smoke—" He aims an escorting hand at me, and I slip by it. "I know one thing." He finally lands it on my arm as I'm headed out. The hot chocolate pours down from his eyes. "We can't do it alone."

What is he? A marriage broker? I must frown my perplexity.

"We can't do it without Jesus."

Uh oh!

With all Forrest's hints and accusations, what nags at me, waiting at a stoplight for Ze Lemon to spurt, is when. If Fawne was calling around for Ariel, why didn't the phone ring? And if she called earlier, while I was at the hospital, where were they, and why was she still so sick?

I have to wait to confront Ariel the next evening. She's up at dawn at the mirror, prepping, and leaves without a word. Breakfast belongs to Dash. Usually I'm gone before he hits the table, so when he sees me sitting there with my glass of orange juice and my mask of iron he can guess what's coming. It's hard to be original in this line.

"It's *them*!" He's immediately screaming, like I'm driving him to the wall with my magnum. "What am I supposed to do if some loser scrub punches me in the stomach?"

"I'm sure you didn't do anything to provoke him—"

"I swear—"

"—never even opened your mouth, right?" Now all I have to do is guess exactly what he said, and I win the Buick. "Ms. Williams tells me you're *trying* to get into trouble—"

"That's bull—"

"Then why would she say it?"

"You don't understand."

"I'm trying. Sit down."

"Why don't you get on Ariel's case like this? Look what she did last night. Do you say one word to her? Do you ground her? Oh no! Not your precious Ariel. She's the good child and—"

"She gets hers tonight. Sit."

He goes to the refrigerator. "You don't want me to face the day on an empty stomach?"

"In light of your recent difficulties, sounds like a good idea."

He takes out the milk and puts it on the table, finds cereal, bowl, spoon. The cats besiege him for their cut, and for the first time in recorded history, he simply gives it to them. All this with the clatter and fuss of breakfast on the ark.

"Listen, Dash, I am nine months pregnant with an alien who eats boys like you. Talk to me. What is going on?"

He swags me a smile, tossing the can opener in the sink, and finally consents to the chair. "Aw, Ma, I'm sorry, really—" And how should I take the suddenly humid eyes? "—but you don't know what it's like. They're all so stupid!" His fingers clutch the air.

"—and you have to tell them—"

"I know I sound—"

"And you're so smart? You're the one about to be suspended—"

"What am I supposed to do? Like every day, every day, there's this kid in my gym class, and he kicks me in the exact same spot, hard, and he tries to take my wallet off me, like just take it, like I'm nothing—"

Who would want to be a boy? (Quick! Call Freud!) "Can't you tell somebody?"

"Mr. Allred? Allred is his neck. He chews, mom. While

72

you're talking to him he's got this wad in his cheek, and if you're outside, you know? he spits."

You pack and I'll gas up the car. But then I remember the vice-principal in charge of delinquent boys at my high school. Mr. Goodman. His trademark was leaving none. Nowhere to hide.

"What about Ms. Williams?"

"She's black—"

"So what?"

"You gotta understand, this kid is black." Dash leans on his elbow, claps his hand over his mouth, and stares down at the empty cereal bowl. "I don't want them all over me."

"Them?" The orange juice turns to bile and bolts up my gorge.

"And Allred? Well, trust me, I've seen his work. It's better I take care of it myself." He's hiding some urgent, some essential depravity or nobility, and whichever it is, or is it both? (he doesn't know, I don't know), he's ashamed of it. His ears are on fire.

"Them?" We need to settle this. My heart is racing.

"You don't know what it's like." He won't look at me. A tear rolls over his hand.

My lips are numb. "Them?"

He commits to the leap. "You don't know how much they hate us."

I let him fall a ways before I say, "I can imagine. They have cause." I want him to know he hasn't landed. "How much do you hate them?"

He colors. "Wouldn't you hate to get beat up every day? And cursed at and laughed at and— Ignorant, mean, and loud. 'Gimme gimme. You owe me.' You don't know. You live in another world. I gotta take care of myself." He shakes some flakes in his bowl. "How come you took karate?" He fills his mouth the way a plasterer fills a crack.

The question waylays me. Elspeth—and it was beautiful—and it felt good—and I wanted to do as I pleased. I do live in another world. Now I'm ashamed. "Not to beat up on people." Then it occurs to me: "You know, guys with attitudes, experiences like yours, black and white, used to start lessons hoping to get back at people who'd hurt them. There'd be all this tension when they had to freefight with somebody of the other race." Not to mention with me, sole representative of the female persuasion. "But after a while, all they cared about was the move. 'How'd my backkick look?' 'Did I surprise you with that flying roundhouse?' Then we'd all go out for ice cream together." This is oversimplified. I would occasionally hear hateful remarks meant to pass as humor, and of course the guys acted circumspect around me, and the whole thing was very self-conscious. But the ice cream is true. And it was something. "It was neat."

"Neat," he mocks me. "Groovy, even, I bet. Swell. You think I could take lessons? Ariel gets horse—"

Where is he coming from? He's prodding his lower lip down with his spoon, and his eyes are fishbowls, a guppy in each. "Not if you think fighting is any kind of answer." But it could be. The way of the empty hand. Maybe it will teach him what he needs to know in spite of what he thinks. It'll do for now. "You're gonna have to show me something. First you talk to Ms. Williams."

The guppies up and blup.

"I mean it, Dash. Today. I see her Monday, and I will ask. You're in for a real education. And talk to your father. Get through tomorrow and next week clean. Saturday, we'll start looking for a dojo."

Can it be this simple, this mechanical? Saturday we have to visit my father. And how the hell will I come up with the money?

Dinner is over and I'm sitting on Ariel's bed, waiting for

her to do a math problem and give me her undivided attention. Her room is the partially finished attic, up a ladder that swings down from Dash's ceiling and is an occasion for violent territorial clashes. The lath walls are hidden by posters of lumpen male rock stars in sadodrag—one of them has his finger completely wedged up his nose—and glossy thoroughbreds, some with foals, romping through fields of buttercups. Every stuffed animal she was ever given lines the perimeter like a totemic firing squad. Her clothes hang like dressing room rejects on a rack beside a big mirror, both acquired when we converted the first floor of a downtown department store into a barbecue joint. Her desk lamp illuminates the fine powdery texture of her cheek, the curve of her neck, her split ends.

I got home late from work—nothing dries in this damp—and we kept to neutral topics at dinner—Is there any hope the U.S. will avoid military intervention in Kuwait? What should be done about hazardous waste disposal? What if drugs were legal but guns were not?—so I only know from a brief exchange over the dishes that Dash survived the day without fighting, and Ms. Williams says that any time he feels like he's going to explode, he can sit in her office. She's pretty cool. She thinks the karate is a great idea. I am feeling *veni, vidi, vici*. The Bruce Lee of adolescent crisis. Bring on midlife!

Ariel bounces down her eraser and rotates, drawing up her legs and hugging her knees. "I guess this is about last night—" Her voice sounds like what happens when you forget to add liquid to your stew.

"Fawne's father—"

"Stepfather—"

"Stepfather, okay, he had a different version. He's positive there was no bottle of Thunderbird in the house. He says Fawne was sniffing a soda bottle filled with burning dollar bills because you told her she could get high—" I slice her a look that scythes her open at the mouth.

"Total lie! Did she tell him that? Burn money to get high? Hey, Mom, I may not be as smart as you, but I'm not stupid. The girl is psycho. Or it's him. She could put anything over on that turkey. Hide a bottle? No sweat. He couldn't look every single place, and if she put her mind to it—"

"She couldn't hide her poems—"

"Maybe she didn't want to. She *likes* the attention. I don't know. You don't believe it?" She exposes her eyes on me. I can hear the timer ticking as they focus and darken.

I pull the note out of my bib pocket and pass it to her. I track its shadow over her face as she reads.

"Where'd you get this?" Her eyes hit bottom. "You searchin' my stuff now?" She's scrambling for a purchase. Shaky ground.

"No. Should I? Right now I don't think that's the point—"

There's a long pause during which I imagine her testing her excuses, flashing them like some ghastly forensics slide show to see how they play. What I could never have imagined is the face she raises, tense with leery humor. "So what is the point?" She looks five thousand years old. Past it.

I'm blown away—both blasted and lightened at the same time, like the bomb blew me into next week, when the war is over, and the mopping up is on. "I mean, how do you explain that? How do you feel about it?"

"I don't feel anything at all." Dead eyes, both barrels. Raising her eyebrows is a tremendous effort.

I'm chilled to the bone.

"Next time you want me to tell you I'm goin' over to Jennifer's to drink beer and screw? You don't."

I don't.

"You know I'm checked out on birth control and AIDS—"

Jesus! "Are you? Is anybody?"

"Mom, it's like now a word from our sponsor. You, dad, Elly, the school, it's like we're nothing but open legs and open mouths. Before I go out I pat myself down for keys, matches, quarters, Tampax, condoms. I don't do drugs because it's stupid and gross," gimlet glance, "and I don't drive drunk, I don't *get* drunk, I just have a taste now and then so I don't have to hear what a goody-goody I am." She lifts the note like a surley waiter lifts the check. "You can believe what you want. I was just making it sound, you know, for Fawne, because she's always raggin' on me about how lame and boring I am. You know what happened that night? We rented some videos, ordered a pizza, and necked. This Michael? A jerk." She picks at the worn denim over her knees. "He had nothing I wanted." She rests her cheek, and her eyes sadly come to rest on me. "None of them do."

"Just don't ever let them do anything you don't like—" The plane is taking off, and I'm running alongside it with a sandwich and a Thermos.

"Oh, I liked it," she shrugs. "It's when his tongue was in his own mouth he got kinda tiresome." Small, hard, clever eyes. Flints. The same damn eyes that watched my clumsy diapering. Look who I had to get born to— "You know what I'm sayin'. You've been there."

Sure. But it took me years on the chin. I admit, "I do." We sit in this cold bright moment, breathing and glowing, like coals. "But this is not something I could easily convey to Fawne's stepfather," I observe.

"For-rest!" Ariel's head dangles back, and she laughs. "I once saw him—" She snuffles. "He was going fishing?" Snort. "And wearing this hat?" She can't go on. Thirsty glugs of laughter. Infectious. "It had these like feathers?" she plucks at her head, "and an elastic band under the chin?" I see him— Baby Huey! I'm gone. "He looked like this great big stupid baby—" I'm on my back with my chest bonging. She's doubled up in the chair. Our faces liquefy. Finally, she sobers enough to say, "No, I can see that," and we're off again.

We recover slowly.

"Well!" I shift onto my side. "But Fawne! What are we going to do about Fawne?"

"Why do we have to do anything?" Her fingers harrow her hair. "After what she's done to me—"

"Ari—who's she got but us?"

She tugs her bangs straight up as though she's got a razor in the other hand.

"She reminds me of me at that age," I press on.

"Figures." She clenches her legs as if she has to fit inside a safe, handcuffed. "But she's no good for me. She's gonna land me in deep shit—"

"If you habitually speak like that, people will—"

"Aw, not now, okay? Look, I don't want to have any more to do with her. She's too stupid to live. I just don't need this."

"But she could be in serious trouble. I think I have some idea what she's going through—"

"*She's* in serious trouble?"

"Well, all this talk about suicide. I mean, not everybody who talks about it does it, but everybody who does it talks about it." I have to walk back through that to make sure it came out right.

"She's just showing off—"

"But it could get her killed or thrown in the booby-hatch. I mean, we have our problems, but nothing like that. We're okay. I just think we should be there for her. She's got to get out of herself, see that smart, hip people can live normal, happy lives. Now how? We need a plan. Is she interested in riding? Ooh, can she drive? You could teach her to drive!"

"She was in two wrecks in D.C. Rolled a VW. She says."

"Well, what was all that about art? You think she'd like me to—"

"I don't believe you." Her eyes are volcanic.

"Maybe we could—"

"You know? You know?" She appeals to some audience concealed by the boiling reflection of the desk lamp. "You are so stupid. So blind!" Her hands thrust at the mirror. "You think you're so smart, you think you know more than anybody, but everything you know just gets in the way of you seeing what is so plain to everybody else." Her hands cup over her eyes as though she is enduring some antiquated medical treatment. The seconds weigh in. "Well all right." She looks up into the mirror and seems to find something small and beautiful that bites. "We'll play it your way. Help Fawne. *Fawne.*" She has to sink deep to retrieve her. "We'll save Fawne. From whatever."

"Ariel." I want to smile, but I'm not sure I do. I'm suddenly very tired. "Seriously, I know this is the right—"

"Seriously?" She rocks forward to plant both feet on the floor, and her arms wind around her midriff. She looks like a diver, shivering at the edge of the pool, listening to coach explain what she did wrong on her inward three-and-a-half tuck before she has to try it again. "Seriously," she says. She chuffs the same laugh of disbelief that used to charm me in her father until it began to make me feel freak.

"Trust me." I stand up, exhale. My ribcage aches. The laughing?

"You want this?" Ariel holds the note by a corner like a dead mouse or something we might want to frame.

I realize that if I read it again I may notice details that still don't make sense. That it will eat at me. I realize I forgot to grill her about the timing, but my timing was off, the time is gone. She could say something like, "I drove her around for awhile. I didn't know what else to do." It's easy to predict. If she says anything I predict, I'll suck on it like a coldsore. I'd rather leave it like this. Working together to rescue Fawne will bring us closer and more in tune than any "truth" I can extort from her with this sordid note. I shake my head. She moves it over the trash can, lets it drop. It falls like a parachute, a handkerchief. She watches it like a message in a bottle putting out to sea. She shows me that ironic squint. Right pair a ducks.

How wrong can I be?

5 Fixing a Hole

So why am I uniquely qualified, you're asking, for the repair and rehabilitation of suicidal high school maidens?

Let's get this over with.

Friday night Rice-a-Roni Festival at Alan's. Zatz had me draw flyers we distributed to all comers in the street. In solidarity with the people of Southeast Asia and Tantric Buddhists and dharma bums everywhere, the guys learned how to make vats of various flavors of Rice-a-Roni, all tasting like the package, but they forgot it would have to be eaten off plates with utensils. Maybe not. Zatz threw a fistful against the wall to see if it was al dente, and didn't he play third base for the San Francisco Treats? ding ding, which set the tone for a sophisticated approach that found Alan frantically vacuuming at midnight before his parents came home. His father had bought headphones, our first, and Zatz settled me under them, in this chrome and black leather sling the old Sinatra sybarite got to go with them, to listen to "Revolver," just out. I felt like I was having my head done, Zatz the beauty operator, smiling, stabbing his fingers at the stunners. I'd had a couple of tugs at a joint from a nickel bag Billy procured in a Bay Ridge candy store. On the return trip, he was chased to the subway by what he

called philistines (and we knew were Italians), wielding bicycle chains and baseball bats, and he escaped unscathed
simply because he was carrying so much less. He mimed
this adventure for me to silent laughter. Because I could only
hear the music, I felt deaf, mute. I was a big pair of disem-
bodied eyes. I had my sketchbook, a black finepoint, gray
for shading, and tried to get everything down with insight
and spontaneity. Dan moved pretty things into eyeshot.
Francy applied glitter forget-me-nots to my cheekbone with
Elmer's Glue-All. Alan, drinking the 59-cents-a-gallon Gallo
chianti we could order delivered from the pizzeria, read me
a very long poem by Charles Olson.

Paul showed up later. I was dancing. He was in a sports
coat, button-down shirt, narrow knit tie. He moved through
the crowd shaking hands, backpatting, becking the cigarette, to slide his arm around my waist and spin me into
him with the smooth remove of a game show host. He was
no dancer. He pasted one on me, then roved to the corner
where Beverly Turteltaub had her skirt around her pupik
demonstrating Yoga positions, while her boyfriend, Jack
Lowry, who never said anything to me but "*The Grapes of
Wrath* is my favorite book" until he disappeared, stared at
the steel toes of his engineer's boots.

People were playing I Ching with pennies and scribbling
Mad Libs. Andy Pasternak proselytized for the Du Bois Club
by impugning the masculinity of Young Socialists. Michael
Raymond was using me to practice his grind. Periodically,
Paul would strum the air at me. I heard him say Proust; I
was reading Proust. "Picasso is a slob," he told La
Turteltaub. With his connections, he didn't like to spell it
out, but he could get everyone tickets *and* backstage. He
mentioned obscure makes of cars, pricy stores, his sister-in-
law; how a friend almost died snorting nutmeg on a ski
weekend at Killington: a laugh riot. Zatz cut off half his tie
and presented him with the tail. Then Vedro tuned his banjo,

Alan and Ruth their guitars, the spoons we couldn't have
for Rice-a-Roni were produced for percussion, and Dan,
Zatz, and Billy, what were they then? The Slithy Toves?
Creatures of Habit? it changed daily, broke into "Skin Flick
Kick," "Goin' to Tibet," and a ballad that asked the senti-
mental question, "Why Are All the Bad Guys White?"

Around ten-thirty, Paul appeared at my side—he had
this way of surfacing as though he swam under opaque
water—to ask if I'd like him to walk me home. I knew what
he had in mind. It was considered bad form to neck at these
parties because so many of us were unattached, not to say
unaffiliated. We'd find a bench outside the park or the bo-
tanical gardens where we could smell the bread baking at
the Bond Bread Factory and the spices from the adjacent
spice factory, and I'd crook my legs over his, and we'd kiss.
I loved kissing with Paul. He made me feel delicious. I also
hated to take the shuttle by myself at night; all those creeps
with three thumbs, and once a kid pulled a knife on me, but
luckily he was just crazy, and when the doors parted at
Franklin Street, I took off.

It was a beautiful night, warm, ultramarine, shot with
stars, a moon like a bone pick, transparent white, crisp.
Billy, Dan, and Zatz walked us part way, leaping parking
meters until Billy busted his balls. At Church Avenue they
split for Ocean Parkway.

> Well, I went to see my mother
> To ask her for a sign. She said,
> 'I'm gettin' ready,
> And I haven't got the time.

> Be-cause I'm goin' to Tibet,
> Goin' to Tibet, goin' to Tibet, my friend,
> Goin' to Tibet, goin' to Tibet,
> To find the better end.

Oh, I went to see my dentist—

It echoed between the hands of the buildings long after they were out of sight. Later that night, they were accosted by a couple of Puerto Ricans, who were flinging them into parked cars when the Baggie fell out of Billy's pocket. "Amigos!" they cried, and they all sat on the curb to forge the Youth Culture Pact on what was left from Billy's brush with the darker side of sports equipment.

Paul and I stopped at the Dutch Reformed Church across from the high school. Boys on the steps sang doo-wop, harmonized "Pretty Little Angel Eyes" to the teased Theresas and pomped Toms in purple shirts. Paul put on his greeting display, steering me like a classic pink Cadillac down some narrow slum alley where he'd grown up. We halted among what looked to me like the inmates of a holding cell. Then Paul excused himself to speak to someone who signaled him from the shadowy recesses of the record store. "Silhouettes." The fine, full voices poured like sugar, cream, and coffee. I closed my eyes.

"Whe'd ya get dose shoes?"

This girl was wrestler material, her arm slung over her boyfriend's neck as though she stood on a crate. I checked her shoes: meathooks. I had on tap shoes. She hoofed, Donald O'Connor style, boyfriend in the headlock like a third breast. A razor blade twined in her rat's nest caught the streetlight. "A Thousand Stars in the Sky."

"So wha aw you, a boy aw a goil?"

My hair was very short. Still, the secondary sex characteristics were a dead give-away. I was also wearing a skirt, eye make-up, six-inch earrings, Francy's forget-me-nots, and it could be of no material interest to this slime under any circumstances. Their hair fascinated my hands the way a chipped tooth lures your tongue. The guys' was like oiled tire tread; the girls', brittle domes of wire wool in which blades gleamed. "Book of Love." The hoofer pulled out her blouse, arched, and wabbled her shoulders to imitate prissy walking, the boyfriend stuck in the stocks.

"Wha happens we rip dem earrings outta you head?"

Run! Where? When Paul cinched me to him, and I slipped into his jacket like a clam into the shell and clung. He gave the boyfriend a light off his smoke, bending me forward into their warm, garlic-sweat-English Leather hunch, their chins glowing faintly green as they puffed. I looked quickly down from their click of eyes.

"So whe you been?"

"Fabulous party." Paul always scanned the horizon in conversation, like Balboa. "Wine, grass, you name it."

"Chicks?" Quasimodo chuckled and got rung by the Hulk.

"Snatch? Natch." Paul smiled inward and then looked up to gauge the appreciation. "Everybody was there. We got smashed."

Laughter. He said nothing about the Rice-a-Roni. I thought maybe he'd been to another party. "In the Still of the Night."

"Wha happent to you tie?"

Paul flipped up the ratty end. "We've got to be running. Got to get this little girl home before midnight."

Somebody cronked on "little." We were showing our backs when somebody said, "You shu she's a goil?"

Over his shoulder. "Positive." Did he wink?

Somehow in the course of the evening I'd changed from a pair of big eyes to a pair of big tits. I felt logy, like I was being squeezed out of a dropper. I hid my face in the smoky ribs of his corduroy.

He took me around the block and through the gate into the graveyard where I often ate lunch, while Billy was Cassius, Dan a grudging Brutus, and Zatz a natural Curly, and we wondered how Dan's mother let him get away with balloonbread-and-Hershey-Bar sandwiches. Paul spread his jacket under a tree in dense ivy, a little apart from the crumbling headstones, like decaying molars. "Earth Angel." "Where Are You, Little Star?" The leaves brushed and brattled in the soft respiration of the wind. Cars out on the street slished by with the alternating lights. Paul kissed me. His tongue darted, flitted, filled. He drew back for breath, and his eyes faltered as if I were as thrilling as a rollercoaster; his mouth fell, plucked, seized. His hand rolled gently from my belly to my breast, which strained as if my thumping heart wanted out. My eyelids fused. My mouth sought the pressure that both wrings and springs. My arms tensed, my hands stretched against his lean sides. His leg pressed into this clutching and caving; my legs shifted to ease him exactly where the pressure felt most, felt best, oh and then shit! the old squabble about unhooking the bra. I had this harness, hard to rehook, of course without any help afterwards, and I got stuck with it around my ears while my big awful breasts slopped like sandbags, as in "left holding the—" Then his elbow dug into my breastbone, and his hand clamped, crushing my voicebox, I was choking, I couldn't breathe, gagging, and his knee was a maul, splitting my thigh. It wasn't about the bra anymore. My eyes broke open. He was wrenching my skirt up and my underpants down and shoving this oversized rubber eraser into the wet and aching pocket of me, and he was rubbing me away. His face was insect. I flailed hands like paddles on wooden arms, I thrashed my pinned legs, but silently, silently, silently, because I didn't want to get into trouble, because I could never explain what I was doing in the graveyard with him, or how I liked it until one shaving of a second ago, because I'd never been really hurt before, and I kept thinking he would stop, he had to stop, I didn't want to prolong it, and because who would come to help me? not Dan, not Billy, not Zatz, and because oh because because because because I have had plenty of time to think about why I was silent since then. "Sincerely."

When he subsided, with an abrupt jerk of his hips and a stifled screech like disk brakes, he slumped on me, his thick bituminous curls greasing my chin, and he cried, soaking, blackening my shirt. I had sticky glop on my stomach. My thighs were cut on the bias by the twisted elastic of my panties. My skirt was impasted with mud and grass. I didn't know there was blood. How would I get past my mother? I fell running? For the train? Down the stairs? A puddle? How bruised was my throat? "For Your Precious Love." "Only You." "Will You Still Love Me Tomorrow?" Moldy oldies. Somebody should turn these guys on to the Stones. "Look at that Stupid Girl." "Off the Hook." "Heart of Stone." The headstones like an old man's grin.

We took the bus. While Paul professed his undying devotion, explaining how the lust I inspired overpowered him, but at the last moment he was able to shake off its grip enough to pull out so I wouldn't get pregnant—and you could watch him listening to himself and preening, pecking his feathers back into place like a sparrow after a bath or a meal, so that he even considered lighting up until he realized we were on the bus—I worked on a credible story. I made him loan me his jacket. The silly scissored stump of tie stuck out of his chest as though *his* heart had been ripped out by the root. I was in for midnight curfew. My mother was watching *Stella Dallas* with all the lights off and a tissue to her eyes. She didn't look up.

I never bothered to tell. I didn't want to hear what it sounded like or what anyone had to say. For a while, I didn't talk at all. It's interesting how long you can get away with making faces, smiles, motions, simply flashing response like a cursor. I continued to go out with Paul, to go down with Paul, so I wouldn't have to talk. Because it was easy.

And I was afraid I'd lose my connection to Elspeth. The

cloak project got as far as a shopping trip to Macy's. She wore a picture hat with enormous old silk flowers and veiling like chicken wire, so beautiful and serious that people felt impelled to race up and shout "Motherfucker!" at point blank range. We found a pattern, got a good deal on blue velvet, we bought notions, frogs!, but then she had to get a full-time job so she could hire a professional to handle Rathbone at the Westminster. She thought she was too short, that they looked like Sonny and Cher. She'd met a tall, skinny guy from the Heights with two hounds he drove around like French starlets in a white convertible '56 Thunderbird. Everything went well—if you discount the arm and a leg it cost her, which Larry's own hounds, not to mention the T-bird and the Heights, wouldn't permit—except once, when he was driving her home, Elspeth stopped to buy them all plastic sunglasses, and Rathbone showed Larry some tooth.

Only Paul would have had the gall to ask her if we could come to the Westminster. He probably had a high society agenda to notch, was accumulating his state dinner chat. We cut school. It was held at the old Madison Square Garden, where I'd only been once before, to the circus, and had been so appalled by the sideshow and the general reaction to the sideshow, I don't remember clowns, spangles, or trapeze. That's probably why I was so antsy in the almost empty arena, waiting for the Best of Breed judging to begin, not listening to Paul hold forth on Rathbone's chances. The competition pranced in circles, rehearsing their sweeping turns. They all looked weedy and bleached to me, splat of foot, short of snoot and neck and sight, and if they beat Rathbone, it would only be because the mediocre always triumphs—look at Miss America, student government, Herman's Hermits.

I was turning to locate a clock when I saw Elspeth under the cavernous overhang of the staircase, like a tender morsel in a giant maw. She was yellowish gray, even her lips, and drawn to a knot. Her clothes mocked her. Larry had put glasses on to read something, and Rathbone bit through his hand. Gouts of blood; ambulance; surgery. We recovered Rathbone from a cage—Elspeth's misery lent us the power of the invisible—and took him out on the leash, now positively cheery, ears riffling, tongue flapping, coat sheering in the cold wind like the chiffon rags on some bit player in *Kim*. Paul hailed a cab and rode in front, smoking, occupying the driver. In back, Elspeth cramped my hand. Rathbone rested his profile on my knee. I can still feel the delicate, silky box of his skull in my palm. His beggar's eyes.

My father would never let us have a dog because if something happened to it, we'd regret how much we loved it. What should this say to his kids?

Paul dropped us off; he had an errand. I held the leash while Elspeth fumbled the keys, took the keys when she crumbled, and let us in. Rathbone trotted to the bed. He sat at the foot, erect, staring out the window into genetic memories of brown sandflats and knobbled mountains until he tucked his chin to his forepaws and slept. I didn't know he would have to be destroyed. I thought it was all over. Elspeth curled up beside him and wept, the sheet jammed in her mouth. The quoits jingled softly.

I sat on the tortoiseshell settee. There was a postcard on it—cherry blossoms against the full moon—addressed to President Johnson, telling him to end the war, and a nineteenth-century anatomy book with tinted fold-out overlays of the organs of a pregnant woman. She had no head. The fetus, as full and white as the moon, floated upside-down at her core, its lips and eyes serene crescents. A new painting, of a baby playing on a dusty floor in dusty Venetian-blind-striped light, the canvas shaped like the trapezoid the window cast on the floor, gathered dust. I watched the light leak out of the day. Elspeth wanted me gone before Joe came home, so when she rose to wash her face, I left. I took the postcard with me to stamp and mail. I felt almost happy. Swollen with it, like a breast with milk, tender. It frightened me.

Then, toward the end of my junior year, Paul sidled up during passing with a paper sack he wanted me to bring him at Hammond's after school. Hammond's was a cafeteria on the corner, diagonally across from the Dutch Reformed Church, where a lot of kids on early session took a bag lunch and bought drinks, dessert. We didn't have lockers, Paul never carried anything, I had two minutes to get to my next class, so I stashed the sack in my big, squashy, black purse. When I told Dan and Billy why I had to stop by Hammond's, they got quiet and wanted to come.

Hammond's was packed, loud and smoky, stinking of sour milk, shoestring potroast, and teenagers who weren't allowed to shower after gym. Billy spotted Paul first. His arm weighed on me, and his long fingers clenched the ball of my shoulder. I skated his gaze to Paul's triangular mask, like a plastic cootie with the cigarette in his yap, and his hand in the collar of Jackie Pollard, Miss Congeniality of the pills and needles set. What threw me, what fuzzed out the mill and the din to a buzzing with yellow and purple explosions, was that I knew he'd set me up. He couldn't just call it quits, he had to show everybody on whose terms. I was jilted, pathetic. Billy's sympathetic arm and Dan's rigidity, taut as caught line, told me that. Poor, fat, pitiful Cee. He'd beat me to the punch, one more time.

I could see one way to go: straight. I threshed the chairs, tables, legs, books, bookbags, to stand over them. Faces, propped on fists, peckish for a whiff of the bone of contention, tracked me. Jackie prigged a sick ripple of smile and looked at Paul. I dumped the paper sack. "You wanted this."

He twisted to me, at the same time casually dropping his arm over the bag and sliding it off the table—the old shell game—and wormed a smile through the smoke. A look

of such intimacy—we were on a pillow, within an eyelash—
of such complicity and salt—he knew I understood and congratulated me for it—hooked into me and tore down the
length of me, and the soft stuff in me started to mush out.
"Carrie, thanks. I believe you know Jackie—"

"I do. Next time you need a pack animal, ask her."

Billy and Dan overtook me in the next block.

"Whoa! Wait up, wouldja?" Billy caught hold, panting.
We all three banged into each other like pingpong balls in
the airstream of one of those pneumatic lottery machines.
He peered into the face I was bearing like a curse, like
Medusa's. "You okay?"

Only my armload kept me from pushing him. "Okay!"
I screamed above the heave of the busses. Old men with
fretted cheeks, worn women toting shopping bags frowned.

"You wanna be alone?" He bobbled like a beachball in
heavy waves. I wanted to run, but the air was water. "She's
not handling it," Billy told Dan.

"I don't believe that prick!" They stormed along behind
me, Dan drumming his looseleaf. Joan of Arc on the road
to the stake, with Monty Python beating a tattoo. "That
ass-wipe, that scum-sucking motherfuck. He uses you to
carry his shit, I mean, who knows what the pigfucker is
selling? meth, smack, for Christ's sake, anything— What if
Cee got busted with it? Jesus. You know they picked up
Lauterbach—cops pulled him out of the coat closet in
Muraskin's room third period. Imagine what they'd do to a
girl. And then he's there with that whore. The guy is a pervert, I've been trying to tell you seems like years. I'd like to
kill him, I swear, I'm not kidding, he needs killing, I'd like
to—"

This went on. Perhaps you'll see the humor in it if I tell
you Dan was a National Merit Scholar who got an 800 on
the physics board without ever taking a class in physics. I
couldn't stand it, and I couldn't get away from it. They trailed

me, not only to my door—managers, roadworking their fighter—but to my apartment; they came in and poured milk, I don't know, put out cookies. It's possible Dan made tea. They tried to convince me I should be glad, I was well out of it, this was the best thing that could happen to me. Get back on that bicycle, Mama, and ride! Billy wanted to know if I had plans. Did I want to sit through *Dog Star Man*— eight hours of silent, double-exposed, 16mm art film—on folding chairs in a basement on Fourteenth Street with them and Zatz tonight?

Paul was an actual dealer. I hadn't suspected. I felt so abysmally stupid. A dealer. Did everybody know but me? What must they have thought of me not to say anything? Or did they tell me, and I was too stupid or deaf to get it? My gut writhed, nerves fired all over my body. Blasting darkness rushed up over me. Billy got Alan on the phone.

"Listen, asshole," Alan barked, "if you weren't worth it, we wouldn't bother with you," and he hung up.

They refused to leave until my mother got home, and then they exited like harem girls, backwards, dropping for my eyes.

"So which one is the boyfriend, already?" my mother teased.

The dealer. The scumsucker.

"When I was your age, I could pick and choose too, you may be surprised to learn."

I went to my room. I expected to cry, but I had dried to a husk. I lay down, but I was running. "Got nowhere to run to, baby, nowhere to hide." The air stank of meat and onions, packed my nostrils. I found myself at the medicine chest. "When I look in the mirror to comb my hair—" Aspirins and laxatives, Bromo Seltzer. I took out a razor blade and felt it against the ridges of my thumb. "Sorry about the clean up—" Clearly, no note. They would both be asleep by one. "Because it's so deep, so deep, inside of me—"

When the phone rang. My mother frowned and clapped

the receiver to her chest to say, "It sounds like a teacher. What did you do?"

It was Elspeth. "Come over right now."

"How did you—?"

"Oh my dearest girl." Her scratchy laugh.

"I want a full explanation." My mother looked pickled in the kitchen light. "Where do you think you're going? What you doing for supper? How you getting home? It gets dark, you know. Wait till your father hears about this—" She chased me to the door, whipping at me with a dishtowel.

I glided through the pelt of questions like a wraith. I sat on the train, and to its ca-chung, over and over, I heard, "I, and not an angel . . . I, and not a seraph . . . I, and not a messenger . . . I am the Lord, I am I, and no other." I had no sense of blasphemy in this association.

Elspeth let me in. "He's just leaving," she announced as we were crossing the hall. I felt something like a contraction. She stroked my arm.

Joe's narrow spine. He was at the table in the luminous cup cast by the lamp. He looked so much like Paul my gorge rose. There were three empties crushed to hourglasses, and he was shaving his cigarette ash to a cone on the lip of a fourth. He watched me coldly behind hornrims. Happily, the new Afghan, El Aloof Mayven, known as Goofy, ganged me. Aloof he was not, a golden boy in puppybrush, big, dense, and genial. Even so, I drew the line at slurp, but I couldn't push away his grinning muzzle. Finally hearing the edge in Elspeth's voice, he rocked down and lolloped for the bedroom with a knotted sock in his chops and a come-hither look.

"If you want them to live in an apartment, you will have to teach them some manners." Joe's voice was sonorous and careful, like a bootblack bucking for butler, Sheepshead Bay aping Shepherd's Bush. "Don't you learn anything? I can well imagine your children—whiners, mongoloid, short, fat, and filthy, sticking to me like flypaper— Bring me a beer. Make yourself useful."

"You said manners?" Elspeth held in the middle of the room as though measuring the space around her, like a hostage in a ransom videotape. Behind her, the mantel mirror still yelled, "CLEAN ME!" "Where are mine? This is Cee, she's—"

"Some gash my degenerate little brother is boffing—"

A new painting on the easel in front of the windows. Chasidic rabbis confronting Mayor Lindsay—she was working from a newspaper photo—on a black and white television in the right foreground. To the left, a naked woman in a blue horsehair wingchair stared at the wall.

"—probably looking to get knocked up to really get her hooks into him—"

The walls reflected in the faintest shadings some movement outside—

"—because it's obvious that otherwise, she's—"

—lit by the television and by the light from an unseen window that somehow, you could tell, was high up and boxed in—

"—exactly like you, another of your sick surrogates, and why the fuck you've got to—"

The sheen on the horsehair—

"—except for your barren womb and you moronic excuses and your sick, frustrated—"

—perfectly rendered—

"—every sad excuse for a—"

There was a perceptible curve to the tv screen.

"—I don't know. Maybe if you weren't sitting on your ass all day, playing in your own excrement— What does a man have to do to get a beer around here?" His chair hit the floor. Protracted metallic chatter—the beer cans. Goofy bounded in, nudged Elspeth, and made eagerly for the door. Joe kicked him as though he was the door, locked, nailed.

Goofy flew up, bowed, whacked on his back, his eyes looked peeled, he cowered along the wall to the corner. Joe slammed out. The slam shook the furniture; something brittle shattered.

"Don't mind him," Elspeth said.

We stood, breathing. Then she was in the corner, soothing Goofy, palping the bag of him until he got up, and she was satisfied with his gait. She righted the chair and began picking up the debris. "I didn't think he'd be here. He seldom comes home, and when he does, he's usually in a big hurry to leave. Or he passes out. Would you like something to eat? We're having a special on the taste of ashes."

I shook no.

"Come on, sweetie, sit down. I'll make tea. Constant Comment. It's delish. Sit where we can talk."

She pointed, and I parked across from Joe's chair. He was still in it.

"You look peaked," she called from the kitchen, filling the kettle. "You're not on some kind of deathy diet?"

"I should be," I got out.

"I know how hard it is to focus all your cells on being other than too fat. How you lurk like a crazed beast and pounce on your fat when all else is in a position of extreme strength, and let all your enemies have a handle on you. I know that even after you reach a healthy weight, every meal is a quagmire. The childhood fat cell theory is widely accepted—you grow these things in infancy; they swell in adulthood; they must be starved relentlessly. So—never backslide. But if you do, don't notice it, as backsliding leads to abandonment. Hop on scale daily. Realize that all things double—chins, tums, thigh blobs—are not really part of you. They goooo awaaaaay—" haunted house voice, hula hands, "leaving a thin person who looks like she was never fat. Life isn't fair in handing out favors. You have to say, 'well, looks like I get to be hungrier than these born-thin cocksuckers. How about that?'"

She set two orange-scented mugs on woven placemats. "Some cheese? I got gorgonzola— Fruit?" She pushed the bangs out of my eyes as if taking my temperature. "You got to let it go, child, the sooner the better."

My feelings sat like a cake of soap in my throat, and I couldn't tell whether spitting them up or swallowing them would sicken me most. I bent to my cup.

Picking a thick paperback off a pile on the floor, she joined me. She had to reach to plant her elbows. "Joe found this." She slid it to me. "Maltese-English dictionary. Open at random. Read aloud." She folded her arms. Child Lama has tea with the governess. The light cast a crown on her lacquer-black cap of hair, contained us in a warm circle.

Maltese? I cracked it open. I ran my eyes down the page. Whoa! "Okay—it means brooding hen. What have they got to brood about?"

"Egg futures. Crossing the road. What else is there?"

"Q-r-o-q-q-a," I spelled it out. "How do you say it? Like dile?"

"Like shit? Try another."

Was she going to Malta? Where was Malta? All I knew was the falcon. "Look at these words!" *Xwejjah*. "It's like they got a markdown on all the seldom-used letters."

"The lessers!"

"Here's a good one—*fartas*: 'he makes bald.' I'd like to see that. Oh, and look at this, is this fair? *Xemx* means 'sun.' They must want their kids to feel dumb."

"They are dumb. They live in a place with no soil."

"What about *bodbod? Bluha? Boloh?* Baby talk! And here's an expression that might come in handy—*Nirrah jikser saqajh!* 'May he break his legs!'"

Elspeth's laugh rumbled up like a motorcycle in a parking deck. I read off words, *twerzaq, fuq, skiddjat,* incomprehensible definitions—"two tumoli?" a "mattock?" until my lips rebounded like trampolines. I put my face on the table and laughed. Elspeth struggled the book from under me and read sample sentences from the grammar section. *Jekk niezla x-xita, il hwejjeg qea jixxarbu* (If it is raining, the clothes are getting wet.) *Mar il-knisja u s-suq. Hu l-habs* (He went to church and to market. He is in prison.) We sighed and then laughed at ourselves sighing. Goofy wanted in on the joke. We chanced restorative sips of tea. Elspeth's glasses puddled up, and she wiped her face on the sleeve of her t-shirt. Her upper arm was mottled with deep blue and brown bruises.

"Oooh, what happened to you?" I blurted without thinking. Whenever I speak without thinking, I sound just like my mother. Tight knapsack, shrunk my slave bracelet, chute caught on the Chrysler building. I reached to touch them as automatically as a mother. My hand hung in the air.

Her eyes crinked at me, and the pilot lights came on. "Can we pick 'em, or what?"

My mouth laxed like the seat of an easy chair. My stomach released. My heart started ticking quietly, like a clock, again. Not the first, not the only, not the most, not the worst. Not for long. Not forever. Not again. I was healed. Delivered. I thought she might melt in the love I looked her. She seemed to flicker.

"I would like to hotly deny I ever spoke vows with this needledick bugfucker," she was saying. "No internalized conscience, and of course he's having it off on the sly with some pokerthin pinbrain bleachhead—and, God willing, he's all hers," she twitched her sleeve, "but it's wounding to be preferred in the sack to tapioca when you know you are a top performer. It is all so—ucccch, acccch—" Wriggling in her skin like a pupa. "But if you knew my parents. Joe is so much better'n 'em it has taken me all these years to notice how bad he is. My parents are truly nuts, sadists— When I think about surviving them, my thinker goes on emergency alert. And do I blame them? Yes! A thousand times!"

I was ready to follow her into battle, scimitar in teeth. She smiled sadly at me like a crippled veteran. "That's why kids are out for me, a laughable non-possibility. Listen, sweets, if you would avail yourself of Mother El's hard-won advice, in choosing a male, remember, the fascinating, the glamorous, the amusing, all pale before the kind, the compassionate, the good. It is only the astigmatism of late adolescence, in the squint of which most marry, that makes the opposite seem true. The fact is, no matter how sexy he seems before his toothbrush has been cosied up to yours for a year or so, the minute you doubt him, he becomes a total dud, ten-inch cock, pretty face, snappy repartee, and all. You can only allow yourself sinful abandon with people you can trust. Failure to heed this has resulted in an epidemic of frigidity to which no one admits. Let the decorative drones be sucked up by their female counterparts. Hold out for soul. If my sad experience can prevent you making a complete hash of your life, it will have been—still not worth it." Her laugh rumbled down the alley and struck all the pins. "But so listen: the upshot is I'm getting out. Scaring up the money to go to Mexico and divorce his popish ass. In the meantime, I have a great big favor to ask—"

"Anything!" I sent Rashid skitting from a sound sleep to the top of a kitchen cabinet.

"Can you look for an apartment for me? I have to work night and day, and he's cut me off from what old friends still live in town, and he can't suspect. I'll tell you my requirements—must be Manhattan, must come cheap, must allow pets, colorful neighbors a plus—and you gad about in pursuit. Whenever you find it, I'm home free, but if it takes a while, I'll have more money. Would this be a detestable chore for you?"

"I would love to," I assured her. "Places to go, people to meet. This could be character building."

She closed her eyes and steepled her hands. "Please let it be in the Character Building."

I pictured myself scanning newspaper ads in coffee shops, using payphones, grabbing a hat, walking up thousands of steps in Cuban heels and seamed stockings, sniffing closets. For some reason, I saw myself as Jean Arthur, Roz Russell, hey! Nancy Drew. Independent career girl. I would learn how to move out.

"You're sure?" Elspeth jogged me. "My motives are entirely selfish. What will your parents say?"

"I don't care. I'll tell them something. Why would they have to know? No, I'm positive. A mission. It's just what I need. You know—you know that—" I wanted to say I broke off with Paul, but somehow such defensiveness felt like he'd won. I also couldn't lie to her. "I won't be seeing Paul anymore."

She smiled and held out her tiny, star-shaped hand. "Put 'er there, pal." We savored our firm clasp, the neat snap of our wrists. "But we won't be s.o.b.-sisters no more," she lamented.

"We could cut our fingers and mingle our blood."

"We could get lockjaw!"

We opened our traps and, soundlessly, we laughed or screamed. Who could tell?

6 Easier Said

Another fine mess I've gotten myself into. It's the Wednesday before Thanksgiving, and I'm taking Ariel and Fawne to hear Eric's band—half-assed attempt to compensate Ariel for sitting through the SATs one last time in the vain hope that by some miracle her scores will ascend (can you see this painting? it's by Titian: heaven is pale green, dominated by a very dry eye at the apex of a pyramid; Ariel, dressed for success in blue suit, floppy foulard, Nikes, and attache case, soars; I'm bottom left, on my knees, telling a rosary of penciled bubbles) and as Step One in the Great Leap on Fawne.

Of course I'm no longer up for it. I've seized the reins at Retro Revert (my title should be "Prevert"), which means I get to nag and scold, scheme and scrimp, tease, appease, fret, threaten, and punish, oh, and shop—what do you know? I'm a mother. I feel, in every sense of the word, wasted. I run home, and all I want is to *make* something. Trouble.

Tomorrow I get to make Thanksgiving dinner for my father on his first jaunt out of the rehab center. I've built a ramp to the porch, cleared wide swaths around the furniture, cleaned, and removed the bathroom door and its sill.

Three days of continuously feeding the woodstove like the engine in the Great Train Race have taken the chill off the sty. I'm planning elegant and elaborate variations on the traditional dishes. Eric has provided a turkey so fresh he can call it by both forenames. There will be four pies. Good wine. My brother and his brood are flying in. I'm shooting for the culinary equivalent of the Ode to Joy. Let us rise.

And I know they'll glom it in fifteen minutes. Push away from the table describing how stuffed they are and precisely how they'll pay for it. My father may or may not speak. If he does, what animal will he most resemble? How often will he remind us of destitution and decay? Who will he reduce to tears? My mother will apologize for me. Harold will grandly overlook Eric and quickly confirm by subtly questioning my kids that he won the gene pool. Someone will make a gratuitous racist remark. We'll be lucky not to lose a child to the fire.

Talk me out of it.

Dash is staying home tonight to keep the fires burning. Since his conference with Ms. Williams he's been sullen but contained: prisoner of love. He goes to her office and sits glaring out as though she's all that's restraining him from mayhem; he strolls off when he wants. A vivid woman— she looks like a Pointer Sister—with a ready laugh that cuts the acid of her observations. She sees him as a downed antelope lashing at the circling pack. She tells me to show faith in him. It sounds too easy. It's what I want to do. "Faith is blind," I answer bleakly.

"Love is blind," she fires back. "Faith is observant."

Wow! It lodges right between my eyes like a spore from space. My immune system scuffs against its hard, smooth surface. You know what it means to be positive these days.

As for the karate lessons, I rejected the former Marine into helmets, stick fighting, and trophies; also the snow-white flakes at the Life Enhancement Center. We're currently combing by neighborhood. Dash watches me handle all this like my parole officer. Right now he's lying inert on the floor by the stove with his face on his arms like It at tag, counting my failings, the minutes misspent. I wish we could slip out before he looks up. Ready or not. No bums rush me.

The girls clop down from Ariel's room spilling giggles. Fawne in ragged drab as postwar waif. Her ears are so hung with doodads they look like come-ons for skeeball. Ariel is rosy and bright-eyed. They've cut off her hair, possibly with a nail scissors, possibly with an electric fan, and moussed out the remaining sprigs. Her jeans are slashed; her t-shirt says, "So?"

"Whoa!" Dash opes a jaundiced eye. "Termites gettin' outta hand!"

They tilt around him like Japanese concubines, on murderous shoes shaped like ocean liners. Anxiety, derision, truculence ripple under Ariel's flush. "How do I look?"

"Goosed by a moose," says Dash.

My hands want to walk her bone structure like calipers. "Surprised."

"She hates it," Ariel confides sourly yet gleefully to Fawne's shoulder, as if they're commentators sharing a mike. Bob and Weave.

"No, no, I like it," I hasten to assure. "I was just thinking the other day how great you'd look with short hair."

"Now she wants the credit," says Fawne.

I throw up my hands. They laugh.

"Where'd you get *that?*" Ariel chins at my ancient purple panne minidress. The black Keds and stockings with palm trees up the calves are new.

"You're ashamed to be seen with me?" I can't get a reading.

"No. It's cool." Ariel compresses her lips. "Killer."

"Very Prince," says Fawne. They break up.

It's definitely time to go. Fawne's coat is like a tramp's;

she never removes it, and Ariel flatly refuses to put one on.

"Don't forget to smash the state, dudes," Dash calls. His father always says this—always—minus the "dudes"—on parting. He said it falling off me into sleep. He tacked it on his love letters, lullabies, the divorce settlement. And he was the one who forgot! Thank goodness I captured him on DNA! Dash tries to heft an enormous log from the recline. As I close the door, I imagine him convoking fiery hordes to consume the sty. Let them cook the turkey. He turns the REM up to window-rattling.

"Evenin' ladies." The toastmaster genital, perched on his porch rail even though it's nine p.m., drizzly, and forty degrees. He squeals, "Lookin' good eeeee-nough to eeeeeeeat!"

Quality control at the female factory. I wish he'd catch his tongue in the conveyer belt.

"Shove it up your ass, zobo!" Fawne yells.

He sucks off his beer. "Up yours any time, sugar." His voice is low but, well, penetrating.

"You happy?" Ariel mutters. "You want dialogue?"

"Don't be such a wuss." Fawne thwacks her. Ariel stumbles. "You got to fight for your rights, don't you, Cee?"

"Maybe Fawne is right," I suggest. Have to start the big build-up somewhere. Why not with the first act of aggression?

"Let me guess, and I'm wrong," Ariel pouts, rubbing her arm.

It can't hurt that much. "Give him a taste of his own medicine," I muse. "Maybe we've been letting him—"

"YOU'RE A SICKO PSYCHO REDNECK ASSHOLE AND YOU NEED TO BE NEUTERED!"

"—although I don't think I'd have put it in exactly those terms—"

Fawne cups Ariel's ear. "Listen. What do you hear?" Ariel jerks her head away. Again, like a nervous filly. They both look at me as if I'm the mediator, and they've just discovered I've privately made them contradictory promises. "Nothing," Fawne goes on, supported by my total blankness. "He can't take it." She wants to share this. "HE CAN'T TAKE IT!"

He's probably just stepped inside for his assault rifle. But, hey, death? Where is thy sting? The old lady across the street, who rakes every morning in a green pompom cap, red high heels, and a walker, raises her blinds to let them crash down. Encouraging Fawne is going to take touch.

The neanderthal discharges a Roman candle from waist level. It scorches perilously close to Ariel's ear and bursts in the street in a shower of sparks. We duck after it's long gone.

"Incoming!" he exults. "Happy New Year, ladies, a tad early. Just drawin' my line in the sand. Never let it be said I oppose women in combat. Come in right handy for all sorts a purposes. Kick a little butt, like the man said."

We've afforded him a great deal of amusement in addition to the patriotic opportunity to quote our eloquent president. I cover Fawne's mouth and haul her to the truck. I don't want to be here when the cops the old lady just called show and want to know who started it.

Since I'm the designated drinker, Ariel's behind the wheel. "I could feel the heat," she says, checking for permanent scars or damage to her look in the rearview mirror.

"Sideburns," says Fawne, elbowing me.

I laugh. "We're certainly off with a bang."

"I don't see what's so funny." Ariel is wan, skittish, her eyes seem muzzy. She catches my concern and scowls. "If he fires off another one at the truck—"

"You've got no sense of humor," Fawne tells her, "*and* you're a wimp—"

"Because I think it's stupid to—"

"Look at your mom, she's not—"

"Oh, I haven't had so much fun since the last time I was maced. I'm just glad nobody was hurt."

"I wish he was hurt," Fawne growls.

"Oh no, just hospitalized, say, for a month—I'll take a week, a day. Are you okay to drive?" I ask Ariel. She looks spent.

"I don't know how I let myself get talked into this." She turns the key.

The radio brawls on with the ignition. "I want to sex you up—"

"How can you listen to this monkey music?" Fawne bangs at the buttons.

"Take what you can get," Ariel peels off, "because Generic is pathetic."

Eric's band. Supposedly cofounded with a guy named—you guessed it!—who blew for the mountains to play bluegrass. Apocryphal, if you ask me. Eric's excuse to keep wardrobe costs down to cheap and readily available black and white.

White on black is the billboard coming up as Ariel guns onto the bypass. "Abortion is Murder." A marshmallow toddler in a Baggie. Agitprop of the Womb Invaders, the Chumps for White Patriarchy, the We Know Better Party. I'm cautioned again, as if our recent send-off wasn't enough, that I'm only a poor relation on this planet—a woman. I pull the pin and toss my imaginary hand grenade.

"Ooh, I hate it too. It makes me so mad. Is that what you'd do?" Fawne asks me. "Blow it up?"

"She's just showing off. She wouldn't do it if she didn't think you'd agree with her." Ariel passes a Volvo. She drives much too fast, especially for someone I carted around like a fifty-pound Ming vase filled with nitro for years. When I clutch the armrest, she speeds up. "Why do anything?"

"Your standard answer," Fawne grouses. "You wouldn't say that if you were—"

"You don't know what I'd say," Ariel talks to the road. Almost inaudibly, "because I don't."

Fawne flicks me up and down with her charcoal lashes. "I mean it," she tells me. "What could we do about it?"

I want to exclaim, "Let's have a play!" "Just don't get her into it," Ariel cuts in. "We went to that big demonstration last year? She wanted us to 'experience' it, you know, 'living history' or some such, and she wore this headband that said 'Anti-Life' and tied all these ratty ragdolls and Holly Hobbies and cabbage-crotch kids to her and dragged one in each hand by the hair. She'd have drug us too if we'd let her. Really, she made paperclip chains. She looked like a bag lady."

"Cool," Fawne coos. Is she for real?

"I thought you enjoyed it." I'm miffed. "What about that guy dressed up as the Pope? 'If men could get pregnant, abortion would be a sacrament.'" They laugh. "Or those girls from UVA you went wading with? Or the old women from Florida who kept feeding you sips of beer until you thought you knew the words to 'Bread and Roses' and tried to lead us in song?" And when the solid crowd mashed us against a wall, and I couldn't move and couldn't breathe, Ariel blazed a trail to some shade, dispatched Dash for ice, and sat stroking my temples. I remember this moment in the same shimmering haze as Beth's death in *Little Women*.

"I wish I'd been there with you," Fawne sighs.

"I thought you were." Ariel's face flanges from road to Fawne. "Didn't you tell Graham that—"

Fawne stares ahead. "Wrong."

"Wrong again," says Ariel. "I thought you told Christie that you were against abortion, so when you told Graham—"

"See," Fawne explains to me, "my mom figures if she had to have me, everybody has to suffer. And Forrest, you know, he's real high on telling other people what to do. Plus they'd never let me loose in D.C. Unless," her eyes widen like baking cookies, "maybe they'd let me go with you. Man! You as the chaperone? I hope they have another one of those things this year! It's still an issue, right? We could stay with my dad—you'll love him—he's the sexiest man alive—and of course he'd *love* you—and we could—"

Ariel veers sharply to make the exit, toppling Fawne on me.

"So what would you do?" she insists, wedged to my side, her lips tickling my neck, smell of mothballs. "Burn it down? Blow it up? I mean, what would your people have done?"

The merry men, I take it. In the golden days of the Symbionese Liberation.

"Come on." Ariel stops for a light and pulls out a smoke. I fake coughing before it's lit, and she rolls down her window so it takes several tries, and we're all shivering. "It's got spotlights on it. A thousand cars pass it at all hours. It's probably wired to the police chief's—" she drags and exhales out the window, "desk." Hanging another quick right into the lot where we always park. "Get real."

"I am real." Fawne pushes out of me, none too soon. I feel like I'm being forced to tango at gunpoint. "I'm serious."

Ariel gears down and pulls the keys.

"You know?" I jump into the cold, followed by Fawne like my breath. She's a bubble I'm blowing, my thought balloon. Speaking now not merely for myself, but for a generation: "Look at it: it's got about the same number of letters and, see? A-B-O, S-M-O, and then you change the R to a K and the T to an I, black out a little here, white in there—get it?" We trudge along, welded at the elbows for warmth and stability. "'Smoking is Murder.' And the fetus still makes sense." Ariel takes a last drag and flips the butt into the gutter, littering. "It would drive the entire community—"

"BANANAS!" screams Fawne. She does a funny dance,

like wiggling in manacles, firing pistols in the air. Ariel can't hide the smirk behind lips bent like staples. You should know that the city fathers, under heavy pressure from the tobacco company, rejected an ordinance to limit billboard advertising earlier this year. Around the same time that the black secretary of HEW blasted the same company for targeting campaigns at blacks and nubile women. And that a state advisory panel on substance abuse ordered all references to tobacco omitted from a brochure on causes of infant mortality.

"We've got to do it," insists Fawne. "It's fantastic. It's the right thing to do." She imitates the avuncular gent on tv who pitches fiber.

It even seems possible. If anything, it's too easy. Here I'm ransacking my brain for some clever way to lure little harry-Carrie back from the precipice, and all I had to do was bait the old political hook? *Un*easy. I could turn around and find myself bound to the billboard, wired to go off.

"But we really have to do it," she presses, "or die trying!"

(What did I tell you?)

"And guess who winds up holding the ladder?" Ariel grumps.

The club, called Hog Heaven because it's above Johnny's Pork Palace, is in our derelict downtown, in a beautiful 1929 Art Deco building from which a department store fled a decade ago. Retro redid the barbecue joint—padded, glossy, with Johnny's snide photos of the New South and, over the bar, a plastic pig that lights up an obscene pink. But I haven't been to the club. I don't often come out to hear Eric; something about seeing him at a distance disturbs me. The lobby, for all its swank cool, is warm and dry, scented with hickory-smoked pork, and makes us sound like the Ronettes. The hobbled teens tail me up the stairs into a clog of bodies, somehow looking dewy rather than drowned and damping my threats of flu. I'm stuck in a raincoat.

Either the band has a lot of friends and relations or the locals really need to get their yayas out before the puritan family festival of gratitude and gluttony. Everybody gives everybody the once over, pretending to be interested in whatever the shouting is about. Fawne takes the unofficial weird-off hands down, and although she knew it before she came in, she splashes in it, prattling to Ariel about an infinitely superior club she went to once in Washington, "My dad took me, but it was more like a date, and you wouldn't believe—" Ariel wears the martyred look of someone waiting in line for the bathroom behind a tour of grandmothers, jiggling her legs, recognizing no one. I try to assess if I'm the oldest person here. Someone moos.

Finally, we muscle inside. I'm paying the cover, about to explain that the girls won't be drinking, when Fawne dishes out a phony ID and clearly expects Ariel to do the same. Ariel overplays annoyed incredulity. I can't hear what she says to Fawne. They hiss and spit like cats. The gatekeeper settles for stamping their right hands; it's the normal procedure. I check my coat; not Fawne. It's like her attitude: her glum.

"My dad let me use it," Fawne argues, pocketing the ID. "He says kids in Europe drink all the time—"

"This ain't Europe," Ariel points out dryly, shouting over the taped Little Feat, the bawl of the loosed mob.

"He says that's how you learn to handle it, like why Italians and Jews—" Fawne irons out a smile. To me: "I was just trying to save you the hassle."

Oh, I know, and come off worldly. Somehow I've got to get across to her that I'm Ariel's *mother*; I need to be shielded. Do I have to tell her parents about this?

I had expected a dance floor ringed by tables, red candle-glasses in fishnet, cocktails with fruit and parasols. No. In the middle of a vast, dingy hangar, the bar is a round island, probably once the perfume or jewelry counter what with all the mirrors at its hub. Mirrors in a bar are a mistake. Mirrors also cover the walls—hiding what?—yet the light, projected from cans in a dropped acoustic ceiling, is dim, casts bags under our eyes, chins, and breasts, lengthens our noses—the Ten Years After Room. The floor is the color and texture of chewed gum. Booths out of some defunct diner line three sides, but the crowd is on its feet at the front where there's a platform made out of pallets, presumably so the music will have to compete with the street noise. I buy a beer and two Cokes, a sustained effort since the bartender doesn't respond to the higher vocal registers. When I finally succeed, the girls are gone. Abducted! Block the exits!

But there's Ariel, slowed only by her shoes, disappearing into the crush. I'm swept back in time: waddling after them in my orthopedic oxfords, crying, "Wait up!" Maybe I should just go pig out downstairs until they emerge, divorced and pregnant. Ariel's friends, like the rainbow coalition from a particularly unsanitary detainment camp, hug her as if she's returned from a failed interview with a sponsor and feel her bristles. Fawne stands apart, paws in pockets, twisting her neck until she spots me and eagerly motions me over. She accepts the soda like it's an Oscar. My stare eventually bores through Ariel's skull.

"What's your problem?" she asks, taking the Coke I'm jabbing at her.

"Flat-leaver."

"So childish." She folds into the mockery of her friends.

"—your *mo-ther?*" a girl exclaims, as though nobody has one these days.

"Your mother!" Comic expletive from a boy with Gabby Hayes's neckerchief on his head.

I can't tell what the looks mean except I may have a future with Madame Tussaud. They keep their bottles at their knees.

"She's got every right to be here; her boyfriend's in the band," says Fawne. "You know what your problem is?" To Ariel, fist on hip. "You don't really appreciate your mom. We should trade for awhile. Then you'd see."

If we're doing the tango, that was the dip. She positions herself staunchly beside me as if I have a hideous deformity. I smile, and her face flowers.

Soon we're engulfed, like stranded crabs by the sea. The noise is at high tide. Tsunami! A chloroform of scent, sweat, and beer socks in my nose. Where are the exits? How can this place meet code? Firetrap! Ariel lights up, swigs from a friend's bottle. All I see is her wet mouth. The guy next to me, trying to bung in front of me with his hips, is waving a cigarette entirely too close to my eyes. Flaming asshole. I see this fleshed out in flashing neon. I could sell a million of 'em. What to give the man who has everything or hang over the boss's door.

"Watch your cigarette!" I holler.

"I'll just put it out in your ear."

"Sideburns," comments Fawne.

A man maneuvering his date like a forklift sends Ariel sprawling into a preppie damsel who wallops her backward, and three girls dodge around her from the right. Idealistic youth. A line of men with arms folded over their flannel chests, louring like the Palisades, butts in behind us. The hairs all over my body erect defensively. Shields up, phasers on stun.

"Don't," Ariel warns even before she regains her balance.

The flannel men set like teeth.

"Is this fun?" Ariel asks me. "Was Woodstock like this? We really owe you one."

The tape stops. My ears roar. Voices surge. The Flaming Asshole signs to his buddies there's room over here, where I am.

The band walks on. Jonesy climbs into the drum-saddle; Dave scrabbles the keyboards; Steve picks up the bass; Alston, a big black man from Birmingham, totes in his sax, which he calls Lurleen, so he can tongue the erstwhile Alabama governor out here in front of God and everybody. Eric, bent as though by buffeting winds, turns his back to tune, to test the amp, faces around to check the mike. Feminine flutter. He surveys the crowd, his specs slipping down, and his white eyebrows up over his pondwater gray-green glint. What does he see? Newborn birds, I think, blind, clamant gullets. He sees me, winks, ticks his index; it's his lounge singer parody, Eric the Rad. The preppette thinks it's for her. "Rick!"

"Hey—he's *her* boyfriend," Fawne informs the world, nodding at me.

"Oh Lord." Ariel closes her eyes and pitches her head back, ready to be gathered to His bosom. Her friends look from me to Eric and back as if this is the matching portion of their IQ test. Then they thump Ariel, laughing. A pimply boy whispers something that makes her groan.

"So that's him." Fawne's crusty eyes crackle and pop. "Wow! Do I get to meet him? Is this cool or what?"

He looks great. Of course the humor that blooms off the knobs of his cheeks. His cornsilk ponytail sleeks against the black turtleneck to his waist. Sleeves pushed up, white hairs swirl down his tan forearms to his finely turned wrists. I feel my nipples poke up like groundhogs sniffing spring; that little pile of oily rags at my center starts to smolder. I see through his painter's pants to the soft gold fluff that furs his thighs, I smell the salty almond warmth of him, I take one of his pennsy-pink balls in my mouth— Whoa! Jump back, Loretta!

It takes me a moment to refocus. I really do smell burning. The Asshole has singed my hair in apprising some crinklecurled wench of his proximity. Fearing for my sight,

I flap about madly and fling his cigarette into the chest of one of the flannel lumberjacks.

"Whad-ja do to my butt, lady?" the Asshole snarls.

Laughter—the wages of singe. Ariel's friends simper at her. She's waiting for a celestial chariot. The lumberjack puts the lit cigarette into the gaping hand of the Asshole, who screeches like the monkey house. Bellies up to Jack. Chins jut.

"You're not going to fight?" I appeal. "This is like *television*."

"Yeah," says Fawne, "The Battle of the Glands."

I throw an arm around her neck and hoot. The pallid face in the crook of my arm oozes happy sap. "We're a good team, Mom," she whispers.

Uh *uh*.

Generic bite down on "Jim Dandy to the Rescue." Indeed. They like to prove they can rock steady before launching into their more esoteric original compositions, like "How New Brand Name?" a recitation of the products in the Kroger gourmet section interspersed with the names of places people are starving, which, according to the liner notes on their EP, is "a stinging indictment of consumerism." Or "Herbal Wrap," where Eric rhymes his favorite plants to a slap bass and random slaps on the synthesizer. Hey, it's better than "Loving an Older Woman Gets Older Every Day." Jangling the big final chord, Eric leaps in the air, plunges to his knees (splinters!), and unplugs his guitar from the amplifier. He is left diddling this silent cigarbox between his legs. Big hole in the noise. Jones tosses his sticks at the cymbals. Dave shuts the lid on the keys and makes as if to leave. Alston farts into the mouthpiece. Oblivious, Steve keeps running the bassline. This is really powerhouse. The crowd whoop the rebel yell regardless; when they die, they'll be a rebel dead.

Eric stands up and reconnects, returns to the mike.

"We're Generic!" The mike wilts, flops over. "Why do I feel like an eighty-year-old man?" He crooks an eyebrow toward where he knows I am, which is behind the Asshole. The ladies yowl their demur. He eats it up. Covers the mike to joke with Alston. Pushes up his glasses. "And we've got one message fo' y'all: Die, yuppie scum!"

The crowd hurl up their hands and carry on like crash on the commodities market. Eric must be thinking of all those folks for whom he plants rhododendrons. His ordinary speaking voice is the color of cognac; this voice is Wild Irish Rose. "So buy American, and to the public, for which demand, inflation, under guard, indegradable, with bribery and corruption fo' all! Buy the FLAG!"

"Brand Name." It goes on for hours. The Asshole brandishes his freshly lit cigarette like an enthusiastic Hitler Youth. Preppette rags out on an invisible rowing machine, regularly bashing Fawne and chafing Ariel's akimbo like an oarlock. I can't tell if Lumber Jack is feeling me up, bearing the brunt of an assault to his own rear, or dancing, but I can no longer ignore it without appearing to cooperate. I spring forward, into the Asshole, who bowls me back, and those old karate reflexes propel him into the oars. Mixmaster! Two birds, one stone. Fawne slams Preppette for my approval. Now I'm leading a *Putsch*. Everybody's headbanging. The Asshole is acquiring the ability to swing.

My daughter's look slits before it shrivels me. "God, you are so fucking *weird*," she deadpans over the din. "What is with you? I ought to have you locked up. You ought to be put away. You are sick. I mean it. I used to feel sorry for you, but now it's just embarrassing. I can't wait to get rid of you."

She absolutely means it. I have wasted eighteen years on this creature. I have poured love into her as copiously and carefully as champagne into punch. It's the love that makes me want to slap her, and only my equally genuine disgust prevents me. I shove off Fawne and whatever it is she's blithering, I push through the lumber, the giddy girls and gassy guys, trade my empty for a scotch, and plunk in a booth for this too to pass. I'm shaking. My mouth is dry and my dress is wet. I calm my breath by the numbers. I work at perfecting a speech like a poisoned apple, beautiful, polished, that she will swallow and choke on. Why should I be fair? Let her live among dwarves. I salute my clever reflections.

By the time the band breaks, I've reduced the poison to a single precious drop that shines in the apple of my eye like a shard of mirror. Ariel's headed for the bar, bunkered in friends, untouched. I realize that nothing has happened to her. It hurts like hunger. Rage ignites along my circulatory system as though it's packed with gunpowder. Fawne lectures her, panning the room for me, and when she sees me, she tugs Ariel almost to dislocation and twiddles me a shy, idiotic, and most endearing wave. Ariel turns and gets everything, and, yes, I'm impressed at how fast. She turns to stone. She turns on Fawne, tearing her arm away and yelling, "Quit it!" Her bloodthirsty friends bark their endorsement. A regular lynch mob she moves with. Fawne tunes them out, trying to read the static between Ariel and me like a ham operator intercepting garbled U-boat transmissions. Without a word or a backward glance, Ariel stalks to my booth, the fuddled Fawne in tow. A worthy opponent. Should I take any credit?

"What do you want me to say? I'm sorry? I'm *sorry.* But you're so—"

I negligently chuck her money for Cokes. She bucks off to buy them with the grace and suppressed power of a brahma bull.

Recorded music returns—Lynyrd Skynyrd—rube rock. Eric puts in beside me, glossy with sweat, trailing a wake of sighs and seductive eyes. I haven't seen so much back-arch-ing since the Weeki-Wachee mermaid ad went off the tube. He licks my lower lip, then the bump in the middle of my upper, then tests deeper waters. He pulls back smiling, pushes up his specs, mouthes his forefinger, and holds it quizzically in the wind. It don't take a weatherman— I want to sink my hands in his hair and go under, probably to clapping and catcalls, side-betting.

But Fawne is sitting across from us, humbly studying her hands, knotted on the table, like a controversial guest waiting for "Meet the Press" to go on the air. Almost humming with excitement. I try to picture how Eric looks to her. I introduce them.

"Cee! It's *Fauve*! You know? The Beast? Didn't Cee tell you about me?"

Eric smiles, sipping his beer.

Furrowed, she brings her voice down an octave and asks him how he'd compare Generic to The Doors.

"The Doornails, you mean." Running his hand up my thigh. "Dead as. Dee-pressing. What's wrong?" he asks me. His eyes scrunch behind his lenses as though blotting my astringency.

I think this sort of get-it-all-out-in-the-open bit is fatuous and false. Play it as it lies. "Slight hitch in mother-daughter relations. This is some classy joint. It reminds me of, I don't know, the Bayonne bus station waiting room. The common room in a women's prison."

"Yeah, and how 'bout the sound system?" He lets it go for now. His beer is in a big styrofoam cup, and his lips taste yeasty. "You're right about bus station. What if I reel off the stops on I-40 from here to Barstow with my head in a waste paper basket?"

"James Brown, 'Night Train.' Where was his head?"

"Co-ol!" hiccups Fawne. "And I was here when you thought of it."

Is this ironic? Our eyebrows raise like drawbridges as it

barges under. Hers flatten, and she peeks up to see where she's going. Little stowaway.

"You need to move away from lists." Ariel whacks down the Cokes and the change, shoving on the bench by Fawne. "They just go on and on."

"Say hey to you too, ace rock critic. I don't have to ask if you been enjoyin' yourself; I know you been torturin' your ma."

"She tell you that?" She slaps her mouth. "Anyway, you stay out of it."

"Yeah," I tell him, draining my glass, "stay out of it."

"Ain't it grand how I bring 'em together?" he asks Fawne, who is acting out her name. "Love the new look, Ari-elly. You got your ma's great bones." He puts his big hand around my neck, and I rest my head against it. Holding my neck seems like the most wonderful thing anyone could possibly do for me.

"Thanks," grudges Ariel. "Or should I thank the bone-donor?" Eyes lowered, Uriah Heep delivery, "Everything I am I owe to you."

"It was my idea," Fawne offers. "I did it."

"You did it," Ariel says quietly, "but it was my idea."

"I thought it would be more heaven, less hog," I say. "Like rock heaven. Do you remember that song? I must have been really young, I had one of the first pocket transistor radios"—gift from a neighbor who fondled me once in the elevator. To pay for my silence? He had that. Imagine the horrible fuss. And my avoidance. Running up stairs is good for you—"and I'm listening to WABC, teasing my hair—"

Ariel to Eric, "Before we were born—"

"Junior high. Anyway, this song was popular. We're up in the clouds, and there's Sam Cooke, there's Buddy Holly—"

"That's not the one, 'There's Got to be a Rock 'n Roll Heaven, Cause You Know They Got a Hell of a Band'?"

Eric shakes his head. "Some things I'm ashamed to know."

"Maybe. Anyway, that's the gist of it. That's what they ought to do here, make it rock heaven. I'm thinking about the Baptistry ceiling in Florence—mosaic, incredibly detailed, God and the Devil and all these tiny naked figures, it's really dramatic, scary even—I've got slides of it somewhere. Anyway, can't you see it? Bessie Smith is God," before anyone can contradict me, "because she looked like God, and Elvis has to be the Son—"

"Sun Records," Eric agrees.

"Sideburns," puts in Fawne.

I chuckle. "And who's the Holy Ghost? The dead Rolling Stone? Brian something."

"Jones," Eric shrugs. "Ghost name. Generic."

"Jim Morrison!" Fawne reproves us as if this is the right answer. We must have skipped catechism class.

"Nothin' ghostly 'bout him. What about Lennon?" Eric waggles my head to tell me he's got to let go.

"Run a contest." Ariel can't resist putting up a good shot even if she's watching the scenery to prove to any interested on-looker that she's not with us, she's just stuck at our table. "Free pass opening night says you can't pick the Holy Ghost. I go with Sid Vicious."

"In your dreams," Fawne sneers lewdly.

"Where else, dork?" Ariel returns. "We're talkin' dead."

"Or Janis J. Keith Moon. Bob Marley." I'm trying to see this.

"Nothin' ghostly 'bout any of 'em," Eric muses. "More alive than most. Kinda unsettlin'."

I'm boggling over. "It's a wonder there's anyone left to make records."

"You know that one by the Jim Carroll Band, 'Those Are People Who Died! Died!'? We do a cover of it."

"Of course," snipes Ariel. "It's a list."

"I'll see if the guys wanna play it next set. Alston wails

on it."

"There you go!" Ariel baps the table, and the bottles bop. "A theme. People will be killing themselves to get in. You got you a house band—better change your name to Genocide—now see if you can't get a license to put arsenic in the drinks."

"'I'll have a Blanche Taylor Moore, and make it snappy,'" Fawne mugs, drumming her fingers, "'I haven't got all day.'"

We laugh.

"Yeah, see? Expand the concept. Death Land! We're talking big money. Have rides like, oh, say, chicken running, where you can really, really die!" Ariel speaks to an imaginary audience of sane people who are everywhere but at this table.

I address the mirrored wall. "I'm seeing this so clearly." I sit up, clear my throat. "It's a nightclub out of a Hollywood musical. The walls and the floor are like white patent leather. Shit, you know? I could paint it right on these awful mirrors, in enamel? oil? alkyd? lots of gleam, but perfect perspective, real depth, and the smoke—" I swirl my hand through the blue air. I'm hoarse from shouting over the noise. "Bessie, Elvis, and, I don't know, Karen Carpenter"—Eric gags—"are up on a white stage like a mound of pot cheese, fronting a band, all the greats, in white tie and tails? and the others are at tables or dancing—"

"You've got to do it!" Fawne sounds like my agent, looking up from the latest bank statement. I awake to the finite realities: to time is money, to limitation, to death—in my cell(s), as it were. Now she sounds like the Virginia who wanted Abraham Lincoln to vouch for Santa Claus. "Could you really do it?"

If I say no, it will convince her there's no reason to grow up, that dreams can't come true, that inspiration is the mother of frustration, and anything to the contrary is just shining you on. You *can't* get no— Ariel is holding her breath. She will be delighted. She will know everything. Fawne will concede—how much? I look at her tense quiver, like a fear-frozen bunny. Game, set, match. Love means nothing. La Sagrada Familia will crumble. Angkor Wat never was. "The Waterlilies" close. Sister Juana shuts her trap. "The Wizard of Oz" fades to black. Miles Davis never shows. Why go to Tibet?

And I can't help it, I *see* it. It's dazzling, heartbreaking. Youth caught in ice. The Snow Queen's palace. "It would take forever. Lots of research, finding good photos to work from— I suppose I could make cartoons at home at night, then pounce them onto the mirror—" I demonstrate pouncing with seasoning jigs of my fist. "Or maybe scratch it on with—"

"Why would you want to?" Ariel's jaw drops as though she's got the bends descending to my level. "We are talking pit here. Out of business in two weeks, and besides—"

"Your eyes look like oysters," Eric whispers in my ear.

"You've just got to do it." Fawne leans forward over her arms as if she has a stomach cramp, as if she's finally broken down to confess a terrible secret. "You must. And the thing is, I can help. The research, all that stuff you were saying, tracing it on the mirror, I can do that." Her grubby paw, on which she has doodled in red ink, darts out of her sleeve to pinch the thin skin on the back of my hand. It looks as though it's come through barbed wire. "It would be the greatest thing that's ever happened to me. It would totally change my life." The paw darts back into its hole.

I wish I'd held onto it. My reflection holds steady on the black pools of her eyes. This could be the main chance for both of us. Such economy argues warmly.

And I remember that during the time I searched for an apartment for Elspeth, after school and then after my summer typing job, I achieved my full height, took up karate, and lost some twenty pounds. I learned first-hand why you can't judge a book by its cover. I discovered buildings in New York where you have to share the hall toilet with the displaced of three continents, where stews are thickened with plaster. I saw insects of a size to make you ask what they could do for their country. I finally found a place on Third Avenue in the twenties. The kitchen and the bathroom were the same room, the room you came into, quite a challenge to decorum when Elspeth started dating. I was there almost daily to help transform it into the showplace of the East Side. We nailed scrounged hubcaps around the tub and painted the fixtures, appliances, moldings, and floors aluminum, the walls and ceilings black, and the Oriental furniture red. The inadequacy of apertures encouraged Elspeth to a series of hinged, oil-on-wood, acute triangle triptychs, predating shaped canvasses by years. I remember this as among the happiest times of my life. I'd fall asleep breathless and wake up revved.

One evening the phone rang, long distance, for me. "Olé!" shouted a rusky voice and hung up, cackling.

"It's ridiculous." I have to swallow. "I really want to do it."

Eric peers over his specs like Ol' Possum, the Practical Cat.

"You have to talk to the manager, please, right now." The white intensity in the carapace of coat, the shaved and charred hair, the black eyes—Fawne looks like a mad monk. She chews her thumb. "You have to."

Eric frowns and feels my cheek. "You already got too many irons in the fire."

"Much as I hate to agree with *him*—" Ariel throws her head back to the ceiling. "This is such complete bullshit. I just don't believe you. You goin' through the change of life?"

"What's his name?" I ask Eric. "The manager. Owner? Would you ask him to talk to me, or should I call him myself tomorrow?"

Arguments prowl his face like thunderclouds over a corn-field. He pushes up his glasses and grins. It's my funeral. I grin back. This man will be drinking to me for years after he's gone, and the further I get, the better I'll look. A real rock 'n roll love story. When he gets up and takes off, it's the same view of him tucking in his shirttail as when I'm in bed and he's dressing to leave.

Fawne wants to talk technique, like her John Nagy draw-ing set just came in the mail. Her animation makes her frothy. Ariel fumes stress, burnout, who'll do the cookin'? who'll pay the rent? What about me me me? I see the seethe at the door—Belushi is the bouncer—Billie Holiday's gardenia, Marvin and Tammy, eyes locked, twining arms to drink champagne. The bubbles tickle my nose. I try to concen-trate on how to peddle it to the owner, but will I do table-cloths—ice-white napery with blue shadows in the folds—or formica with grooved chrome and bases like tar spills?

The owner is my brother's age, short, brown, balding, in a soft Hawaiian shirt blotched with parrots and pants with so many pleats it looks like he's wearing a laundry bag. Like a black Phil Collins, the living dead rock star.

"Nate," Eric the Rad again, using his hands like model-ing tools, "this here's the girl with kaleidoscope eyes you've heard tell of. Carrie Krasnow, Nate Transou."

I blink at the extravagant compliment and offer my hand. Nate nods, searches his pockets for hands, can't find any, smiles at the floor.

"Why don't you ladies come on up front and let Cee do a little wheeling?" Glasses up so he winks me the big eye. "I got to get ready to rock."

Fawne has to plow Ariel off the seat. Finally, she grabs her cigs, untangles her legs, sighs all over me, and stalks away for her friends. Fawne decides to follow her only after Eric's trace has grown over.

Nate dips into the booth and asks if he can buy me a

drink. I say no and ask if I can buy him one. He smiles no and caps his hands on his elbows. Bracing himself for a hard luck story.

I start with Retro because Johnny downstairs will speak well of me. Nate keeps smiling at the table: cut to the chase. But I feed him some c.v., hoping he won't ask how much work I've actually sold. "Look, you call this place heaven, and what do you see? Mirrors. Hell is the place for mirrors. Who's the last person you want to see in a bar?"

"My ex."

"Myself."

He sneaks up to see what I have to fear from mirrors. Checks his own reflection. The smile is a tic. "Hog Heaven," he says. "Little witticism. Toyed with Blind Pig." He tilts toward the crowd. "Too young."

I'm falling in love. "I want to paint heaven from one side to the other. Rock heaven. On the mirrors. It's a posh nightclub, and everybody's there: Otis, Elvis, Jimi, Janis, you name 'em. I can render them instantly recognizable."

Now he really slants me one, but I radiate sincerity; I can't help it if I'm good. (Let it be true.)

"I don't know what you have in mind for this place or what your investment in it is. Maybe you won it in a crap game. Maybe it's a stop on the road to Atlanta. Maybe you just work here. Me, I like to make where I am as good as I can. Why not make it heaven?"

"How much will it cost?"

I slop back against the seat. The raucous tape goes off. Generic starts creeping up on "Tell It To The Judge"—excuses Eric heard in traffic court. I haven't given money a thought. I want to say, "Nothing." Nate looks up. "Fifteen hundred," I shout. It sounds both audacious and like peanuts. "Plus materials!" I add hastily.

"Okay," he says. Somehow he can talk under the music. "I'll think about it. Maybe you can show me somethin', a sketch, a piece of it. Give me a timetable. Say next week?"

If I didn't have to roast Tommy Lee, I'd've had it yesterday. I have to stick with the storm-at-sea voice. "Sure. Great. Next Wednesday? What's a good time for you?"

"Suppertime. Six, downstairs." He holds in his shirt as he skims up from the table. "Pleasure."

"Yes! Oh, and is it okay if I come by sometime to take measurements?"

"Sure." The hands are back in his pockets, he wobbles on the sides of his shoes, he studies the floor. "When you say rock heaven?" He frowns. "Music heaven. Monk at the piano."

"White piano. Black hat. The porkpie."

He agrees with his shoulders.

Now where do I put Professor Longhair? I've got to get me some mirror, I think, and fast! See if it'll take paint.

"What did he say?" Fawne slots into the booth like a bowling ball into the gutter.

"I've got to show him something next Wednesday."

Fawne's eyes bulge. "Can you do it?"

"He loves the idea."

She spazzes a clutching gesture that could be a stunted hug or a strangle.

I smile and reach across to squeeze her shoulder. "I'm counting on your help."

"You got it. Man? This is so crucial. It's magic. Like the first real thing to happen to me. Do I get paid?"

I nod. I am a union maid.

"I can't wait to tell my dad. Maybe they'll let me call him tonight. You know, he told me, if I just—"

"Are we leaving?" Ariel. She seems to be looking in an invisible periscope.

"He loves the idea," Fawne squeaks, as though she's been sucking helium.

"I just don't believe you." Ariel looks like she's going to

fall over. "This is like Ethel and Lucy paint Ricky's club. You're always saying how you don't have time to take a shit. What are me and Dash supposed to do while you're fixing up the clubhouse?"

"What do you need me for?" I ask her.

I expect her to roll her eyes, but instead her face seems to tear in half like paper. "Can we go now?" She almost doesn't get it out.

"Do you want to?" I'm ready to buy a round for the house, teach these kids to boogie, but then I think of daubing the King's pompadour on my reflection over the bathroom sink in various types of paint. "I wanted to tell Eric."

"You know he'll come over after—"

I sure hope so. I also want to whip him into stiff peaks with my desire wire.

"Besides," Ariel prods Fawne, "didn't you say you had to be home by twelve?"

"I'm sorry, Cee, I know it's a bummer, I lost track. Forrest is gonna have a cow. I guess no call to dad tonight—" Forlorn.

"You should have told me." Shouldering purse. "Look, I'll come in with you and tell them what happened."

"And about me helping you? You'll get their permission? Ooh, and D.C., you remember—?"

"Let's just take it easy. One step at a time."

When I open the door, making straight for the paints and greatness, Dash is sitting in a chair he's placed directly in the way. He's gray and greasy as if smeared with newsprint, he's wrapped in a blanket with Victor on his lap and Nancy on his neck. His eyes are flares.

"What?"

Tears well and fall like hot wax. "Oh, Mom. It's Grampa."

"When?" I spin toward the door, grip Ariel for her keys.

She pulls away with a grunt.

His head sags forward. "He's gone. Gramma called. She's with the Dorns. She says she's okay. She said call her tomorrow."

Gone? Where? How? I twist toward the door. Toward the phone. Toward Dash. Toward Ariel. I twist until Ariel pushes me down on the couch. We all sit and watch to see what I do next.

7 I Don't Want to Spoil the Party

What I do next is soap over all the mirrors, a Jewish mourning custom. So that four days later, when I race in after the funeral to splash cold water on my face, I can't see the result. My mother, dabbing on powder, painting frowns she pulls at an advancing and retreating compact, says I picked a funny time to get religion. Ariel goes out to the truck to repair her mascara. Dash reminds me he had to shave in the reflection off the toaster. "Why wouldn't God want us to look decent?" Ida asks. Who was Jesus's tailor? I think. I don't know what God wants, but the mirrors are suddenly keyholes on heaven, and if I look in, I may not be able to look away.

I'm thankful I was so prepared for my father's home-coming. A mere eight hours slavish attention in the kitchen last night, punctuated by my mother's disheartening meta-physical questions—"Why did he leave me?" (The raise.) "How could he do this to me?" (Sat in one place and ate pastrami for seventy-five years. Smoked like Mount St. Helens.) "What will I do now?" (Punt.)—and I can feed the mob at our heels. Eric, wearing an apron over his white shirt and skinny black tie, his hair braided and stuffed down his tight collar—why not two braids wrapped around his crown and a dirndl?—skipped the burial to lay out the feast, apportioned in perfect mouthfuls, surrounded by bouquets of fresh herbs. He's brewed four octanes of coffee and tea and arranged a flock of folding chairs and nesting tables in what I'm sure he thinks are "conversation groups," but which I know will degenerate into "pits." And still the man is wringing his hands. I back him into the refrigerator. We rub chapped lips and hug like sprockets, then quaff a quick one. My mother sanctimoniously refuses her usual Bloody Mary. She clicks shut the compact like a hymnal and purses it as the first limos disgorge my two maiden aunts and my brother Harold and family.

Harold steams in the door. He looks harried, even though Diane is the one herding their four grub-pale children. Harold married, at a prudent thirty-five, a business major some fourteen years his junior, and as soon as they had amassed an adequate portfolio, he let her take leave to found his dynasty, the three girls and, at last, Prince Hal, now two. Do the girls realize they are only failed attempts, as Ida so often told me, chortling, as though *we* had no gender, at the little paragon making with fiendish intent for the cat asleep behind the woodstove? Probably. The nine-year-old, Brooke (Ashley and Morgan; Wysocki, mind you), has her dainty Stride Rite set to pitch him ass over ears into the fiery furnace.

"No-oh! Ho-ot! Ba-ad!" Diane croons distantly, like Rudee Valee to the rafters with a megaphone. Her face has that unlived-in look. She plotzes on the sofa beside Ida and grasps her wrist like a piton. "I don't know how you're coping," she wonders wearily, as though Ida's coping were something like jumping rope, and, at her age, she ought to stop it.

"Well, thanks," sniffs my mother. Diane not only started life as a shiksa (she's supposed to be retooled by Harold Jr.'s bar mitzvah), she's *management.*

Meanwhile, I pluck the undaunted baby badger out of danger, earning a dirty look from Brooke and a kick in the crotch from this screaming resistance the color of raw steak. Harold says, "Look at her! The liberated woman. Couldn't wait to get her mitts on the baby." I think of hurling Snooks at him. His hair is completely gray. He's getting jowls. With contortions of the brow, I enlist my two to take charge of his nippers, who adored Ariel and doted on Dash at first glimpse of Their Hipnesses, and who surrender to them now with an alacrity that makes me want to sedate them. Dash puts Prince Hal on his shoulders until a few impatient whacks from those stout boots threaten his windpipe. "Giddyap!"

Harold sizes up the spread, then, swatting Hugo off the seat with a napkin, plants his pumpkin in the big chair. "I'm starved," he announces. Diane stands up.

Enter my father's older sisters, ninety and eighty-eight, helped by my cousin, Yussel, and his wife, Trudy. Luba can hardly see; she worked over fifty years as a proofreader. Fritzi is almost deaf; she was a court stenographer. They've lived together forever, and they loathe each other. In 1963, the blind Luba asked the deaf Fritzi if she was about to trip over a rug that had a curling corner. Fritzi didn't hear her. Luba tripped. She hasn't spoken to Fritzi since, although she is the garrulous one. Does Fritzi know it? She keeps asking, "What? What?" Anyone trying to explain the whole business to either of them is assumed to have been taken in by the other's wiles. "She can hear all right when *you* do the talking." "She has no trouble watching tv." They live in a tiny apartment, crammed with phony gilded white Louis Quinze and shaded lamps the size of palace guards, in a neighborhood that terrifies them. They are very frail. Luba is still recovering from falling off a ladder. Fritzi can't shake a cold she caught taking the subway into Manhattan for a white sale. They are both wearing woolen turbans with feathers and fake jewels, silver mink stoles over their sensible coats and heavy handbags. When did they get so short? They have the same face, and it is also my father's face, and someday it will be mine. Why soap the mirrors?

Yussel and Trudy brought them down on the plane to thwart their hitchhiking or rustling horses, hang-gliding to get here. Yussel holds Fritzi's arm; her foot dithers over the doormat as if it were a fathomless fissure. Luba hurtles ahead, "What's the holdup?," barely restrained by Trudy from flattening Fritzi. Yussel is an electrician; also a fence. Trudy is a buyer for Bloomie's. She rolls her eyes at me. At the cemetery, Luba flinging herself at the grave like a varsity tackle and cursing my father for abandoning her, Trudy sharply tapped my shoulder and ordered, "Get your mother out of here," while Yussel battled Luba back. Now Trudy mutters, "Don't ask!" before I open my mouth. We get Fritzi seated and help her off with her things. The hat stays. Eric peels Trudy in one deft spiral and whisks the coats away. "Wow," says Trudy, leering. I probably blush.

"You'll have to speak up, Carol, darling, I don't hear so good no more," Fritzi tells me.

I peck next to her dark Joan Crawford lips to avoid her pointy glasses. She lights up like a Coleman lantern. Whoosh! Who does she think I am?

"Is it Carol?" Luba lands her cane on my left foot. "Let me look at you!" Her eyes swim over my face like cave fish. She takes a big plug out of my arm. "You're so skinny! What are you, sick?"

"I lost some weight—"

"Forty pounds," says my mother, bobbing her head as though everyone disputes it, "and she's kept it off!"

"About eight, nine years ago. You remember, Aunt Luba." I kiss her chamois cheek. She still smells like gardenias. "You're looking well."

"I didn't remember you was such a liar," she snickers, tweaking my chin.

"What are they saying?" Fritzi demands.

"CAROL LOST WEIGHT," shouts Trudy.

"FORTY POUNDS," Ida yells.

"Well anybody can see that. She looks beautiful." She says "bee-yoo-tee-ful" in the lingering, caressive intonation of my yoot. "What's your secret?" She pulls out a cigarette and snaps her lighter at it.

I stop myself cracking the "near-death diet" joke in the nick of time. "I run!" I pump my arms, point at my ears. "With earphones!"

"Is that why you're talking so loud? Those things ruin your hearing. Where are the children?" Luba cocks her head toward the noise from the rear of the house like a lion downwind of playful infant wildebeest. She probably has a Spalding and a broomstick in her pocketbook.

"They'll surface for food, I'm sure."

"I can't hear a thing." Fritzi shakes her head at her folded, jeweled, freckled fingers, ribboned in smoke. "So where are the children?" she asks Trudy.

"Aunt Luba, please, sit. What can I get for you all?"

"Did you hear that?" Harold lurches in his chair. "She's picked up the accent."

"You know Carol—she's a sponge," says Ida. "You should hear her children. They sound," she mouths soundlessly, "black."

"Cream and sugar," says Fritzi.

"Put me near my darling Harold," Luba commands Yussel, who is tailing her with a chair, sweating in his overcoat and fedora. Using Harold to block out the stove, he prods her the long way around. He could really use a whip with that chair.

Diane collapses into the sofa. "I'd love some coffee." She looks like she needs it intravenously. "How about you, Harold?"

"We've got regular and decaf," says Eric, finally getting

hold of Yussel's hat and coat and tossing them in the bed-room, "also tea: high test and herbal."

"He's got regular and decaf," Diane repeats.

"This is my good friend, Eric Austen," I say tartly. They have been introduced. More than once.

While I'm still speaking, Harold tells Diane, "I'll have the regular," reluctantly conceding to dire necessity.

"I've got wine, beer, liquor, and soft drinks, if you pre-fer." I've got a bottle of Chivas left over from when dad sold the store, fathead.

Diane smiles tolerantly, as though in one of my peoples' sacred primitive rituals I have offered her a steaming mug of sheep's piss. "We'll just have the coffee, thanks. With cream," she sinks lower and murmurs to Eric, "and do you have any Sweet 'n Low?"

"No, but if you hum a few bars—" Eric, juggling cups and spoons.

"I'll have a martini," says Luba. "I see you hired a waiter."

This is the one who can hear. "My friend, Eric. He's a landscape designer and a musician. He's helping me out."

"A musician! What's he gonna play, Taps? You're too old for such foolishness. He'll use you up and throw you away. Find a steady man your own age and settle down." Luba was engaged during the 1950s to a "theatrical agent"— I was terribly impressed by the way he whistled for cabs— but her glamorous career in publishing—she wore a natty visor, like a cardsharp—came first. "Wait! What happened to your husband? I saw him around here a minute ago."

"What is she saying?" cries Fritzi. "What is she telling her?"

"WHAT DO YOU WANT TO EAT?" shouts Trudy.

"What have you got?" Fritzi asks stolidly, although she is the one who can see.

Car doors are slamming up and down the block. My

parents' friends, card partners, and neighbors from Heartwood Acres straggle along the sidewalk, the path, search-
ing in vain for a railing to help them climb the steps or the
ramp. My former husband, Karl, and his wife, Elly, pass
them hand-over-hand, like marshals at the crossing of the
Red Sea. Heat pours out. The furnace roars. The aunts shiver
and want their coats back. Next door, the neanderthal is
stationed on his porch like a star-fixated assassin at a pre-
miere, with six-pack, radio. The Retroverts lean against their
cars, waiting for the old folks to file in. Pearly Gates! I start
spinning like a dervish.

But at some point, everybody is sitting or standing with
a full plate and cup. Cousins, uncles and aunts, the
Heartacres, the Reverts, Susie and another nurse from rehab, Lou's pet physical therapist with distressed eyes and a
drawl that pulls like taffy. My mother does a headcount
and seems pleased with the turnout. She has a sign-in book
at the door like "What's My Line?" so later she can find out
exactly who her real friends are. Her food sits untouched
on the coffee table. Dash and Karl lean against the wall
talking to Karl's plate, shifting or scratching or enthusing in
syncopation. Elly swivels to spot someone more out of it
than she to chat up. Did I say she's a social worker? Their
son, Adam, little Lord Baden-Powell, is at day care, and she
studies the other children to see if she's deprived him of a
vital learning experience. On the floor, surrounded, Ariel
demonstrates how good she is with children, like Maria von
Trapp, complete with convent haircut. Every now and then
she stabs a look straight for Karl's soft core, with a sigh to
imply Dash isn't doing his share. Even the cats come into it;
she poses over a nuzzle of struggling fur. The room smells
like a tropical colony: spices, flowers, tobacco, coffee, chocolate, sweat. Eric and I are lodged in the doorframe to the
kitchen, drenched, panting, butler and maid in our generic
funeral black and white, an ideograph for "the help."

"It was a lovely ceremony, Ida," Mrs. Dorn says. "The rabbi spoke beautifully."

"He was eloquent," agrees Mr. Fragiacomo.

"Very good. And so young!" says Aunt Sophie.

"I thought he was glib," Harold frowns, sitting forward. "What was all that crap about Dad's love for the state of Israel?"

"Your father was a champion of the state of Israel." Luba hoists her chin.

"Well," says Ida, trying to include everyone, "maybe he wasn't a religious man, but—"

"He cared," nods Mrs. Murphy.

"He cared," nods Mr. Wright.

"That's right," says Uncle Phil.

What he actually did was ape the rabbi in funny voices on the Day of Atonement when we beat our hearts and re-peated, "For the wrongs we have done we are sorry." He put my transistor radio in his breast pocket to listen to the Series throughout the High Holy Days and accepted sym-pathy for the putative new hearing aid. He wouldn't give me the dime to hand in at Hebrew school on Arbor Day to plant a tree in Israel. He once let an orthodox friend mis-take pork for chicken, and then he *told* him. And us! Laugh-ing! But hate Arabs? With a vengeance.

"He didn't give a good goddamn about the state of Is-rael," objects Harold.

"He was a saint," Aunt Luba says, and that's that.

A tottering old man I don't know hauls a chair to the buffet table. No jacket or tie, sleeves rolled up, his shirt hangs open, and I can see under his u-necked skivvy his thin, yellowed chest. He grumbles at a woman with red cot-ton candy hair—I'm thinking of her as Miss Kitty—and she heaps his plate. He makes a noise in his throat, and she slaps mustard on rye for him.

"Yeah, okay, a saint, I'm with you, but what about the

military bit?" Harold punches his pointer down on invisible notes: auditing. "I mean, Dad was in the army, sure—he was drafted!—he was no hero, and that was forty years ago—"

"Sir! A man's military service brooks no reproach!" Foghorn Leghorn, he even has the big beak, unbuttoning and buttoning his jacket, crossing and uncrossing his legs, to display preparedness. "Do you know what it was like at Guadalcanal, son? Do you know what we had to eat?"

"I bet he tells us," mutters Trudy.

"What?" asks Fritzi.

"Well, I'll tell you what. If a man found a cockroach in his rice, he was glad of it." Emphatically, "It was meat!"

"Barf me out the door," says Dash.

"What?" Fritzi begs.

"HE ATE ROACHES," Trudy yells.

"Did you have to tell me?" asks Fritzi.

"And that's nothing compared to the siege of Leningrad, where—"

The old man at the table grunts, and Miss Kitty laughs and says, "Oh, it sure is!" and helps him to more turkey.

"I'll tell you one thing." Ida ties her arms under her breasts and hefts herself higher against the couch. "I'm so glad we bought the prepaid funeral package. It made everything so easy for me. I just called them, and they went into action."

"You think they jump into their pants?" Trudy asks me. Eric stifles a guffaw. Karl doesn't. That must be the difference. Elly twinkles at him over a moue of disapproval.

"Sign me right up," Diane murmurs to the ceiling. That couch is quicksand.

"Oh, I did, I got one for myself, and so should you," Ida rotates her head to tell Harold, then me. She has puffs under her eyes like waterlogged cottonballs. "That way, at a time like this—"

Julie Edelson

"You don't have to be bothered," says Mrs. Trivette.

"That's right," says Mr. McConnell.

"You don't have to think," sighs Mrs. Clark, a recent widow.

"Such a relief."

"So how much did it cost?" asks Aunt Cookie, who never knew any better.

Ida pauses. She can't think of a withering retort, so she simply tells her.

"What are they saying?" Fritzi asks. Trudy gives her the gist. "Hasn't that Cookie got a nerve on her?" gasps Fritzi. "So how much?"

The old man belches, and Miss Kitty says, "Of course!" and spoons him more Indian pudding.

"He was a wonderful man." My mother's brother Phil calls the meeting to order.

"An angel," says Mrs. Brown. "So polite."

"Such a dear," Mrs. Dorn agrees.

"That's right," says Mr. Carter. They all nod.

"He was always immaculately dressed," Aunt Luba intones. Her watery gaze and the turban make her look like a medium. Harold catches my eye and moves his lips along with hers, "Never a hair out of place—"

"What there was of it," says Cookie, "and there wasn't much."

"Why, in summer," Luba drifts on, and Harold doesn't miss a beat, he's built his reputation on cracking me up like this and then pointing the finger, "he used to change his shirt, twice, three times a day."

"LOU WAS NEAT," Trudy answers Fritzi.

"Ach, he drove us crazy, running his shirts to the Chinese."

The old man hacks a long, wet scroup. "He'd just love a piece of this." Who is she talking to? "Mind if I—?" Miss Kitty cuts a wedge of Mrs. Bacalini's sunshine cake and a slab of the chocolate cheesecake.

"And hard working," Ida quavers. "He worked every day of his life except Sundays and holidays. And even then sometimes he'd—"

"Sure, he didn't know what to do with himself outside the store. Except play cards and go for the newspaper. If he was the guy goes out for a packa cigarettes and never comes home, we wouldna noticed for weeks. Years!"

Why is Harold being such a stickler? He must pride himself on his candor. Ida is a clench of vexation. This is not that singular marvel of whom everyone has heard so very much and to whom their own offspring have been so unfavorably compared.

"It put you through college, young man," Luba, in the voice from beyond, "and your sister."

I hear the Wicked Witch of the West saying, "And your little *dog,* too!"

"—these kids today have no idea the sacrifices we made for them—"

A paroxysm of nodding. "That's right!"

"—the things we did without so they could have." Luba is leading the villagers to drive out their own children! I see them collecting their pitchforks. Run!

"I'll have you know I was on full scholarship," Harold informs us.

Everybody looks at me.

"Hey! Brooklyn College! Regents Scholarship! Thirty-five bucks a semester!"

"Ease off on the treble, babe," Eric whispers.

"Yeah, but you have to admit, that year in Florence—" Harold hectors.

"Summer jobs. I *made* money!"

"CAROL BANKRUPTED LOU," Trudy tells Fritzi.

"Lou was always a tightwad," Fritzi assures me, lighting another cigarette. "Good thing your mother handled the money. We'd give him carfare and lunch money, and he'd walk, have a glass tea at the automat, save the rest. And for what?" She hacks the exhale. "A fortune in shoeleather."

"He never lied, cheat, or stole, not even when the neighborhood was overrun by schwartzes." Turning into an Old Testament prophet: Lubadiah. "He was a pillar of the community, a generous provider, and devoted to his children!"

"Oh, get off it!" Harold rears in the chair as if it's hydraulic. "I remember one time, I musta been about thirteen, he met me coming outta the shower, I was in a towel, and he took holda my chest and squeezed," he grapples the air, "and he said, 'breasts like a woman.' Hell of a thing to say to a boy that age!"

Harold's been dragging that one around a long time. Maybe he's trying to cheer us up by convincing us it's good Lou's dead. He looks to me for support. I keep thinking about Lou's smell, shaving cream and Chesterfields, about how his shirt felt against my cheek when I curled under his arm for hours, watching tv, and our clasped hands in his overcoat pocket when I danced along at his side on those trips for the newspaper, and about his voice, wooly, scratchy. About the way, when I was little, I could suddenly, and for no reason I ever understood, delight him. But then because I never understood, I'd work myself sick trying to do it again.

"I don't know." Ariel has Prince Hal clambering her thighs and grasping her earrings. "I agree that was a horrible thing to say to you, but I think Grampa was tired a lot. I think he got tired sooner than a lot of people and much more tired. Like bored and tired. So he'd get jumpy and, like, push." She pushes Hal back to her knees.

Elly draws Karl's attention away from Dash's run-ins with security for skating in private parking lots to Ariel's fine sensibility, and he looks up, glows at her, puffs like a pigeon. I don't think he heard what she said, but if Elly liked it, he must have had something to do with it. Ariel basks in their regard, sternly pretending not to notice.

"—and I vowed to myself that when I became a father," Harold holds forth right through Ariel's remarks, "I'd be exactly the opposite of him. Take time with my children. Enjoy them!"

Diane rises slightly to say, "He gets right down on the floor and plays with them. In his good suits."

"You shoulda seen Karl," my mother says, smiling at him coyly and wiping her seeping eyes. "He was like a woman with them kids. Changed the diapers, fed them, give them a bath—Lou useta say, 'Those kids don't have a father; they have two mothers.'"

Karl half-smiles, smoothing his mustache down the sides of his mouth into his beard. Dash stares challenge in his ear. Then Karl levels on me eyes as warm and lively as embers.

"Lou was a perfect father, a wonderful man, and the prettiest baby you ever saw in your life." Luba's eyelids descend like the Tablets of the Law from Sinai.

"Not to mention an excellent poker player," says Mr. Dorn, frisking himself for cigars. He hands one to Mr. McConnell, and Karl takes one.

Another wind shakes the darling buds.

"LOU WAS A PRETTY BABY," Trudy shouts for Fritzi.

"He was a royal pain in the ass from the day he was born," Fritzi says, and, through the smoke, her smile breaks like sunlight.

It's that old tv show, "This Is Your Life." You'd be brought to the studio on a pretext, and everybody you ever knew would reminisce about you. Only this is your death, and some people are spiteful. Can I market the variation for the '90s?

The old man sits back from the table and burps the scale. He holds his stomach between his hands like he's wondering how to mail it or shoot it through a hoop. He motions

to Miss Kitty and produces unintelligible sounds like a crowbar prying up a tread. I'm thinking, "He can't eat any more!"
when Miss Kitty addresses me. "Carol? I just want to tell
you how much Gut has enjoyed the food."

"Not *The* Gut?!" mutters Trudy.

Karl spurts smoke. Dash hoots. Eric hides his face on
my shoulder.

"Gutmacher," Mr. Dorn supplies.

"He says it is just superb, and so it is. He hasn't eaten
this good in a long time," exclaims Miss Kitty. "And do you
know what else he told me?"

He loons up with his jaw dropped. No teeth.

"How much he likes Carol. That's a fact. How he likes
a gal with a little meat on her bones. What a firecracker she
is."

My son turns to the wall to vent his risibility. My daughter is positively leading the children in scorn. Brooke, in
fact, is screaming. The Reverts cover their mouths.

"Why, I'm downright jealous." Miss Kitty swats Gut's
shoulder, and he rocks around the fulcrum of his knees.

Karl squints through the smoke at me. Suddenly, it's our
wedding. Karl has hair on top of his head again, and the
belly's gone, and I think, "fire-breathing," like I did when I
first walked into the storefront to ask about the silk-screen-
ing job, and he was hustling donations over the phone, and
behind him, these great Cuban posters of Ho Chi Minh and
Che, local lithos of Erica Huggins and Malcolm X, judged
his performance. Che—the cigar.

But Karl smoked a cigar at our wedding too, sweating
and expansive as though he'd hit his number. Everybody
came. Karl's rabid Bronx relatives who took to mine like
Gilbert to Sullivan—when they weren't arguing, they made
comical music together. Karl invited his Harlem scout troop,
and the old farts kept asking them when they were going to
perform, and they'd look at each other scared. Francy made

it, and Billy, Dan, Alan, Sharon. Zatz, slipping joints to the guitar player and requesting "Good Golly Miss Molly," "Great Balls of Fire," "Work With Me Annie," claimed the mike with the original Toves to ad lib a ditty they called "Kiss My Nuptials"—theme music!—until my mother muzzled him and made the guys they'd hired play the Hokey Pokey and Hava Nagila. Karl's scruffy comrades came, however pissed off about marriage, sex, religion, art, partying, and pigs-in-blankets. And when everybody was leaving our apartment the next day, after a whole lot of Tavola red and pizza, I thought we were all married, like Moonies, and Karl had to pull me in off the fire escape, from which I was pelting them with blossoms off the swiped floral arrangements, calling "Don't forget to smash the state!" in my nightie. Elspeth was there with her new and vastly improved husband, Russ, and Sharon's awful husband asked him if he was ever unfaithful to his wife, and Russ said solemnly, "In every possible way, on every possible occasion." Else and I waltzed so she could relate this, scandalizing the aunts. "I think you both got great bargains," she said. We spun around laughing like girls in the schoolyard. Karl and I swore to treat each other fairly and share responsibilities and give each other space and not forget to smash the state. And he kept kissing me and I kept laughing, which made the Justice of the Peace lose his place, and we never to my knowledge actually said, "I do."

My father looked really happy that night. Maybe he'd thought he'd never get me off his hands. Maybe he was glad with one big party at cousin Morrie's dive in Bensonhurst to repay twenty years of social debt. Of course, he carped, hitting each table like itching powder, but as we were going, he took my hands and said, "Well," and he kissed me for the first time since I was eleven. "Don't be a stranger," he said.

Right now that seems the saddest thing imaginable.

"Anyways, it was a beautiful ceremony. I don't say it couldn't have been a little warmer—" Ida smiles bravely, and they all nod with her.

"Ah, but you know warm spells can be treacherous," warns Mrs. Brown. "You can catch your—a bad cold in weather like that."

"Didn't it happen to my brother? He went out without his coat one of those freak warm days last January? Well, he was gone before Easter. Just like that."

"I'm telling you."

"It's those kerosene heaters kill so many in the winter. And now they're saying you can get radiation from your electric blanket. I swear! If the bedbugs don't get you—"

"—the killer bees—"

"I read where they killed a horse—"

"At least it didn't rain," Aunt Sophie inserts with determination.

"We need rain," says Mr. Evans.

"—livestock, entire herds of cattle. They're aggressive. You know how a bee won't sting you unless you mess with it? Well, these *will*—"

"'Was you ever stung by a dead bee?'" I ask Eric, but Karl's the one who's seen that movie, and his smile reminds me how soft his lips can be.

"They attack in squadrons. They say they're due here any time, coming up from Texas—"

"Take cover!" Dash drops.

"But it's dangerous out in the open like that," says Mrs. Brown. "So many people are struck by lightning. Especially on the golf course."

"Did we bury Lou on a golf course?" Trudy asks indignantly.

"There was a hole in one," yuks Karl, prodding her.

"And now I heard tell of flying cockroaches!"

"Meat!" Dash rejoices. Karl needs to squelch him, but

he's convulsed.

"Oh no!"

"Yes! My neighbor had them in her hanging begonia—"

"Yes, but what you have to be so careful about—Carol, I want you to listen to this, what with all these cats, and you too, Harold," Harold and I snap to attention with Rockette timing and earn a frown like a bobbypin from our mother, "is ticks. They can kill you. They get on the kids, you can't even see them, and the next thing you know—"

"It-th coitainth!" Dash slobbers, drawing his thumb across his gullet.

"Well, but that's nothing. There are these frogs in South America, poisonous ones, big as coons, can give a dog rabies."

"Isn't it a shame about those dogs attacking that boy jogging?" Mrs. Clark starts the heads wagging sideways.

"The very next day, little seven-year-old boy was bit by another one, same breed. Didn't rip his throat out like the jogger, but it sure did mutilate his—"

"Well, I'll tell you, it's a fact, there is nothing more dangerous in this world than a mother pig. Of course you know she'll eat her young, but if you try to interfere with her, she'll tear you to pieces. Isn't that right?"

"What are they saying?" Fritzi asks hopefully.

"I give up." Trudy claps her hand over her mouth.

"HOW ABOUT MORE COFFEE?" I venture.

The door thumps, and two Reverts leap aside to let Fawne crash in. Under her filthy, scrawled, Vietvet psychocoat, she's wearing a black spandex miniskirt, laddered black stockings with exposed garters, combat boots, a torn black Iron Maiden t-shirt, studded leather dog collar and wristbands, and she's blacked her lips and eye hollows. Her ears are reliquary. You'll remember the hair. Her nose. Where is she changing these days? The Hop-In? Everyone gapes at her as if she's fraught with meaning. She searches for me, and flinging out her arms, she groans, "Major bummer!"

The raven quothed. The bell done tolled. I don't have to ask for whom.

"My God!" blinks Fritzi. "Is it a stick up?"

"HOW ABOUT MORE COFFEE?"

Those tongues are really parched. Eric and I circulate with pots.

"Now they're saying decaf is bad for you—"

"—and oat bran isn't that good—"

"I heard a man had to have it surgically removed, it was packing his intestines like ce-ment—"

"You know what's supposed to be real bad—"

"I wrote you a poem, Cee." Fawne has extracted a folded piece of notebook paper, edged in black marker, from her pocket. Biting her lips, "I want to share this with you all. It's called 'Dead/Dad.'" She says "slash." The Reverts are already laughing. It reads rhythmically, like rap, and somewhere into it, Dash starts chugging in time.

dark dank
drip down
cold cold old old
ground ground ground

your dad is dead
    how long?
he's gone to bed
    like forever man

no more boredom/
broken bottles/
barren bedrooms/
bad breaks/back seats/
bare bones/
blues/blackmail/betrayal/
bullshit/
for him no sir

i don't know if he beat you
or if he was good
don't let it cheat you
he's worm food

So don't be unhappy
do something wild
death is your father
life is your child

"That was very nice," says Mrs. Clark, clapping softly. Aunt Sophie fixes down her wig like a British judge about to sentence.

"I had to write it in kind of a hurry, you know," Fawne pleads, "but I tried really hard to be honest and put in everything I was feeling." She passes it to me, smiling anxiously. "I almost said, 'I am your child.' Maybe that would have been better. It's yours, for keeps."

The black edging comes off on my palm. Actually, it's DEAD. Economical. "Thanks." I don't have a free hand to caress her. I'm both appalled and deeply touched—it sounds like the thesaurus, I know, but doesn't it also sound like young Cee? My little black dress has no pockets. I stash it in the sign-up book.

Ariel shucks her clinging charges and moves to Fawne's side as readily as if they're soon to be blindfolded and shot.

"This is my friend, Fawne," she grits out. She pulls and lights a last cigarette. Do your worst!

"Fauve," Fawne corrects indulgently.

Ariel bites the filter.

"Come sit by me, dear, and tell me of your native homeland." Luba waves a vague arm.

Ariel tugs Fawne in the other direction.

"I brought something for you too, Ari." Fawne pats her pocket. Hard, flat, in a brown paper bag. Ariel's eyes scramble. "It's the Sylvia Plath," she tells me with twitching lips. "You probably have it." Back to Ariel, "Should we take it upstairs so it doesn't get messed up?"

"And how did those two meet?" Harold asks me sweetly, holding up his cup, "In *stir*?"

It's tempting to pour the coffee over him. His daughters watch Fawne disappear up the ladder. They want badly to poke, scratch, sniff. I give Harold another year, year and a half, before they just say no to him. My girls return, I'm surprised how soon, and after a raid on the kitchen for drinks and victuals, camp in a corner. Ariel seems afraid of missing something, but I don't know what. She looks like she's been crying.

"Lately, there've been cases where people have swallowed the bay leaf and perforated their—"

"—well, and these frogs have got, like, what do you call it? hallucenogenetic drugs on their skin, and you lick them to get high—"

"Who figured that out?" Trudy asks Karl.

"Guadalcanal vets!" Dash seems inspired.

"I say it's your own damn fault if you leave this wonderful country and go gallivantin'—"

Yussel rises. "It's time to go. We've got a plane to catch, and Ida must be exhausted."

"Oh, no, I'm all right, please, stay." Ida huffs to sit up straighter.

Yussel proceeds to the bathroom and then for the coats, while Trudy sees to the aunts. I should have rented a jiffy john. Elly steers Karl to the corner where Ariel is repelling boarders with her cigarette, deaf to Fawne's earnest efforts to help her accept death. Elly is as wide-eyed and smile-ready as a mail-order bride. If Karl had a hat, he'd be turning the brim through his hands. Ariel switches from perk to pout when they engage Fawne; she sticks her nose in her cup and puts out to sea.

The Reverts have no trouble trampling the old folks to scram. "Sure are sorry. Don't worry about work; we get along fine without you. Always thought you were kidding about the sty. You know? paint job, repoint the brick, and it wouldn't hurt to blow in some insulation. Save you money in the long run. Well—"

The hospital staff stoop to kiss Ida. They shake hands with me. "He was doing so way-ell," the physical therapist laments, trailing that bewildered "way-ell" out the door.

"Keep an eye on your mom," Susie cautions.

Although my mother is now up on her heels, she looks shrunken. Each of her friends steps aside to let the next graze her cheek with his lips or cradle her hand. They inch the floor as though it's slippery; they touch as though they're made of sand. They speak of tomorrow, next week, a phone call, another visit, others who will visit. As they file past me, they stroke or kiss me and tell me how sorry they are, what a good daughter I am, what a good mother I must be to my lovely children. I feel like the old bag of blood in my chest is red silk, trimmed with lace.

Gut, layers of garment hanging open on him like robes and towels on a trounced fighter, droozles up at me and makes a noise like a rusty hinge.

"He says he never ate this good at a funeral before," laughs Miss Kitty, "and he's made the rounds, believe you me."

"So long, Slim." Mr. Dorn pats my ass, and I kiss him.

"You take care of yourself."

"Take care of those beautiful children."

"Your mother—"

Aunt Cookie presses me to her bosom and asks how much rent I'm paying. "You bought it?" she marvels. "They say it's so cheap down here, but I say, pay a little less, get a little less. You must be in hock to the eyebrows. What's your mother pay on her place?"

Yussel envelopes me in his coat. He's skunky from nervous sweat.

147

"We didn't have a chance to talk. How you doing?" I ask. His pinkened features seem buried in sallow, sagging flesh.

"I been better. You okay?"

I nod. "It was swell of you and Trudy to bring the aunts."

He shrugs, fitting his hat down on his temples. "They should be in a home, but try telling them. Listen, you or your mother need anything—money, advice—you call me."

"Don't worry about us. It was good to see you."

"Under other circumstances—" He dredges up tissues and snorts.

Trudy hugs me. "Any time you're back in the apple—"

"Thanks for everything—"

"Not so fast. I'm still trying to leave them here. Dump them on darling Harold."

Luba pegs me with her cane. "It's no fun getting old," she says in that oracular tone: a voice from the front. "If you knew what would happen to you, you'd never let it go this far."

"Consider the alternative," I suggest.

"All things considered," she says firmly.

"Consider the source," mutters Trudy.

"Carol, darling, take good care of yourself." Aunt Fritzi smacks her fresh red mouth into my neck.

"You too, Aunt Fritzi."

"I don't know what Luba told you, but don't listen to her." Her smile rushes like headwaters. "I never do!"

Dash holds the door open for them. Fritzi pauses to ask, "Do you know who I am?" She can't make out his answer.

"You look just like your grandfather at this age," Luba tells him, pinching. "Those long golden curls." Dash's hair is short, straight, and brown. "We wouldn't let him get a haircut until he went to school. He hated us for it!" she laughs.

Only when their fragile backs are turned does it hit me I

may never clap eyes on them again. Their crazy hats bend to their labored steps.

Diane has finally jammed all her children into their outerwear. They have stopped complaining about leaving and started complaining about how long it's taking to go.

"We sure appreciate you taking all this on yourself, Carol." Significant look at Ida. "I don't know how you manage."

I put my hand in Brooke's tousle, and she freezes. "It gets easier."

Diane looks puzzled.

"The older they get," I explain.

"The older *you* get," says Diane. The four-year-old Morgan has Sluggo swinging from her shoulder seams, trying to dance with him. "Put down that nasty cat. You've got fur all over your good coat."

"If he was nasty," Ariel calls out over whatever Fawne is telling Elly and Karl, "your kid would be shredded right now."

Diane flashes me some gratified pity.

"Goodbye, Carol." Harold has the heir apparent perched on his forearm, sucking two fingers and pulling his earlobe.

"Are you tired?" I brush the plump petal of his cheek.

He hides in his father's lapel, smearing a smile.

"Of course not," Harold booms. The child jolts. "We've got a long way to go before *we* can call it a day. I've got to get to work bright and early in the morning." He jounces his arm. "We're going on an airplane." Hal's face curdles like custard, his eyes shut, his nose goes hard and white as a cherry pit, his mouth yawns, and after a long, tense silence, he explodes. Harold tries to josh him out of it, but then there are two blasting Klaxons. He dumps him on Diane. "Change him," he says.

"Did you bring your wand?" I ask her.

She glares at me over Hal's ranting bunt.

"Well, so, Carol." Harold puts his hands on my biceps

and pulls me forward, pushes me back, like the prototype for a hugging robot. "Let's not go so long between visits. Our kids don't know each other. Maybe they could come down here and spend the summer." I must show alarm. "Oh, not here. Of course not. They don't have all their shots." Har, har. "They can stay with Mom. She'll want the company." He bunches Diane to his side. She's still bundling the rowdy infant Hulk. "And we could use a little time to ourselves. I've been thinking Club Med. I've always wanted to scuba. Well—"

Sometime during this interchange with my brother I must go into a tunnel because now that he's gone, it's suddenly light again and much quieter.

"Can I clear a room, or what?" Fawne is saying.

Karl and Elly put their hands out at me.

"It's a rite of passage." Elly coddles me in her big molasses eyes. "We all go through it sooner or later. You can comfort yourself knowing he led a long, full life—"

"How about we take the kids off you for a month or two?" Karl asks bluffly. "Would that help?"

"I don't know, Karl," Elly ponders, "you don't want to deprive her of her support system in a crisis. Then, too, who knows what the children are going through? Death isn't easy at any age. They may need the reassurance of a stable home setting—"

"Why don't we play it by ear?" I interrupt before Karl can make anything out of that "stable." "They'll come to you Friday unless I call. Is that okay?"

"Sure." Karl mellows his voice, narrows his eyes as though fitting a secret note through a slot into me. "I'm really sorry about Lou. I—" He pauses. He's discarding phrases one by one as meaningless. That's going to have to do it. He hugs me like a mitten. "Don't forget to—"

"He always liked you a lot," I'm moved to say. "I was remembering our wedding. I think you were the only thing

I ever did he approved of—"

"He had a funny way of showing it. 'She married a bum, she lives in a slum—'" Karl breaks out his big laugh. "Your aunts!"

"The aunts!" I stumble back onto a chair, laughing. "Luba!"

"What?" my mother asks.

"The aunts!"

"Oh, I know. They're losing it." She pushes her shoes off with her toes. "Every Friday night for how many years did I feed them? Gewalt! I hate to think. I just hope to hell they don't see no vacancy in my apartment."

"When she thought Fawne was like from Outer Slobovia." Ariel nestles next to her grandmother and induces her to eat a buttered roll.

"Fauve," whispers Fawne, only she's got a whisper with an echo. She edges nearer and stands, picking at a hole in the upholstery.

"When she thought Fawne was staging a holdup?" Eric cartwheels into the armchair where Harold has left a trough. "Your money or sixteen stanzas of 'The Ancient Mariner'."

"That's the other one—Fritzi." Karl humps over the arm of the couch. He puts his hands flat on his ears. I put mine on my eyes. I have no doubt someone covers his mouth. You pick.

"What about that guy—what was it?" Dash slides his butt along the floor to lean against Ida's legs. "Gut." He laughs like bells. We all chime in. "He *had* to be an alien."

"It's the only explanation," I can think of.

"He lives in the building," Ida explains. She reaches for Ariel's cup. Ariel swigs, looks in it, turns it upside down, crushes it, opens the woodstove, chucks it in. She gives Ida a carrot stick, slivers of turkey, until Ida closes her eyes in demur.

"What if he wasn't saying what the old bimbo said he

was? What if she was making it up? And he's really saying, 'Help me! I'm being held captive and forced to stuff myself by this ditzoid redhead!'" This kid has watched a lot of tv.

"Youse guys are just awful," Ida says, catching her breath and sniffling.

"Your brother is awful," Ariel says to her nails.

"Harold? Oh, he's not!" Ida looks around for an ally.

"That's what they're saying about us," I tell Ariel.

"He's a genius at business! And a real brick! Now, her I got no use for—"

"That Trudy is hilarious," Eric says.

"Trudy. At our wedding, Trudy, she grabs holda my arm and sorta, what can I say? appraises it. Like in pleasure units. Then she whispers something so—" Karl waggles his eyebrows. "I was at a total loss—"

"You? Ha! A first! As I recall, you drank. Vast quanti-ties of—"

"Look who's talking? Pot, ahem, to kettle—"

"Who wants a drink?" Eric hops his legs up under him like a hallucenogeneric frog.

I raise my hand. So does Dash. I slap at it.

Karl tumbles onto Ariel. "We got time for a beer."

"Okay! Ida—? Good. How 'bout you?" Eric doesn't know Elly's name. Only she and Fawne are still standing; they strike me as dangling. She shakes no. She looks at her watch.

"What do you all want?" I ask Ariel.

"I think you people are absolutely so amazing the way you make everything a joke," Fawne blurts, arms thrust out like a town square statue. "I sure wish I was a Jew. I don't care what anybody says about money-grubbing or Hollywood or killing Christ and all that." Her smile is a clearcut. "You people are just so warm and," it comes to her, "earthy!"

"Uh, honey?" Elly frowns, "For one thing—"

"I'll have a Pepsi," says Ariel, "and so will she."

We listen to the ice and the glasses and Eric and Dash working together and at odds. I love everybody for not uttering one single word while Fawne broadcasts abashed benevolence at us until they return with trays and set them on these helpful little tables.

Dash, easing back into his spot by Ida, kisses her knee and says, "Let's talk about something that doesn't kill you and isn't dead."

Much, much later, Eric and I are in bed. I'd wanted to undo his braid and brush his hair by candlelight, to get a back rub in return, but he comes at me with his tongue hanging like a dog loose at the beach and pounces me like I am a dream deferred. I'm numming his clean slice of chin, and he's gnawing the insulation off my wiring. My clothes are just off. I work my finger into the knot of his tie, and his shirt flies away, his pants can't keep up with him, he could vault on that boner, he strips his socks while one knee pins my armpit as though he is dragging me from a torrent up a steep, slick bank. He is that breathless. His eyes twist to a tight, bright focus. He works my breasts like clay; my nipples are firing. He slips to lap my clit, burrowing his hot head against my thighs, and when I moan, he clucks. He clutches and releases my flesh as though appreciating its tilth. He comes into me with such bounce I think of salmon, and we rock and roll from our hips to his back to my back like stunt pilot and plane: tailspin. Needless to say, I am asluice with juice. When we splurge, we burble and shluck, our tums unstick with a loud sclop and splock back together like suction cups, we're in stitches, still sealed with sweat and spunk, we splutter like mudsuck, splooge like slush, and when I snort, we simply dissolve.

Banging from the floor above. Oops.

We huckle up. He licks my tears and blots me dry with

kisses. I put my arms around his neck to the elbow and stretch like baby bear to just right. His face on the pillow is so open and kind. I soar in his eyes like a hawk until they close. I am light and happy, relieved, bereft. I wheel over tomorrow, surveying its promise. How I will wash the soap off the mirrors and begin to paint heaven.

And then I wonder what my children will make of us laughing. I see my mother alone in her big bed, her two tiny black eyes in an immense snowscape of sheets. I see my father, dead, and sort of laminated, in that high-gloss polyurethane box. And then I wonder where the hell to start on Fawne.

8 Easy Come, Easy Go

L ook at it. It's almost done.

I'm up on my scaffold in Hog Heaven, the day after Christmas, around four, five p.m. Ariel and Dash are spending the holidays with Karl and Elly because they have everything I don't: enraptured child, toys, a tree with lights and glass ornaments, a dog, land, two full baths, an entertainment center, spirit. The weather has been unseasonably warm, and I keep imagining them frolicking—moving out for that long pass in fresh winds that spiff and slap like a shoeshine, darting through birdsong pinewoods, leaping sunstippled creeks, and laughing constantly like the families in laundry detergent commercials. Maybe Karl will capture the magic with his camcorder. I can watch it in the dark getting drunk playing "Irene Goodnight" over and over as I lapse into senescence. They gave Ariel a VCR; Dash, a computer. We have only so many outlets, so many amps. Where will they plug them in?

At Karl and Elly's?

Eric's in the mountains with his clan, pickin' pig, pickin' string, dropping by the resort clubs to pick up with old buddies and all those old flames to whose daring, beauty, and imagination he's so reverently and frequently given tongue.

My mother is cruising the Caribbean with Mrs. Clark. ("Is it too soon?" she asks me. Yeah. Better wait till *you're* dead.) Retroversion has been suspended pending the New Year. Who wants to party in rubble?

(You think you're so smart.)

I've been here for days. On the plank. My brush dips into the colors, but when I touch it to the glass it seems, not to lay them down, but rather to melt the film that hides the colors that are really there. "CLEAN ME." See? I mix iridescent gold, copper, bronze with the flesh tones like fairy dust to spark their breath. I streak their hair, pearl their sweat, star their eyes. Behind me, the room is glacial and obscure. Before me, pink spotlights warm the smoky gauze; candles glance off smiles; dresses glister; silk shirts gleam; jewels; drinks. I hear laughter. I can't stop to eat—these paints are deadly poisons, and it takes too long to clean up. I just keep adding the retarding medium. Time slow dances. I'm on air. "Kind of Blue" on the box.

Fawne was supposed to clean up. That was the plan. She'd race over here after school and set up, and at 7:30 she'd clean up before showtime. No task too gross. She was zealous, on fire. I could have got her to take Baghdad with a scrub brush and a tank of Lysol. Her parents' opposition yielded like snow to sun. Fawne showed them my rough draft of the King and twittered how later, if she proved herself, I'd let her transfer it to the mirror. She compared the project to The Last Supper, of which they have a reproduction, framed, no glass, dusted with Pledge, in the dining room.

"Well, Carrie, I just don't know," said Forrest, tilting back, lighting up. Fawne stood, like a raingear-clad contestant on "Truth or Consequences," in readiness. Lacey and I sat forward with our hands tied on our knees. The Pelvis twitched on the carpet, orbited by the pekes. "A club, you say? Is it the kind of place a white man can take his wife?"

The pair of ducks quibbled over my shoulder. "She wouldn't be there on her own much, would she? With all that temptation, if you see what I'm sayin'."

I knew he meant the liquor, but it brought to mind a Columbus Day Parade I bumbled into once where a Harlem high school band in maroon uniforms marched by to the strains of "You Were Temptation," and talk about your jungle fever! Santa Maria! And then I envisioned an interracial last supper of peanut butter and banana sandwiches in the Jungle Room at Graceland, and I could hardly open my mouth to say, "You can come with her if you want to."

Fortunately, Fawne was running the defense. She'd blocked each of his feints with a fast denial and was saying, "Cee'll *can* me if I don't do the job. She *needs* my work—"

"Mrs. Carswell," Lacey insisted. I wondered if she'd actually changed into those designer jeans, heavily accented with gold jewelry, to cook and wash dishes. She must have renewed her lipstick after supper. Fawne stuck out her tongue and crossed her eyes at me, and I bit back a smile.

"Of course, I'd have to check into it personally," Forrest said.

"I declare, it's the very soul of Elvis," Lacey said, looking down at what amounted to a blown-up fashion sketch. "You are truly blessed with a God-given talent." To Forrest: "This could look good with everything else on her college application. Well-rounded." To me: "You won't let it interfere with her school work?"

Forrest bomped to the upright. "Well, Carrie, we'll talk it over and let you know our decision directly." Then they began to discuss transportation. Fawne said she'd get Ariel to drive her, and I told her the number of the bus and where it stopped, and Lacey cried, "The bu-us!" and Forrest smiled indulgently and offered to spring for a new set of wheels if they could trust Fawne not to abuse the privilege.

Fawne sprigged after me to the door like one of Heidi's

goats.

"Lucky I didn't bring the Otis Redding," I said.

"I forgot to tell you she loves Elvis—'everything but that trashy hillbilly stuff'—'Hound Dog'—" She did that squirming, shackled dance. "It's all going perfectly! And I'm getting a car! Can you believe it?"

"I thought you lost your license?"

"Between here and D.C., I never got one. You know how Ariel gets these things mixed up." She looked me some exaggerated compassion, although I was just as glad Ariel has more important things to think about than Fawne's biography. "Not all there-iel," she joked tentatively until my chuckle gave her the go-ahead. "Anyway, thanks, Mom!" I watched her decide to throw her arms around my neck and tighten. "You've really saved my life!" I tried to make the affection and immediacy of my hug instructional.

And when we built the scaffolding—Ariel, Dash, Eric, Fawne, and I, with Nate looking on like Noah's neighbor—you'd have thought she never sold lemonade or made a puppet theater in a major appliance box. Back at our place, over curry, she told us, in earnest, this was the most fun she'd had since my father's funeral.

"Jesus Christ!" said Ariel. "Get a life!"

"How about yours?" she asked and looked around to see if anyone was laughing.

But the next day, I took off early and was set up to train her, and she was an hour late, wagging a ferrety boy. She knew I wouldn't get hung up about it because I'm an artist.

"Art is discipline," I pronounced from on high.

"Oh, come off it, Cee," she laughed. Her eyes fidgeted. "This is my friend, Rat. He gave me a lift. He's really cool. I told him all about you, and what we're doing here, and he thinks—"

"We're doing nothing. You're wasting my time." I turned my back. It was as good a way as any to begin the lesson.

"She's not really like this. Cee! Why are you being like this? You sound like Forrest or some bitchy old teacher. I told Rat you were *human*."

"We've got work. He'll be welcome when we've got something to show."

"Cee-eee! This is so stupid!"

"Whenever you're ready."

"I thought maybe Rat could help too, like at least till I get my car—"

Great—now she was recruiting. That's all I'd need—Jack and Jill. Hell, why not the Dead End Kids? Maybe she saw me as Fagin. Rat surveyed the scene hungrily, as if I'd soon find him nibbling at my ankle or the furniture or selling it out of a van. "We have an agreement. I'm not renegotiating with your parents. I'm sure they'd be delighted to learn you were coming over here every evening to swab the decks with a boy."

"What they don't know won't hurt them," she said slyly.

"Go wash your hands."

After a few minutes of forced jollity on her part and some stomp and whomp from him, he was gone. She went to the sink, then boarded the staging. I tried to explain what her job involved, but there was so much emotional noise, it was like trying to teach someone about to hang how the trap door works.

"Look, Fawne." I knucked her chin to lift it. It flopped like Howdy Doody's when she bleated, "Fauve!" I wiped my hand on my 'ralls, but her eyes were the real grease spots, spreading. "Fauve. Art is not what you get at the end, it's what you put in from the beginning. If you don't—"

"Yeah, sure, skip the sermon, okay?"

"Let's get this straight. We both have a lot at stake here. My professional name is on the line. I want to get paid, and I want to work again. I've got no time, too many responsibilities—"

"Yeah, I know, but you don't have to go off on me. If you're gonna be like this—" Her face was a sack of mope.

"I'm sorry. But I thought you also wanted to show your folks you were mature enough to be trusted. And I thought you wanted to—" She let off resentment with an almost audible hiss. I couldn't tell if or when she tuned in. "—find yourself. Find out if this is the kind of work you'd be interested in, or—"

"Yeah, yeah, but I thought it was going to be fun." Her eyes blistered. "I told Rat we were *friends.*"

This touched a nerve. I realized that when she suggested Rat's participation, I felt like a pretext. I felt used, conned, for having believed I had something to give that she wanted. A lot of junk in this attic. Clear it out. Who's the child? "We are friends. And it can be fun, but first we've got to get down to it." I took a breath. "Now. This is cadmium red. It's made from a heavy metal—"

"Speaking of which, can we put on some music?"

"—more toxic than lead, and the fumes—"

"Ariel told me she didn't know if she could get me here twice a day—she was really cold about it—and I don't know if—"

"My arrangement is not with Ariel, it's with you, and—"

"Yeah, but I assumed you'd make her—"

"You assumed wrong. It was your—"

"So when I tried to get something going with Rat, you—"

"Yes, but you—"

"You know, I don't have to be here." She buckled out her upper lip. "In fact, it's a real hassle."

Fists automatically balled on my hips. "I was under the impression you volunteered."

"I was under the impression you needed me to!" Her voice stretched thin. "Didn't you?"

Did I? What was I thinking of? Elspeth. My mind opened like blinds. Light and air. I was handling this all wrong. I was used to working with Dash and Ariel as equals, and Fawne was used to being manipulated and manipulating like a terrible two. I had to get down on all fours with her and make her play nice. "Fauve. You can be invaluable to me, but only if you take it seriously and—"

"You let Ariel get away with murder, and you don't jump all over her."

"Ariel and I go way back. We've worked out a lot of things. And believe me, I let her have it, straight from the shoulder; we don't mince words. Besides, she works really hard. You don't see what she does for me at home or on her job at the stables—"

"Maybe not," she simpered. "Do you?" She was deliberately tickling, irritating as a blade of grass.

"What do you mean?"

"Oh, you know. I mean, who knows? I mean, you can't be sure. If you know what I mean. I mean, you *have* to trust her, right?"

I'd like to see what the Spanish Inquisition would do with this. "Right. So, anyway, cadmium. The point is, don't get it in your mouth, and when you get it on your hands—"

"Are you really gonna let her drop out?"

"Of what?"

"School. She said that's why she didn't have to take the SATs. I mean, it's great how you can accept her for what she is."

I pulled height. She smelled like grape gum. "What are you talking about? Of course she took the SATs. Most recently just before we came up here to see Generic. That was her reward."

"She skipped a couple of midterms, too." She was bringing me this in her teeth like my pipe and slippers or a dead mole. "She skips whole days at a time. I thought you knew."

"Why haven't I heard from the school?" My stomach foundered. Ariel almost always picks up the phone.

161

"Beats me. Well, anyway, I guess you never said she could take a year off either."

"Oh! No, wait, I did say that. Once she gets in, her junior, senior year—"

"I must have got her mixed up with Christie. She's the one who didn't take the SATs, I remember now, she's getting married. I'm still pretty new at school, and I guess I get what all these different people tell me confused." She smiled with her eyes averted. "What I'm trying to say is I think you're great. And Ariel, well, I can see how you might be disappointed. My mom—not my dad, he loves me no matter what, that's why I love him so much, that's why I should be living with him and not her, only, well, of course I get in his way somewhat. But she's all the time—" She trilled, "'You're not leaving this house, young lady, till you bring that B plus up to an A.'" Her eyes leveled with her voice. "That's why I guess I kind of overreacted before. I just wish—" Wistful dimpling. "You know what I mean." Her fingertips fluttered my arm. "We're so alike."

I gave her a lift home an hour later, promising to write up a detailed protocol—"How'm I supposed to keep track of all this?"—and the anvil I'd been toting came off for a moment. At dinner I asked Ariel about the SATs. She asked was I having paranoid delusions now too, stumped up to her room, dropped a lot of shoes, and made phone calls until very late. Lying with me under the blitz, Eric said, "Somebody's doin' a number on your head, but damned if I can tell who. Or what. Or why." I tempered against his warm solidity, and he mooshed my hair. The next day, I called the school. They didn't know off hand, but when the computer was up again, they'd check her records and get back to me on it. Then it was Christmas break.

That first Saturday, Fawne breezed in at eleven. I'd been here since seven. I had to finish her evening's tasks and do the morning's. She overslept; she was sorry. And about last night—she couldn't get out. She really tried, honest! She was inspecting the first panel, middle, near right, where I was blocking in the bandstand. "I'm glad you didn't let it hang you up any," she said dully. "It's fantastic. Only—"

Keith Moon, shirtless, flying apart over the drums. Bird and Coltrane, drawn on their horns as though feeding. A downlight strikes Benny Goodman's lenses. I put Jaco on electric bass, and Mingus on acoustic bass because I couldn't choose between them. Jimi kneels, zooming the strings, zagging slo-mo spectral streamers, zen concentration. Lennon, straight up, the Holy Ghost if for no other reason than that he was always stark naked, as he is here, the Russian icon do, hung with his guitar like a picket but fully exposed and feet hovering six inches off the floor. Monk tinkers at the sleek white baby grand; Bessie leans in its curve in what will be a blue sequined dress, beaming, behind Elvis, center foreground, in jeans and midnight-blue shirt with the collar up, in the characteristic lambda posture over the gripped mikestand, diamond drops whicking off the stiff tips of his plume. Oh, and to the left of Moon, the back-up—Mama Cass, Janis, and Florence Ballard, the dead Supreme. Each has her eyes closed in her own way: serenity, passion, eyeliner.

"Only—" Her voice frayed.

Only it bothered me that I couldn't hear what they could possibly be playing. If she said anything like that, work stopped until we did.

"Only aren't you letting him have too much say?" Her face blighted on Nate's office door.

Blues, anyway.

"I mean, just cause he's paying," she stuffed her paws in her pockets and swivelled toward me, "you shouldn't let him tell you who to put in. He's gonna ruin the whole thing. I mean—"

Blue Moon? Blue Monday? "I hate to break it to you, but it's all my—"

"—just because he's black, doesn't mean he knows any-thing about music. They think they own it, you know? I mean," indicating the gods with a nick of her chin, "who *are* all those fat old n—"

Little ofay ignoramus blues. "Please, don't say that word."

"They say it. Haven't you heard of—"

"Just don't. You're smart enough to see the difference between—" Black and blues.

"Okay, okay. All I mean is nobody's gonna know who they are. Or care. It's not their club, even if—"

Every Day I Have the Blues. What did I expect, growing up in that household, with that shrine to Stepin Fetchit on the front porch? Teach, Cee, teach! I saw myself taking a power drill to her ear. "You really don't know! Wait'll you hear!" Kicking myself to exclamation. "I'll dub some of my records, and we can groove while we work. God, what a treat in store for you. You'll be knocked for a loop."

"I hate old stuff. I thought you were gonna do Jim Morrison." Her mouth was a clot.

And so were my paints. Hard'nin' Artery Blues. Blues Balls! "See, to me, The Doors sound old, but Coltrane, Charlie Parker, hey! Bach, they sound fresh. If you haven't heard it, it doesn't matter whether—" It wasn't the music, and I didn't have the time or patience to excavate all the layers. "You want to have input. You want to do more than clean up." Call me Madame Cee. Her eyelids creaked up, with what sharp teeth lurking in the depths of that dirty water? "So some time I'll show you the general plan, and you'll tell me where to put Jim Morrison," like maybe hang-ing around the women's bathroom with his fly open, "and right now you can glue blue glitter all over Bessie Smith! Would you like that?" Smiling to blue blazes. Blue Velvet? Blue Suede Shoes? Devil in a Blue Dress?

"You mean her dress, right? Listen, that'd be nice, but I

have to go Christmas shopping with my mom." She yawned. Blue Christmas. "She's coming back to pick me up at one. I forgot to tell you. She's assigned to check the place out. Check me out. You. Sorry." Hands in pockets jig helplessness as though they were severed or stuck. Tar baby. "He's not around, is he?" (Nate.) "I haven't let on about *him*."

Baby's in black, and I'm feelin' blue. "There's still plenty of time. Here's the glue, here's a brush, here's the glitter," here's your ass, here's your elbow, "—take off your coat and have at it."

She peeled as if it were her flak jacket and there's a war on. She was wearing the closest thing to a twin set and tweeds they make these days. Miss Fawne. Lady Fawne. "She'll kill me if I get it messed up." She exhibited her unsightly propriety like scabies.

I threw her an old shirt of Karl's. "And I'll kill you if you mess Bessie up." Any Woman's Blues.

I was roughing in the skirted tables around the dance floor—I couldn't see the dancers until I heard the beat—when Fawne inquired, "Uh, sorry, Cee? How do I get the glitter to—you know—" She was shaking it daintily at the vertical surface like someone on a salt-free diet or with a severe neurological disorder.

"You put glue all over the area?" Blues In A Bottle.

"Well, no. I thought—"

"Half?" Half Moon? Baby, half mercy on me—

"Well, see, I—"

"Do half. Carefully! And then take the plastic top off the glitter, and just—"

"Oh! I get you! Great!"

"NO! WHOA!" She was winding up like Nolan Ryan. When do they learn glass breaks? I seem to recall baby Galileos in the highchair. This meant that if I told her to get stuffed, I could expect to see her mounted over the hearth. "Here, wait a minute—" I produced some newspaper and dumped the glitter out on it. "Now all you do is pucker up and blow. You can do that, can't you? Jesus!" I'm making like Bacall, and she's Boreas. "At the wall!"

"Oh, hi!" Behind a barrage of scent, like being mugged with maple syrup, Lacey pulled to a halt, in a pink suit and so much jewelry she jingled like eight tiny reindeer; in fact, exactly as though she was hauling a sleigh with only a few seconds to spare us, she teetered forward over her pumps. "Hey, y'all." She grit her teeth in a fierce smile. Her face was flawless, like wax fruit. "I'm here to fetch Fawnie."

"Mah-um!" brayed Fawne, flunking down glitter and glue in an acidhead's huff. "You weren't suhposed to cu-um uhn-til wu-un!"

"Way-ull, we gots to get us su-um lu-unch, don' we?"

Who were they, the last of the Mohicans? Ugh!

"We've got to get some lunch," Lacey translated for the Jewish Banking Conspiracy.

By all means. Get stuffed.

"This place is a lot nicer than what all I expected—" She must have expected a Turkish toilet. A sty. My reputation precedes me. She locked her fingers and set her heels as though about to recite "The Boy Stood on the Burning Deck," while Fawne doffed her smock.

"Be sure to wash your hands," I cautioned her. "Get inside those rings."

Fawne held up a pinky ring, a skull with red eyes and working jaw. "I meant to show you. Ariel gave me this for Christmas. Picked it up at the mall. Wicked, huh?"

"What won't they come up with?" Lacey showed distaste. "I hope she didn't waste any money on it."

"I'm sure she didn't. None to waste." Fawne scrunched her lips.

"And now I guess you have to get her something equally revolting?" Lacey fudged at me.

I was just glad it's the thought that counts. "Next time,

leave it home. Unless you want to get paint in it and culti-
vate the resemblance. Now, wash." When did I enter the
Mom-Off?
"But I didn't even—"
"Get used to it. Scrub!"
"Cee-eee! You're just—"
"Mrs. Carsnow! How many times must I—?"
Fawne acceded to the wash.
"It's mighty nice of you to take such an interest in Fawnie.
I don't have to tell you I was real concerned at first—" Fawne
hit the head, and Lacey swooped into the confidential. "Just
keep her away from the booze and the niggers is all I ask.
Don't let her out of your sight for one second, cause if she
could do me that way, she would. Her real daddy, in D.C.?—
we moved there from a little backwoods town in Georgia,
and it was the biggest mistake I ever made in my life, I can
tell you. He's a boozer and a shameless womanizer, and the
minute he got away from his family and his church— But
Fawne just idolizes the man, and—well. I certainly got to
hand it to you. Since she started all this mess she han't said
one word about visiting him over Christmas, and—"
Fawne emerged.
"—so this is the famous mural you all are working on.
Cute. And kinda—you don't want our state senator seeing
it. I guess I don't mind a little nudity in a nightclub, but
couldn't you pick a better specimen?" Smirking at Lennon.
"Just keep the clothes on the coloreds, is all I say—don't
give 'em any ideas. I guess their money's the same color's
ours. I still think your Elvis is divine. I can't wait to see it
when you get it all done. How long you reckon it's going to
take you?"
Four hundred years. Definitely—The Wailers. I felt like
I'd been dunked in warm spit, but it had dried so fast I
couldn't prove it, even to myself. Can I get a witness? Fawne
was back in the nuclear mutant coat at Lacey's side, a refu-

gee orphan suffering a photo op with Imelda Marcos.

She showed me her raw little digits. "Satisfied?"

"Yes," I enunciated. It registered. "Will you be back tonight to clean up?"

"We've got a dinner engagement," Lacey said, trying to flatten a spew of Fawne's hair. "The holiday whirl—"

"Tomorrow morning?"

"Church, of course." Lacey smiled at the play of her gold-knobbled hand over Fawne's scrape and thatch.

Fawne shivved her off and looked at me like she was for sale, cheap. "Just don't lay all this guilt on me, okay? I can't help it, okay?"

"Mind how you—"

Okay, so, what? The problem with talking to kids is that you know there *are* right answers. I knew this was not one of them. But it pushed out of my mouth where it had been wadding. "Well, there you go, Lacey, you don't have to worry about the booze and the coloreds because Fawne is never going to be here." I enjoyed her falter. "Fauve." Now I was just fooling with the buttons. "Don't make promises you can't keep."

"I'll be here tonight *and* right after—" Fawne's ravening eyes twinkled, cold as stars, "church."

I coasted past Lacey's distress. "Good."

"But, Fawne, honey, you know we have—" Lacey's hand flitted like a footless bird.

"You have—" Fawne talked to her chest, but she looked up to flash me sweet venom.

"—a prior commitment." Lacey peered at Fawne's head as though the crystal had gone cloudy. The hand clanked down on her purse.

"And I don't? You heard Cee—"

"Mrs.—"

"Did you ask me if I had plans? Do you ever ask me? Anything? I'll miss church," she vowed to me. "I'll be here at eight."

"We can talk about this later." Lacey shoveled Fawne under her arm and turned to me. "I'd have thought you'd see my side of it."

The quiet, tripped up, tired way she said it illuminated her side: a sheer cliff above breakers. And in those shoes! Blues Keep A-Fallin'. As Lacey's temporary crutch, Fawne crimped her sly mouth. Which side am I on? Shit! Look at me: I've got a running shoe over the fence and an orthopedic oxford straggling behind, stiles threatening my tender privates, and I still don't make my move. I had to go clean all that crap off Bessie and start over again.

Am I blue? You best believe it.

Fawne didn't come Sunday, and she didn't come Monday. She seldom came; when she did, she was always too late or too early, too noisy and skittish or pouty and sluggish to be anything but in my way and on my nerves. I learned to love the sight of her back. I sent her to the library—everything was out; nobody could help. I sent her for supplies—she returned with questions, as if, instead of magic beans, Jack kept dragging home the same damned cow, "You wanted me to sell her? How come? This cow? You sure? Can't we eat her? How much do you want for her? Where do you want me to go? How do I get there? Run that by me again?" Anything she did, I did again.

She had ideas, opinions. She wanted mine. She felt sick, she had a test. She crept up on me like shingles, and my brush ripped over the glass. She didn't want to disturb me but. She brought spectators, kibitzers, critics. She bragged on me. She bitched. She needed to talk. She cried and needed comfort. She thanked God for me. She had to tell me: that I should see the way Nate looked at me; at her; that she saw Eric talking to the most beautiful redhead the other day; that she hadn't seen much of Ariel lately; did I know where she was keeping herself? what she was up to? who she was

169

with? If I heard what she said about me. She tried to stand up for me but.

Lacey called to say how happy they were with the change in Fawne. I'd worked miracles. While she was so busy with me, they'd cancelled her analyst appointments. I hadn't seen Fawne in three days. She said she was helping Ariel study for her English exam, since I was so busy.

And I'm trying to accommodate, to take up the slack. I was strangling in slack, and everybody was mad at me, bleeding what time I had left to show me and tell me. Dash blacked an eye defending his board, which wouldn't have happened if I. Ariel had to work late to make money for presents; she'd grab some fast food, which wouldn't be necessary if I. They called, "Goodnight, mother," like a curse. "You're too tense, baby," Eric schmoozled. "Go with the flow." I hated them because I knew they were right and doing their best and trying their hardest, and it was all my fault. I felt as though I'd starved them and run them ragged to make them a huge cake and then eaten it all, eaten myself sick, right in front of them. I hid out in Hog Heaven.

And then I was on my own. Silent night. Wholly night. Blues in the night. Irene, goodnight.

But look at it. The rear wall where Tommy humps the glowing neon pinball machine, while Brian Jones and Dennis Wilson coach and thump encouragement. Tim Hardin, on the phone, covers his left ear, "Don't Make Promises," and Brook Benton lights a cigarette, waiting for him to get off, "Lie to Me." The tables for two hemming the dance floor, where Bob Marley and Peter Tosh indolently pass a reefer five miles long (slightly foreshortened) from Fats Waller and Sippie Wallace, and Roy O anxiously cranes to spot his date, late again. Buddy Holly and Ritchie Valens, grinning, huddle to whisper, and Karen Carpenter looks up, pale as a lily against the black jacket of Sam Cooke, his hand absently skimming her shoulder as he calls to Jackie

Wilson, Otis Redding, Joe Tex.

Up two steps and then two more, in crowded half-moon booths of quilted ice-blue satin, Paul Butterfield, harp to mouth, Mike Bloomfield, hailing more drinks for Lightnin' Hopkins, Memphis Slim, Sonny Terry, and Duane Allman, trying to get something organized, and the noble profile of Muddy Waters by Mary Lou Williams and the other piano players, Professor Longhair, Bill Evans, Count Basie, Teddy Wilson, Eubie Blake.

Whites and blues, black, silver, and gold. All the heat comes from the skin, the subtly deepening gradations of melanin; red and coral lips; the fire in their eyes.

Nate is the one who told me they're playing "Heartbreak Hotel." Of course they'd carry Elvis, in spite of his dragass boneheaded attitudes: this is heaven. We stood there listening to what they might do with "Heartbreak Hotel." A rush—wild wind through a busted windshield, rain howling in on the bed through a window you just can't get up to close. I had to change some facial expressions. Inject that judicious, intelligent despair. Then I could paint Billie, big, luscious, dreamy, in the arms of Duke Ellington, dapper, amused, and deftly dipping her, although for one horrible moment I thought, too bad Lester Young is still alive, the way he used to back her, and I almost got sick. I confessed to Nate.

He said, "What they could never know is how much we love them. What they mean to us. Know what I'm sayin'? Maybe nobody ever knows. Really feels it. Real thing gets muddied up with the hype, the bullshit." He had his hands in his pockets, and his eyes on the floor. He looked up to say with resonant bafflement, a big lonesome bell, "Love," and quickly looked down again.

Then I went a little nuts and put in James Dean, Natalie Wood, and Sal Mineo. Without a cause. Well—tenderness. Try a little.

Julie Edelson

"What the hell?" Nate's tetchy smile. "We got the walls."
Yesterday evening Nate came in from Christmas dinner
at his mom's, after paying a call on his ex to see their kids, a
boy and a girl, ten and eight. He turned on the bar lights,
poured himself a drink, put on Aretha, "Amazing Grace."
He sat in the chair he first set up to watch me paint, and
now and then I'd join him and have a drink so he added
another and a table, and then he started lingering a little
with the waits, so he brought a few more chairs, and then a
white cloth, a vase, and a carnation. Jackbuilt. Now his
reflection fits in heaven.

"Like how you did Kay Kayser," he said when the tape
ended. "Some folks just won't *be* dead."

I didn't have to respond. We've gotten used to listening
together. He likes to play me inspiration. I shed light on a
beer.

"I tell you 'bout the other night? Band was late, comin'
over from Fatalville, and didn't nobody mind. Stood around
star gazin'. Comin' in now just to take a look at it. That's
Abbie Hoffman you puttin' in, am I right?"

I smiled ruefully. "Youth International Party—international youth party."

"Yeah. Put George Jackson with him."

I turned to see what darkened his voice. I don't talk to
enough people who know more than I do. "Yes. I was thinking Huey Newton. Didn't he get shot not long ago? I was
gonna find out. Well, or Fred Hampton, Mark Clark—no
shortage of young black martyrs. And then Woody Guthrie,
Leadbelly, Phil Ochs—another can of worms. Hell, Hall of
Worms."

"You eat today?"

"You know what makes me feel really weird? Every time
somebody dies I'm gonna wanna zip over here and paint them
in. Ghoulish. I've even thought about like leaving room, so
if— Christ!" I knocked on wood. "If I say a name, it might

happen, you know? like the Queen of—?" I put a finger to my lips. "We'll see her start to appear. Or like what if I make a mistake, the person isn't dead—and then *they die.*" I make fisheyes. "It's finishing it. It's freakin' me out."

"Know what's wrong with you?" He sipped and lounged. "Too intense. You need to chill."

I laughed and thumbed behind me. "All in good time."

Which is why we were smiling wryly like wily old athletes when Fawne bashed in. "Am I interrupting something?" Snotty, like one of those early talkie ingenues straight off a truck farm.

"You rather be starting somethin'?" I asked her.

Nate crossed his legs, regarding her blandly.

Her eyes downshifted with her gears. "You ought to be glad I could make it. I'm supposed to be gratefully playing with my electric curlers, too stuffed to move on some kind of vomit pie. Instead, I thought I'd go where I was wanted. I came here to work." Rosie the Riveter. She pushed back her bangs, and I noticed she'd shaved off her eyebrows and penciled in spiderwebs. At first I thought she was riddled with varicosity or had shot up ink. Snuff, I thought, having seen pictures of Tibetan monks with black sinus cavities. "You don't know what I had to do to get out. I'm gonna get skinned."

"Your parents love the new look?" I tapped my brow.

She snorted. Imitating Forrest at his heartiest, "'Is it Halloween? I thought it was *Christmas.* Ho, ho, ho!'" In her own screaky voice, "See, it doesn't go with the outfits they bought me or the agenda they set. It's not *Christmas,* right? Short on mistletoe and puppy slobber. I told them, you know, just take the clothes with you, on the hangers. Make everybody a lot happier. That's insolence. You get eight to twelve in your room for insolence, and no phone."

I laughed. But because I coveted her wit for my dull daughter, it left a bitter aftertaste. And spooked me. "Sorry.

I do like the webs. Glue on a dab of glitter here and there. Dew. Now that you're a pro." I turned back to work.

"Geez, you're almost finished." She came closer. "When did that happen?"

"Where you been?"

"Hey! I'm here now. I told you, it's not easy. You oughta know that by now. Besides, it's *Christmas.*" She couldn't let the word pass without kicking it. "Truth is, Rat was in here a couple of nights ago, and he said you were near done, and I couldn't believe it, I had to see for myself. No matter what." Ferocious. "I hitched!"

Downplaying the drang (after all, I've hitched, and it's *Christmas*—didn't He hitch? and then He squatted), "Voilà!"

She walked the wall end to end. I stopped to watch her. I was suddenly reminded of the Vietnam wall in Washington, the same black, reflective surface, the same intent search for loved ones. I looked at it again. It had gone opaque. Layers of glitter and paint. Waterlilies. God, that pre-Raphaelite horror of Ophelia's floating corpse. Stagnant algae and frog's eggs. My chest tightened. I looked for Nate, but he was gone. Light outlined his office door.

"This really pisses me off." I looked down. From my angle, she looked like a blasted stump, witches'-broom and all. Her gaze was a blade. "You said I would have input. You said you needed my help. 'Can't do it without you,' you said." (Do I twang like that?) "I thought you meant it. I thought you were doing it for me. Isn't that a joke? I thought we were friends. That was more important to me than the stupid painting. I could tell you anything, and you'd understand. I thought you were like my true mother, and we'd found each other, and we'd make everything right for each other, maybe even get my dad back." Shrilling, "You never gave a shit about me!" Tears flew from her eyes as if she'd been punched.

I carefully modulated my voice. "You weren't here."

"You didn't want me here! You made me feel totally unwelcome. I couldn't figure it. It was like all of a sudden you hated me. What did you expect?"

The tennis ball in my throat made it hard to speak. I had trouble keeping track of what my gripes were. "I expected you to be serious and conscientious and to put something into it, and—"

"I was! And every time I tried to put something into it, you let me know exactly what you thought about it. Where's Jim Morrison? Where'd you put him?"

I shuffled. "I put him by the doors."

"Yeah, to the toilets. Did you think I wouldn't notice, or didn't you care? I bet you think it's funny. God. You said you'd wait. You said I could decide. Just that one thing."

"You weren't here!" I choked down my exasperation and pumped a deep breath. Like childbirth. As hard to remember advice. "Look, let's be honest. You didn't want to work. You wanted to gab. And show off. You used me as a way out of your house. I had a job to do. Someone is paying me to do it well."

"The nigger. Your new fuck."

I ignited like guncotton, white-hot, instantaneous. It felt glorious. What did I owe her? "Listen, you nasty little racist guttersnipe, I know your parents fill your head with this shit, but—"

"That's all you care about, getting it on with the nigger. And right under the nose of your boy-toy and your own kids! I guess I got in your way over here. I cramped your style. That's it, isn't it? That explains everything! You must think we're blind. You're the blind one. It drives Ariel crazy, you know? I mean really crazy." She smiled sweetly. "It drives her to drink."

Cheap shot, but it damped the fire. "Come on. You're the one—"

Her face. Something both cowering and taunting in it.

A loose laugh like hacked phlegm. "You're like the only one in the world who doesn't know she's a fucking drunk."

"That's impossible." I finally put my brush down in the jar of water. My righteous fire was out. I sifted the smoking ash. What had I been burning? Evidence. "Ariel hates drinking. She doesn't even like the taste. She only—"

"It's not the taste, it's the feeling." She faked reeling. "Blotto."

"I'd know it. I'd be able to tell. She's never once—"

"She avoids you. You think it's hard? You're never there. When you are, your mind's somewhere else, like on your lovelife. Wait till she hears about this one. What flavor. Freak of the week. She'll stay trashed forever."

"You're crazy." Pins and needles up my arms. The palette fell on the table of paints, and the tubes smattered on the floor like applause. "Fawne, I'm sorry, but you really do need help."

"She has to shoplift so she can save up money to buy the stuff. Sometimes she steals from your purse. You know where she goes?" Her face was bloated with malice like a baby's belly with milk. "You know that big kangaroo slide in Eller Park? She gets hold of a bottle, a case, whatever, she's not discriminating," the hard twinkle, "and she sits in the pouch and gets loaded. Sometimes she takes a guy with her to help her buy the stuff or get home, but she really doesn't give a shit about anything but getting drunk. One time, she got that redneck who lives next door to you to—"

"This is not true." The kangaroo is orange fiberglass with specks of red and gold and random black hairs that make me think of rats falling in the vat. You have to crouch to get inside it, where it smells like piss and glue, and climb halfway up a ladder to tumble into the pouch. It was where I used to find her when I'd been chasing after Dash. With her fist to her mouth and angry eyes: you love him more than you love me. She was already too heavy for me to lift out, nor could I reach in and pet or kiss her. I can feel the places it cut into me when I tried. It made me feel dwarf. "This can't be true. I am home, I'm home a lot. Every night." But she sleeps over with friends, especially weekends. I don't check up on her. "And I think about her all the time. It's certainly not true that—" and now I had something I was sure of, and I held it up to my eyes like a match in a cave-in, "I'm interested in Nate. That's just—" I cast down on Fawne what must have looked like the lunatic triumph of the ship-wreck washing up on Miami Beach, "crazy."

She laughed. "It's amazing how all you can think about is the nigger. Ariel may not be much, but she's yours. God! You know? I'd rather have my stupid, boring, bullshit mother than some conceited Jewbitch who can't even be bothered. At least she goes through the motions. And you know what else? You think you're so great, you think this mural thing is such hot shit, well, let me tell you, it's not. It's just a lot of old niggers and Jew hippies and rednecks nobody ever heard of or cares about and it's old old old. It's a moldy old ugly cartoon." She picked up one of the fallen tubes of paint and gurged it at the mirror. Cadmium light red. She made squiggles like she was decorating a cake, then she splot it like a rubber dagger. She threw it at me. She's not much of a throw. Then she punched at the glass. The pinky ring dinked a chip, and she dug into it until it branched. She looked like she'd disemboweled someone. Laughing.

"You've got to wash that stuff off," I told her. "It can make you really sick."

She laughed and put her hand in her mouth. Nate grabbed her by the elbows and forced her stiffarmed to-ward the bathroom while she screamed racist filth and thrashed her gloppy tentacles. Propelling her like a Dumpster, he shoved her in and followed. Screaming and running wa-ter.

I had to sit down. Eventually, Fawne sputtered out on a

long stream of hate. Nate found me on my scaffold, swinging my feet. I touched his mucky shirt. It was sky blue with airplanes, bridges, and orchids on it and now cad red. "Your shirt."

"Wash up," he said. He showed me my hands.

I looked at them. I don't know how long. I looked at him. "'I've got blisters on me fingers,'" I tried to joke, but that's always seemed to me the cry from John Lennon's heart. "Did you hear all that?"

"Go wash, and we'll talk."

"What am I going to do?"

"Wash. Then talk. Do it right."

Sometime while I was washing he put on Sam and Dave, "Soothe Me." He must want me to fall apart. He played it twice and turned off the stereo. He'd poured a drink for me, Southern Comfort. I looked at it with fear and loathing. I could taste it. "I gotta talk to her," I said.

"Yeah, you do." (I couldn't take his gravity, so I fuzzed at the murk three inches from his ear.) "But first you got to think out your rap. Don't come at your child with guns blazing to find out it's all a lie."

"You're right." But I jumped down and went straight to the phone.

He brushed my arm. "Even if it's true, it's not the end of the world. Other folks been there. And back."

"I can't think till I talk to her." I made the call. Answering machine. Elly noodling on about keeping the lines of communication open. Where were they? Restaurant. Church. The pouch of the fiberglass kangaroo. The beep stung me. I left a message for Ariel to call me here as soon as possible no matter how late. What else? I put down the receiver, and tension wrung me like a sopping towel. My breath slammed like a jackhammer. I sobbed sweat. I wanted to call again. Maybe I did. How many times?

"What're you fixing to do right now?"

I don't know how long he'd been watching me with his hands in his pockets, rocking on the sides of his shoes. He was gauging what he was fixing to do. I looked at the mural. "Work."

"Go home. You need the sleep. I'll drive. We'll catch a bite. You eat a little, then sleep, get your act together."

"Sleep." I couldn't imagine walking through the front door. Going up to search her room for empties. Finding them, and sitting on her bed, waiting for the showdown in the ticking darkness. Finding nothing, and swallowing whatever that means. Ariel still sleeps with a two-foot, amber-eyed bear named Betty. Her smell. It's how my papa smelled in the rehab hospital. I felt hung over. I imagined nailing my front door shut and taking the next bus. The neanderthal waving. I shuddered. "The only place for me to go is in there." My fractured heaven. My ugly old cartoon. My funny valentine. Nate's eyebrows clumped. I hated laying this on him. "Hey!" I tried to smile. "I'm glad I've got *some*where."

He pulled out his hands and fanned them open, letting me go like loose change. "More mirrored panels and epoxy back in the back. In case of brawls."

"In case of fire, break glass—"

He smiled. "Think you can fix it?"

I climbed up and began removing broken bits with my palette knife. Nate brought a box for the trash. I was surprised by the blackness beneath them. I had to tap to test its solidity. I listened for voices. Nate helped me lift and fit in the new section.

The instant it was in place stemware tinks, someone laughs, the music rises. "I Love the Sound of Breaking Glass." It's lucky Fawne could only reach part of the dance floor; the shortage of women had left it rather sparsely populated. I see the dancers so clearly now I can paint them free-hand. I'm so happy to be running my brush over their beautiful bodies again. I turn their faces away so I don't

179

have to know who they are, so hair swirls like veils, a taffeta skirt, an open jacket. I don't know when Nate left. He put on a Monk tape that starts with "Don't Blame Me," the wittiest, the most brilliant stumble over the keys; it makes you question the whole notion of mistake. I turned to glimmer at him for it, but I couldn't see him for the water in my eyes. If he was still there, he didn't answer. I only called out once.

Restoration takes no time, or no time that I notice. I stand back to see if I've worked the perspective in right, if the dancers are in proper proportion. They were never gone; I just broke my glasses. The damage is undone, but even though my arms are aching, my neck is a knot, my brush keeps reaching out. Ariel's face hovers on Karen Carpenter; Elvis sneers like my son. I close my eyes. When I open them, I catch my own giant reflection, and heaven recedes from me.

Everyone I love is out of reach. I let my home, my family, my old friends slip away. I lost Elspeth. I left Karl. I surrendered them to the easy, to the simplicity of silence and solitude, to slide. The fiberglass kangaroo is a slide. My father died. You know I gave up my father long before he gave up the ghost. "Don't be a stranger." And Fawne—how could I be so vain as to think I could save her without going to the trouble to reach her?

Now my children. I've enjoyed these last two weeks without them. No complications, no fears. No loose ends. No heat, no noise. No sticky, sloppy, thorny emotion. CLEAN ME. I see myself in freefall from the planet in dense, black quiet. Slipping into darkness. My cord is cut. I'm moving so fast and with none of the slog and cramp of running. In my thick, white, self-contained spacesuit, I'm smiling.

There's only the lower lefthand corner to paint. My father is there. I see him clearly. I know just how he feels about being here: he's irate. He can't get out fast enough. The music is making him sick. And the schwartzes. I mix the colors of his beaded bald head, the lividity through his cheeks, his liver lips. The steam wilting his starched collar; a mortified shab in a rumpled blue business suit. Why didn't I tell him to dress? He's brandishing the check; he demands to see the waitress. Shit! There's not one single waitress. Wait. Now I see her.

Nate's here. That's how I know what time it is, what day it is. Boxed-in day.

"You still here?"

"No."

"Wise ass. You talk to your daughter?"

I drop everything.

"Hey," he says softly. "Club opens tonight. Some group called White Flight. Can't wait to hear what they putting down. Damn! You're done. Damn!" He shows me a smile so unexpected it feels like the third degree. "It's good, girl, very good. Let me look. Damn! Damn! Love you as the waitress." He frowns. "Quittin' time. Leave that mess for us."

The phone rings. I slide off the scaffold. Nate's already picked it up. He listens for a moment, hands it to me. It's Karl.

"Cee, listen carefully. Everything's all right. You got that?"

"Ariel."

"She's alive. She's hurt, but she's going to make it. There was an accident. The EMS people called, and she's on her way to county hospital. We're headed there now. The sitter just walked in. We'll see you there. You got all that? Say it back to me."

"Go fuck yourself."

"Are you okay? Can you make it?"

"Jesus, Karl."

"We'll see you there. Cee? We'll see you."

See me? Hey. I fold.

9 You're Gonna Lose That Girl

Nate drives me because I'm shaking and the nausea and because however many days ago, I ran to work. I'm running now—eyes, nose, pores, bowels, brain—like an open faucet. Run for your life if you can. Nate handles his nifty sports car with authority at high speed. The speed screams like Little League bleachers. The cold freeze-dries me, stiffens the clabber of me humanoid. It's very blue out. All blues. Christmas lights streak by like subliminal advertising, like blinders, cataracts. A wailing firetruck passes, its lights drubbing. Up ahead and across the beltway, bolts of smoke unroll from a billboard: "Abortion is Murder" is burning. The smoke chokes, tamping our nostrils, forcing tears. The whole world is pulsing balls of flame, roaring with pain. Is it over? Who won? (Not me.) The hospital rears beyond the conflagration above huge mounds of red dirt and nosing yellow bulldozers. Nate swings toward it. My gut roils. I wish I were on the Oblivion Express. Instead, I'm playing Lassie. My poor daughter. If only she could have aborted me. It's giving birth that's murder. Living is murder. This is a travesty.

"Did you know one of Charlie Parker's favorite words was travesty?" I can't tell if Nate hears me.

He has a hard time finding the emergency entrance with all the detours for construction. Destruction. They look alike. We circle twice until he cuts up a do-not-enter. He offers to find parking and join me, but either I can take it from here, or I can't. I make a perfectly graceless exit, and when he doesn't laugh, I know what kind of shape I'm in.

I've never been to an emergency room, but I've watched television, so I'm braced for bedlam, cranking my volume to high. The admissions desk is just inside the second of two glass doors. Tinsel twitters as I push in. It's fairly quiet. Many voices, but no urgency. A baby crying somewhere. A green bottlebrush wreath hangs next to a clock over a very pale ponytailed man, holding his arm at the elbow like the color guard holds the flag, and two disheveled, pasty children, eating potato chips from little bags. A fat woman in a puffy pink coat and matching house slippers is giving information to a steel-curled matron behind a terminal. Her dark brown skin is mottled pink as though it's splitting up from her chin, and the matron keeps her eyes on her keyboard. A smell like pine solvent and eggs. I'm almost visiting my father again. My father died.

A tall, sepia man in white with a stethoscope hangs up the phone and asks how he can help me.

"My daughter—the EMS—" I realize I don't know what EMS stands for, "said—told my—brought her here—"

"What's her name?"

At least one of us is coherent. "Ariel Krasnow." I know. It's a ridiculous name.

"Spell that." He checks a list, phones. "You got a Krasnow back there? Ariel?"

Like I'm at Bimco, the last resort for plumbing parts, and she's an obscure ancient fixture. A duck leg. I'm describing her until he puts up his hand.

A young woman with rigid green-blonde hair sidles into the secretarial chair beside him, looking from him to me to him to get her bearings. "Thanks, Stan, I can take it from here."

"We haven't got her," he tells me. "Must be at Baptist."

I grope for my keys and remember, no car. Brakes screech inside me, filing sparks; I taste the metal.

Stan slights over my sleeve. "We'll call."

The receptionist taps the touchtone with stiletto fingernails. "What's the name?"

Whose name? Searing panic, hot poker up the ass. Do I have the cash for a cab? It's that dream where you can't put on your clothes.

Stan spells Krasnow. "Happens all the time," he assures me. He's writing and scanning the room with eyes that blip like a heart monitor. "If one of us is unusually busy, they just change the call on the way. We've got a stroke coming in by chopper any minute now. We'll find her."

"They say they haven't got her." The receptionist casts up a skeptical scrinch.

The lava in my mouth erupts as tears. I'm clinging to the counter to keep from spinning off. If I start screaming, will they find her any faster?

"She's got to be somewhere." The receptionist pushes up the sleeves of her sweater. "They told you they were bringing her *here*. How long ago?"

"It must be forty minutes, an hour—" My voice sheers for the stratosphere. They called Karl. I don't know.

So what took you so long? She doesn't ask this. What kind of mother would—? No. She just wants to know what happened to Ariel.

"An accident—" I don't even know. I don't know anything. I don't know anything, and I wasn't with her, and I wasn't looking after her properly, and now I can't help, and she's lost, gone. What's divine retribution got on simple guilt? Easy: forgiveness. Grace. In spades. Believers get off easy. So why are they so hard on the rest of us? My brain is on fire. "My husband—ex—Ariel's father—he called me, and—"

"Big guy with a beard? Loud?"

Karl! Or God—?

"Yeah, she's here." She practically twirls the receiver to her ear. "They don't know what they're doing back there." (This is comforting.) "Gets that way some time. Your ex checked her in, sos all you have to do is go on back. I'll tell them you're on your way."

I march for the swinging doors. March? Sure, like a green reinforcement at Second Manassas.

People in street clothes, sweatsuits, with eyes like holes, slung up and down the hallway, nurses dodging purposively among them, a spare gurney with a black pad against the right wall, an IV stand, and a collapsed wheelchair. In the first room on the left, I see Elly. In ten full rows of molded plastic chairs ten across, she's got the only face not staring up at a tv attached to the wall. Anxiously watching the doorframe, her big brown eyes clap over me like suction cups without taking in who I am or what I mean. Dash is flung back in the seat next to her, gripping the legs, mouth open. A female newsvoice describes the damage caused by zillions of bees nesting in a suburban attic in Houston. Honey is dripping through the ceiling, which drones like the 82nd Airborne. Elly bangs Dash's arm like the buzzer on a quiz show—she's got me. He grimps annoyance at her, backtracks the sticky trail of her concern to me; his face cracks like a pack of cards to show shame, misery, resentment. Fawne flips forward from behind Elly with the noise of the slap. Shooting gallery duck. Whoa!—no, she's coming at me, a torpedo. I keep going.

"Cee! Please!" Her feet clack like a baby's pull toy. She plucks fecklessly at my arm. "I gotta talk to you." She cleaves the traffic, the curiosity as noisy as honking, and plants herself in my path. "I was *there*."

Inside her sooty hair and the sputum greenblack menstrual cad-red rags, her dirty, scribbled face, is a child. The lewd, self-centered excitement of a terrified child, something smarmy about the lips, slurring into smile, while the eyes suck inward, quail. This stops me. I fend her to the wall as though we're in an air raid drill. She smells like wet coal ash. She can see I'm chafing toward Ariel, so she speaks very fast, like a shill; her emotions splutter her face like a thick white sauce coming to the boil.

"See, after what happened with us, I had to talk to some-body, you know," eely lips, "and I couldn't make it home on my own, with how I looked, the paint and everything, and I didn't have a ride—" she hears my dial tone, and her eyes drop like bright dimes into slots, "so I called Ariel—"

"You got through?"

"Yeah. No problem." Glint between the lids. Psyching me—was I already dubious at this irrelevance? Hard coins: they say, "Bite." I say nothing. I merely feel cursed. "I told her how you were almost done until I, you know— Like, see, I wanted to warn her about what was coming down on her, but I didn't know how—"

"Go *on*." I beat the wall. I want to stamp.

"Anyway, she picked me up, and she was shitfaced, re-ally plowed, and manic, and if Forrest or my mom got a load of her, you know, I'd be screwed. I had to get her off the road, right? I'm begging her, slow down; you know, I can't drive standard"; undertone, "I can't drive at all"; quick brush up and down, "so I said why don't we go somewhere and make those letters like you suggested that time, to make the abortion billboard say 'Smoking is Murder'?"

A rolling pin crushes down me from my skull to my toes, the dough of me sweats butterwater, and I'm clogged. I have this nightmare every night. I can see what's coming. I have to wake up. My fingers drill into my forehead.

"—and some night we'd sneak over there and put them up and, you know, like that would really impress you. So she drives to your place, and she says, 'Wait a minute,' like she's got to get something; she leaves the motor running. I try to get her to go in, but she won't—when she's like that you can't make her do shit. She runs up the drive, and that guy is baying like a coyote, and I'm thinking, oh God, don't leave me here, but then she's back in the truck, we're hauling ass, and I figure we're headed for her dad's. But then we're on the bypass, she's doing sixty, and when she sees the billboard she swerves off, we almost conk out on the roof, I swear, and she crashes into the legs of the billboard and like totals the truck. And I'm like, oh Christ, now what? I think I'm losing my mind. But she's crazy, you know? She pulls this can of charcoal lighter out of the back and climbs on the roof of the truck, and she's going up the ladder; she tells me, 'Fuck this arts and crafts shit. We got to burn the mother down.' I tried to stop her, really, I swear—" She pauses to breathe. All ears around us—pitcher plants. I feel the hungry hang of those lobes. The hooded eyes. Enquiring minds. She lets them click her piteous smile at me. The sick erotic conspiracy of the spanking. No drug can alleviate the pain of severe burns. "God, it was high. I'm terrified of heights. I thought I'd fall over backwards watching. Finally, she makes it. She thinks she's Jagger, she's playing the Coliseum, dancing, waving up applause, she yells down, 'End of the line, Fawnster. Are we gonna talk about it, or are we gonna DO IT?' I'm looking for the SWAT team, the news team; I mean, my life is over; I *know* that. Then she splashes the stuff around and yells, 'Just say NO!'" Fawne really shouts, here, in the hospital corridor, "'TO EVERY-THING!'"

It's Jimmy Cagney in *White Heat* on those burning oil tanks, "Top of the world, Ma!" I'm helplessly watching the tiny imperiled figure of my daughter, brilliant, fearless, and drunk out of her mind, at the end of her rope against a wall of flame, and at the same time I'm tuned into a fifty-year-old movie on a nineteen-inch black-and-white console. The close-up zooms in: You mother! Someone close laughs.

"And then she lights it. Man!" Fawne's eyes well acid. I see the air around Ariel jellying on their liquid surface. "I thought she was gone." She has to shut them to skim off the scum. I shut mine, but my lids must have burned off or vitrified—I can still see. "I was scared shitless. And then I heard her boots, hitting the rungs of the ladder. I was so glad—you know?" She wants points. "And then I heard this thud." Her fists fly up like clods of bombed earth. I want to touch her, I want to touch someone, but I'm thinking burned skin, coming away on my hands— "She fell like, I don't know, two stories maybe?"

I want Ariel.

"And when the cops and the paramedics and the firetrucks came," she's still talking to me, but I must have crossed some line she won't, "you know what she said?" She snorts. "She said, 'My mom is going to love this.'"

Someone laughs.

"It's not my fault, is it?" she calls after me.

Ariel is in the third room on the right. I see Karl's broad back first, his bald spot, the hairy white rhombus where his pants gap away from his shirt, and I have an immediate impulse to yank up my own pants, even though I've been in overalls for years. His shirt is blackening with sweat.

Ariel's head and feet stick out on either side of him. She's stretched out like the magician's lovely assistant, as if she's about to levitate, or Karl is the Chinese box through which swords will slice without piercing her. Her head is braced at the temples by some orange padded block device strapped around her forehead. Space geisha. Or a giant phylactery. "For the wrongs we have done we are sorry—" Tears trickle slowly down the fine groove by her cheekbone into the brace as if by capillary action. I go faint, both from the relief of seeing her, and not charred, and fear of what I'll see next. I try to get hold of myself. Karl is stroking her brow, hushing her.

"Geez, Dad, cut the shoosh stuff! It hurts! Can't I even cry?" The outburst costs her considerable pain, but she has to add, "Ain't it scout to cry?"

Karl's big laugh sways like a hammock. "You sound just like your mother when she was in labor with you. I'm trying to get her to count, she says, 'What are you, a hypnotist?'" He guffaws. "We're wired on Lamaze, she's telling me, 'It hurts, asshole!' Obstetrician asks her can she push a little harder, she says, 'Come over here and say that, schmuck.'"

This is pure stand-up comedy. I certainly don't remember being vulgar. I do remember pleading with Karl to stop telling jokes because it hurt to laugh. Ariel is not laughing. I take it as my cue. Clearing my throat so as not to startle them and because I don't know what to say, I say, "Hi!"

"Mom!" Now Ariel looks like she's running faster than the eye can follow—flat out—like once up to speed, her molecules will disassemble and regroup well out of our gravity. Karl drapes his heavy arms around my neck and hangs and burrows. I sniff his gamy warmth. Karl hugs, not to give comfort, but to get it; he makes me feel like a hot meal, a stiff drink (Jesus!), a good fire (Christ!), a good mother (my God), and the comfort this gives me is very deep. He raises friendly eyes, and I nest in his whiskers. We turn to our daughter together, his arm over me like a lintel.

"She's just back from x-ray." It strikes me we're surveying her like our flood-ruined spring planting. "That brace and the board she's on are giving her a lotta pain, but they've gotta make sure her neck's not broken—" I flinch; he snugs me, "before they can take them away. Should be pretty soon. Then we'll know something. You heard what happened?"

"Fawne." I lean into Ariel's line of sight. She reeks like a smudge fire. I'm afraid to touch her. "I really love you," it seems vital to say.

"Jesus fucking Christ!" she spouts like a kettle, and her eyes and mouth boggle at the pain. "Don't you think I know that? Jesus! That's just it." She's been waiting for me to unload. "You love me and trust me, and I lie to you and get drunk and fuck up." The tears pump evenly like part of the healing machinery. Her face strains like she's trying to tack it out to dry. "I am such a complete fuck-up. I wish to hell I'd never been born. I wish I was dead."

"Oh Ari, don't. I'm the fuck-up. Where was I when—?"

"Don't," she spikes down on me, "just *don't.*" Her eyes close over something like malice and peel up to show revulsion. "It's not you. It's not about you."

"Oh God! If only I'd—"

"No!" Like watching her sizzle on a grill. "You wanna know, or you wanna tell? I've been jerkin' you around so long, you *can't* have anything to do with it. You don't live in the same world as me anymore. You know I steal from you? I steal from Dad, I steal from *Dash,* the kids at school, the stores. And I lie all the time. I used to think I had to, to cover up. I used to play a little game with myself where I tried to make something true sound like an outrageous lie, and when I was lying, I'd sound, like, caught." She hikes her shoulders, and her mouth opens like a vise, gradually closes into a kind of gripped smile. "I know you don't think I'm too good at anything, but I was real good at that."

"Sara Heartburn," Karl and I say together. Our eyes commune, and he touches her cheek.

"But how did you ever get the idea—?" I'm going on, and Karl is saying, "Maybe a career in acting—?" and we look rank disbelief at each other.

"But then it turned out I couldn't tell *what* was true, and I couldn't remember who I said what to, so I just shut up."

"I can't believe that when—" My memory is running

full-tilt backwards, like the speeded-up figures in the earliest flickers. Her tender pallor, my slip of a girl, my straight arrow. "You were lying?"

"Case closed." She smiles. Karl pats her hand. Her gaze ratchets around the bridge of her nose, tightens the smile. "You didn't have to make it so easy, you know? You could have looked a little harder; you could have listened. I told you I didn't want you workin' all the time, even though it freed me up, because somebody's got to stop me, and I don't know who else. That's why when you started up with Fawne—" Grimace. "She's such a ditz! It was just a matter of time before she made me *her* problem, you know? Part of her icky little soap opera. Betray me and think she was doin' us a big favor. I was so sick with fear every minute, but, like, deep down, I must have wanted to get it over with; I mean, why else did I let her hang with me in the first place? You know how when you're really high up, even though you're scared of fallin', part of you wants to jump? I guess I just went ahead and, you know, jumped." Her chest heaves like a bellows. "But it's not her fault, and it's not yours. Really, I'm so proud of you. I never wanted to hurt you. All I ever want to do is impress you. I *love* you. I just don't know what to *do.*"

"Oh, darling." I wish I could think clearly, but I want to melt over her, a second skin; I want to take her back inside me where the aching is and shoot the bolt. Everything I think to say puts the guilt back on her. "I love you" has become recriminating. "God!" I'm exploding. "I hate my life! I hate myself!"

"No! No no no, please. *Listen.*" She casts her left hand about until she finds mine, and we clench. "It started out, it made me feel better, at parties? it kind of blissed me out and let me loose. And then I was doin' it every weekend, just for something to do, some way to get through the time; I mean, the other kids were too, but I couldn't stop, I couldn't handle it. I got so scared, I was drinking to go numb, to tune out the fear. Now," she closed her eyes, "it just kicks my ass."

Karl puts his hand over ours. "Ariel, honey, you're sick. Give yourself a break. You know, my father drank." He looks at me excitedly. I nod: a morose drunk, he once told me; he died young. "They're pretty sure it's genetic. In a way, it's lucky it came out so soon. We'll get help. We'll lick this thing, whatever it takes. First, we'll—"

Thank goodness for Karl, I'm thinking.

"First, he'll teach me to walk—" Ariel grits. "Jesus! I'm his science project."

A short man in surgical greens introduces himself and pumps Karl's hand. The doctor. He has polished, golden skin and a ruff of white hair, and, in the company of a pretty, athletic, ringleted nurse, I see ministering angels. Clearly, I want to be saved.

"The good news is the spine and neck are undamaged. The bad news is her hip and leg are broken. We're going to transfer her upstairs to orthopedics and let them take it from here. Do you have any questions?"

Karl mentions the board and the brace. They want to move her only the once; it won't be long. I ask about pain-killers when she's been drinking. He wants to know how much. She doesn't know. It's been days. Karl and Elly have a liquor cabinet they seldom open. She's drunk all the clear things she could replace with water and some brown things she could replace with tea. The doctor makes a note.

"Don't look at me like that." Her eyes, cornered, slash at me.

"I'm sorry." I hide my face; I can't change it. "I'm so sorry."

"Jesus! You just won't listen. Let's stop kidding ourselves, mom. It's not something you can paint over. This is it." Her features warp. "This shit." She's racked with pain.

Another nurse appears, and they're wheeling her out of

the room before I can think of the best thing to say. Karl prevents me running alongside them, trying to come up with it, like charades. He and the doctor patter pleasantries over clasped hands. We might have just closed on a house or met at a cocktail party. The doctor leaves. Karl trundles me to the door and down the hall.

"This is great, huh? I feel like a total turd. How long you figure she's been at it?"

I'm not really ready to kick off the comeback.

"If only we'd—well. We don't talk enough." His eyes are hoarding his share of the blame. "Communicate. Listen, I'll take care of the cops and the legal fallout. Elly can handle the social services angle, get her in a program, find a shrink, whatever. All you gotta do is be with her, I'm talking round the clock—"

"I want to. I have to, you know? For myself—"

"And Dash. He's almost as bad off as she is. He's been covering for her."

"Christ!"

"I'm good for the money, you just let me know, right? You can do this, am I right?"

If he cuffs me, I bop his chops. I manage to dredge up thanks. I *am* immensely grateful; I just can't stomach the bluster. Five minutes of communicating, I know why we're divorced.

"I know you can. I have complete confidence." Look at him—do I need bucking up this badly? It's not the first time I've suspected Karl fears for my sanity. Probably since the day I walked out on him. "Listen. They're fine kids. Sturdy stock. Ariel's gonna come outta this. We'll see it through together, you, me, and Elly. Try not to freak."

He should be singing. The showstopper. "Don't Cry For Me—" I search his eyes for the humor I can use to make him cut the crap.

"Although that Fawne," he puts in. "A real piece a work.

Her parents leave her on her own at Christmas to go to London?"

"Oh, right."

He snorts. "That's what she told the cops. Tried to sell Ariel down the river in her haste to dissociate herself from the crime. Implicated you, too, in a kinda buy one, get one free deal. Loyalty of a flea. Thought she might make the witness protection program. Set herself up in Vegas with her old man. Disappointed she didn't get an interesting scar out of it." He wizens. "I bet she's your doing. Ariel has more sense."

Let's go back to the crap.

"You take Dash up with you." He looks in the waiting room and paws at Elly. "We'll take batgirl home and sort things out with her folks."

"You'll love them. Watch out they don't wash you in the blood of the lamb."

"That anything like the hair of the dog?"

"It wags the dog." Our smirks decay. It hits me that that pig Forrest was right about everything. "They've got dogs. Two horrible little yapping rat dogs."

"Three." Karl eyes Fawne. She's attached to Elly but trying something on Dash, probably securing half-interest in his sister's effects or the rights to her docudrama. Dash looks glazed.

"You look awful." I caress his hot cheek up into his matted hair.

"It's the war," he says. "Seen yourself? 'Hee Haw' meets *Chain Saw Massacre*."

I'm Steve Martin's mother. "Ariel's in orthopedics; her leg and hip are broken. I have to stay. You can go home with Karl and Elly if you want."

"I think you ought to stay with your mom," Karl tells him, pulling down his mustache.

"Nonetheless, I think I'll stay with you, Mom." Dudley

Do-Right. He's locked on me, but I don't think he's looking at me. Karl smiles gently, loving himself for being too wise to take the bait.

Elly fumbles for my hand. "Carrie," she says, the way your doctor would say, "cancer." She wields her sympathy like the reflex hammer. "You're being so brave."

How does she know? And what are my options?

"What about me?" Fawne squeaks. "I was *there*."

I suppose I could run, but how far would I get? "Ev'ry step I take, you take with me—"

"Oh, of course!" Elly throws an arm over Fawne. "You've been through a terrible trauma—"

Maybe I should puke all over her.

"You know," Elly tells me, "I can see a lot of good in this. Finally getting it all out in the open—"

What an opening! And then I'd say, thanks for letting me share this with you. I'm really warming to the idea.

"—and now you can all get the help—"

"Too much help as it is," mutters Dash.

Elly blinks at him, cringing smile at me. We must look like welfare cheats. "Facing up to the truth *is* painful, but it works." When this fails to cheer us, she adds, "You're so much better off than you *were*. Look at it that way. You're on the road to recovery." She presses my hand and drops it, slings up her purse. Her next mission beckons. She links elbows with Fawne. Karl yokes her under his arm. She smiles at his ear as though it's camera two, while he buffets me and Dash with bluff, practical reassurances. Who do they think is watching?

"Say, Karl, before you take off, you got any cash on you?" I'm playing my role to the hilt. I wish I had fewer teeth and some spangles. Dye job. Gum. Cigs. "I got a lift over here, and I'll need cabfare to get us home."

Karl struggles his wallet out of his pants and forks over a twenty. "Citroën's not giving you any trouble."

"How could it?" Dash rounds his eyes.

"Is it winter?" I ask.

"It's the war," Dash confides.

"Always an excellent car," he explains to Elly. "Got the highest rating that year in *Consumer Reports*. When you think of its age and the miles on it—"

"And how much it cost and how much we put into it and how it used to drop dead right from the very start—!" I exclaim.

"Cheap at half the price. But at least it wasn't made by fascists." Dash is quoting.

Elly darts forward to peck his cheek and implore a touch of eyes. He sweeps his hand across them to rake back his hair. Elly wakes Fawne out of a trance by again hooking their elbows.

"Can I stay with you tonight?" begs the little matchgirl. "I'm scared of being alone. I don't know what I might do."

"Well, of cour—"

"You gotta face your folks sometime." Karl hitches on. "They must be frantic."

Elly's surprised eyes access his database. She turns to the teen phenomenon with new interest.

"But you'll come in with me?" (What heartless beast would not?) "Give Ariel my love," to me; "tell her I'll call, if they let me—"

They wheel for the doors. The three somethings. So brave. In fact, they walk in step, with a little hop, even. "Don't forget to smash the state!" calls Karl, showing the fist.

Dash and I automatically check each other. He looks like the morning after—grubby, irresolute, exhausted, and disgusted. One look, the house lights go up, and this insane, inane double family feature is finally over. We start the search for orthopedics.

Ariel is in surgery. They're going to put some kind of metal screw in her hip, cut the tissues around the leg fracture to reposition the bones correctly. General anesthetic. Several people have told me we're really lucky, but I can't seem to make out how. Dash and I are in the lounge, sitting on a This End Up loveseat together, even though there's no one else around. Neither of us can get comfortable. We intort and spraddle until he removes his sneakers and sits sideways with his arms around his knees. I do likewise. Matching ginger jar lamps behind us on matched tables; we're a Rorschach test. We both study our fingers.

"So," I open at last, "how was your Christmas?"

"Weird. Kind of like camp. They made us hang around and eat and do stuff that was like scheduled. Ten a.m.: walk in woods, cut down tree, weep and wail over cuttin' down tree, lunch, trim tree. Ariel had the truck, but Elly wanted us to do all this kid stuff together, makin' cookies, playin' games—she didn't want us to go to the Vert or the movies or anything. You know what her theme song is?" He sneaks me a smile. "'You'll Do It My Way.'"

"Maybe it's Adam. With just the one little guy, you try to make everything—I don't know—perfect—like your fantasy—"

"Yeah, well, the kid gets on my nerves. Ought to call him up for Desert Shield; he's ready. G.I. Joe. With her goin' all drippy about the tree, you'd think— She *says* stuff to him, but she smiles. And if we want to rent a video or Ari wants to listen to her thrash on MTV—uh uh, bad for the little angel. And every time we'd get alone anywhere, one of them would drop from the clouds and want to talk heart to heart about some big deal like sex or responsibility like campfire pow-wow. Now that we're older. They had to keep remindin' themselves. You know who's gettin' older."

I love it; he knows it and plays to it. He probably had a great Christmas.

"I mostly worked on my handplants. I'm getting pretty good. Ariel, she—" He stops and reddens. "Hey, we really liked your gifts. Although we noticed they were things we were gonna get anyway. We called to thank you, but you weren't there. Elly made us write cards."

"I liked mine, too." Peacock feather earrings and a fanny pack so if I'm hit by a car running, they'll be notified. "The dojo's just a storefront, but I really liked the teacher. He's Korean, and he made this very quick, sly joke," I chop a knife hand, "without telegraphing or laughing. And the class is racially mixed; it's over on the east side, so—"

"Yeah, well, you know, talkin' with Ms. Williams really cleared me on that. You gotta stop bein' afraid and start dealin' with people somewhere along the line." He lifts his shiny rootbeer lifesavers. "I been thinkin' now maybe you and me can get into tag team wrestling, like with the karate gimmick."

I purse at him. "Sure, what better way to make a living?"

"Call ourselves the International Exaggerators."

I laugh. "A real opportunity for costume."

"Glitter underwear!" he yells. The sludge of silence reminds him where we are. A passing nurse frowns and smiles. He lowers his voice. "And Ariel, well, she was really happy you could afford the good boots." His face shatters. "She'll still be able to ride?"

I don't know. My cheeks must be as red as his.

He looks back down at his hands. "She'll die if she can't."

It's a statement of fact. I'm glad there's nobody bleating upbeat bullshit at us. "How long have you known?" I ask in a coated voice.

"Not long. Since Fawne." His lips crimp severely. "I think it *was* Fawne. You know how she sucks all the air out of a room?"

I know it's me. "I wish you'd told me." I immediately

wish I hadn't said this.

"I wish—" He says, "I had too" through tears so wrenching and brackish his jaw sticks. He puts his face on his knees. I jerk forward to hold him.

Sometime later he falls asleep in my smelly lap—like a week-old catfish—mouth open and snoring. Dash hasn't fallen asleep on me since he learned to walk. My hand stumbles the strange big bony ridge of him as if I haven't seen him since then, as if I'm combing him out of the wool of memory. My children aren't particularly pretty without their eyes on. But then—stunning, beyond any rendering. Is that an illusion of love? Or its source? I know one thing: I see it. Spirit. I see Ariel on the operating table; in all that white and silver and the green of the gowns like the green of thick glass or ice or deep water, the warmth of her buttered-toast skin, her nutbrown hair, coffee bean eyes, her fine, difficult face. Her blood. I want to steal to the door and do a sketch for an oil, after Rembrandt. Or in recovery, on a raised-head bed in an island of light, just as she opens her eyes.

Please.

The heat rushes up, billows the drapes, mixes with the cold air that seeps around the mullions of the window behind them. I feel wiped out. I feel completely to blame for Ariel's drinking, and accepting it levels me like satisfaction. I know where I am: at bottom.

And what next? When her leg and hip are mending (please) and she's caught in the undertow of doctors, counselors, programs, I don't know, cops? struggling for her soul, how can I help her? How can I back her without pushing her? Love without leaning on her?

Maybe I can't.

What am I going to do?

Maybe nothing.

I look at nothing until I feel stifled—a long time? a short

time? Compared to who? Buddha? Donald Duck? I find myself thinking of Elspeth.

10 Easy To Be Hard

It was winter, 1968, Christmas? yes, because the whole building across the street burned orange with electric menorahs. I was sitting at a table, not writing a theme for Eng. 350 (overdue) on Shelley. What was there to say? "Nothing beside remains." I got that. I was also trying to draw my frost-flowered window. What I really wanted was that evening blue steeping behind the waxy crystals, the steam off the radiator, the weave of black branches, the snowy lashes of the streetlight; the orange sweetening it. But I don't paint, see; I just draw. At least I knew my limitations. Lately, all my drawings looked like cemetery gates. I could always teach. "The lone and level sands stretch far away." Lone sand? Crumpled drafts crackled at my ankles like the dry egg cases of insects, like invitations to Miss Havisham's wedding.

And there was a war on. Everywhere.

Sammy came in, threw his bookbag and aviator's jacket on the couch, lifted the needle onto "Surrealistic Pillow," and sat to roll a number. This cold bitch screaming, "Don't you want somebody to love?" Don't I? "You better—"

Sammy was the latest in a series, a graduate student in anthropology (although he'd never been off Long Island for

201

more than two months and that was at camp in New Hampshire and to California with a teen tour). He knew a lot about shadow puppets. He had long, wavy, auburn hair, dead white skin, and eyes like fire opals. It was his album. No matter how often I put on something else, I wound up having to take this off.

"Hey, baby," he said, "you want some a this here mary-jew-wanna?"

I looked over my shoulder. "Will it help my paper on Shelley?"

He considered the litter, lighting up. "Can it hurt?"

I slouched to the couch. It lurched like a kid on high heels. Danish modern, last legs: Either/or.

"How was your day?" I asked on the inhale and sounded like I'd had my trachea removed.

He shrugged. Put his boots up on the edge of the coffee table, which was so packed with arty candles (his) it looked like the Garden of the Gods. In fact, if I'd had a little molded plastic cowboy on a horse, we could have filmed an episode of "Gumby." I started whistling "Happy Trails," but my gulch was too dry. I no more heard the Airplane than if I lived in the hangar.

"Peace Corps," he exhaled. Knit his brows. I'd forgotten I asked about his day. And then I whistled. "I applied today. Malaysia. Or Afghanistan. Think of the drugs."

Think of the rugs. I wondered if he was sufficiently enamored to bring me one. I had better put in my order soon. And include postage and handling. "When?"

For caring when, I was forgiven my previous inattention, but now he whiffed dependency. The nervous half-smile restated those often stipulated reservations. "It takes time. I think they check up on you. Red tape, paperwork. Don't worry." He dragged his thumb down my neck muscle to my nipple and flicked it, grinned. "Of course, all good things must come to an end." His mustache mopped the scoop of my throat.

"You want some tea?"

He nuzzled my clavicle on the way to my ear, his customary overland rut, route! like those timid pre-Columbian spice merchants. Beyond this point lie monsters. Pushy kiss. Lots of double- and triple-tonguing. He needed a mirror. I was the mirror. The couch bucked like a bronc. Gumby and Pokey. I knew I should be working on Shelley. If I was serious about my education. If I was serious about making a living. If I was serious about my future. If I was serious about anything.

"What do you want to do about dinner?" I asked.

His smile stretched like a sunning cat and settled on my mouth. If we fucked now, I'd be soaking pots at midnight, but I'd rather get fucked than say no and hear him analyze why to the same effect. Gumby pokes Pokey in Dry Gulch. High noon. Tombstone Territory. The right front leg buckled, and we plummeted to the floor like boulders. "Baby! The earth moved!" he joked, "Knocked the legs right out—"

The phone rang. I tried to conceal my relief. I hoped it was my mother. Or his! Big show of reluctance before he reached to answer it, as if he was a slave to his passions even in an avalanche. Passed it to me.

"What do you mean, calling me in the middle of the night and suggesting we go to Tierra del Fuego? It'th dithguthting, the whole filthy idea!"

Elspeth laughed, and I was carbonated. We hadn't spoken in ages. I bounced up, and Sammy weltered like he was light in the hold. "How are you? Where are you? What's happening?" Amelia Earhart back from the Pacific! Odysseus from Troy!

"I've gone downhill, East 11th between A and B to be precise, and I can only conclude that wafting good thoughts and longing in a person's direction counts for diddly, or you have not yet evolved antennae. Too busy to breathe eking out a pittance and so horny for yakking with a non-moron, I describe you to the roaches. If you would care to drop by this evening, I might consider not taking poison. Unless, of course, you have a heavy date" (under the circumstances, this seemed clairvoyant), "in which case, hire a wheelbarrow. Make 'em want it! Who was that masked man, anyway?"

Sammy had lumbered off to rummage in the fridge. I lowered my voice to read her his vitals. "And gorgeous." A real testimonial to my hidden inner qualities. I looked forward to showing him off. Then I realized to whom. "If a bit—" What did I have to show? Nothing.

"Scant lecturing from me, kiddo, I just threw out the delivery boy. Not only a ninny, but fattening. Boredom and loneliness do breed strange bedfellows. Still, he liked it, and I've got my groceries, and that's about as close to mutually satisfying as we've come around here for donkey's, masters be johnsoned! Put a move on, child, I'm all adither to see youse."

My energy had evaporated with the brief review of my résumé. I didn't want to see myself through her eyes. "I don't know, Else. Have you looked out the window? I'm not sure I'm up for it. I think I'm coming down with something."

"Over under sideways down. I don't believe I left you a way out. See you, shining Cee!"

I'd described Elspeth to Sammy, recounting in meticulous detail whole conversations, perhaps twice a week from our first meet, as one of my selling points: I may not be much, but I've got a friend who lives in a lamp. So he was right eager to traipse out in the slush, to wait for the intermittent local on a frigid elevated platform, to find her either wonderful or wanting; either way, he'd win. He was also a thrill-seeker. He thought there *were* eight million stories in the naked city. He thought if he stayed in one night, he'd be missing something. I went into a muck sweat over what to wear. My hair hung like limp lettuce. I hoped she wouldn't remember I'd ever lost any weight. I put on long jet earrings and a velvet jacket—black, strewn with yellow flowers and green leaves and made by me so the lining didn't hang right— and buttoning my coat over it, I might have been headed from shtetl to steerage.

Sammy finished milk and a sandwich and set glass and dish in the sink. A drop clung to the soft droop of his mustache. "Am I okay like I am?" he asked, genuinely concerned after my futile flummery.

Definitely. I felt that twinge singe out to my extremities, now that we were committed to the search for the pole. Do you know the difference between involved and committed? Take bacon and eggs: the hen is involved, but the pig— He zipped up his bomber. Take off.

The hall stank of cat piss, bacon, and roach bomb. Someone had written, "Earthmen, we scorn you," on the wall and across her door. Sly had been through here, and the Devil Rays. The doors, the floors, were diaphragms, vibrating laugh tracks, a shrill fight, pots and pans, leadfoot bass. Braced for the onslaught of however many hindlegged legionnaires on leave, I flabbed when the door opened on a circus pug. Elspeth had gained twenty pounds, most of which had deposited along her cleavage, spilling out of the vee of a short cream, orange, and brown kimono she wore over chartreuse stockings. Bright red Orphan Annie frizzle and round red glasses. Her flesh had the dull yellow sheen of provolone and seemed tied in similar bulges. Silt under her eyes. Double chin. Older.

"Else! Where are the dogs?" I asked. "Where's Goofy?" Then I remembered Rathbone. I congratulated my tact.

"I sold him for a bundle I ate between jobs. Ditto cats. Welcome to the wonderful world of single-blessedness. You may kiss me."

I hesitated, as if she were a bedridden, fortune-telling aunt. My lips barely touched. Her black shutters tightened focus and snapped; I was exposed from every angle. She spun a manic smile on Sammy.

"Ah, the well-known anthro-po-pologist." She put out her hand. "What do the natives call you when you're at home?"

He looked at me. Beset by a panhandler. I wanted to push him. "Sam." He inched back, guarded his mouth. "Ma'am."

She looked quizzically at her hand, sniffed it, withdrew it with a shrug. "I'm Elspeth. I'll tell you someday about my battle to achieve a last name. You may want to document it. Wave of the present. I had a donkey skin shadow puppet once, gift from a boyfriend, beautiful, deep, billiard-ball colors." She caromed him the eights. "But why?"

He looked like he was holding water in his mouth.

"—if you only see the shadow?"

He was holding in laughter. He was fourteen, and he'd stumbled into the hootchy-kootch in a squalid carny sideshow, and some sad old stripper had singled him out. The light was merciless. It's called rubbing your nose in it. The television racket: cosmic mocking.

"Well, gee, time's up, and no answer! These zany foreigners—go figure!" She waved us in, pushed the door to, and restored chain, bar, a pitched metal post that jammed the knob, and turned two keys.

I didn't want to see what smelled in this kitchen/dining/whatever. It was as if we'd blundered into the digestive tract of some yawning animal, complete with visceral rumbling.

"Let me take your wraps." She threw them on the floor in a flurry of dust kittens. Sammy refused to surrender the leather jacket. "Sit." She pulled a chair away from the mad tea table, and several days of newspaper swashed to the floor. Sammy sat; I sat; Elspeth pushed the cheese rinds and cracker boxes, greasy plates, cups, and glasses, the red spiral of Schmulke Bernstein salami wrapper, the open Rose's Lime Marmalade with a knife and a cockroach and crumbs in it to the center of the table and sat. "He kept all the good furniture, and he knew shit from furniture before he met me. But it's just as well. I call this building 'Free Lunch' because of the steady conga of junkies toting appliances down the fire escape. I'm working on a painting— correction, thinking of working on a painting—for the little gallery in the hall? A bare hangs-over-the-bar belle, like so—" She posed with shoulder and hip foremost, leg bent up, leer. Her breasts pooched out like two raw Cornish game hens. Sammy sucked in his lips. His eyes kept darting at my dodgers. He was wondering how big a mistake I might be. So was I. "—on a bed of greens. And a chap seated behind her, not unlike, say, de Quincy—"

Sammy lifted brow, goldfish still swimming his saliva.

"*Confessions of an English Opium Eater,*" I supplied. He nodded, smiling complacently as if I were his A-student, acing my orals, and he'd forgotten more than I'd ever know.

"—or perhaps Poe—I'm seeing neck ruffles, but maybe that's a napkin—holds her at knee and ankle and sinks tooth in calf." She mimed the chomp. "Either in the manner of Annnnng—"

Ingres, to you. "Nineteenth-century French realist."

"—or Grünewald." She laughed like a typewriter.

"Medieval kraut. You know those crucifixions with the cherubim snagging His blood in chalices?"

"If I care, I'll ask." Whoops! Class dismissed! His gaze skit the cracked and seeping walls, spattered medicinal colors, the grimy, gouged linoleum, the blacked-out windows. He held himself like squeamish skirts.

"I pretend I don't live here either. I managed to keep an FM radio for awhile by stashing it in the stove until I preheated the inevitable Spanakopita Sylvania. Which reminds me, have you eaten? What can I get you?"

I almost said, "Clean cups." Sammy said, "We just ate."
"Some wine. Tea, surely."

Sammy found his watch. "We can't stay." Played with
the zipper on his coat. I got him into this.

Elspeth narrowed her eyes on me so that I felt myself
compress. If I'd still had on my wool cap I'd have pulled it
down to my shoulders for the rest of my life. Instead, I put
my hand over my mouth and smiled weakly at both of them.
Somewhere in the building a bottle smashed. Bass throbbed
like a headache. Gregor Samsa tore around a corner.

"That's too bad. I was hoping we could go to the Electric Circus later and dance. It's in walking distance."

I imagined the three of us dancing. Slender Sam sand-
wiched between the two gaudy hippos. I was swelling. She
poured white wine in teacups.

"Well, I don't know—maybe." He slanted me the inter-
rogative. "I've never been there. I've heard it's a trip." She'd
hit him square on the hip, as it were. He once told me he'd
like to experience a cockfight. He consulted his wine. "Will
someone be joining us?"

We looked at him, and he looked at the way his knees
were crossed. "I mean, are you expecting someone else?"

"No," puzzled Elspeth. "Why?"

He frowned, tossing his hair back. "It's just—I gotta be
honest with you; I don't like being used. As the man, you
know. Taken for granted. Escort, bodyguard—you know.
I'm sure if the shoe was on the other foot—"

Instead of in his mouth. I could hear Elspeth's smile when
she said, "I'll sit out the cheek to cheek if it bothers you.
But, see, it's like tribal, you dig? Aren't you the anthro apolo-
gist?"

"I just wouldn't feel comfortable with it." Smoothing
down his thighs, the little vamp. Me without a grapefruit.
"It's not that I'm against that sort of thing per se—" He

showed his pearlies. "I just like to do the choosing. And I'm with Carrie." He grazed my sleeve. "You know how insecure she is." He freshened the smile. "Nothing personal."

I felt like they were trading camels for me and one was too much. I wanted to be jettisoned. Goodbye cruel world.

"We are talking about dancing?" Elspeth asked me.

He simpered. "I can foresee other complications. Some guy gets obnoxious— Or you want to split, and we don't. You see what I mean. I like to keep it simple. Mind if I use your bathroom?"

"Such as it is." She looped her wrist, and he swayed off as if sheathed in satin, shooting back a look that told me, "Straighten this out." The door closed. "Simple," she said. "Any good in the sack?"

I was abashed. Had he heard? Was he listening for my answer? Apparently not. I didn't know who I owed what. I felt like an agent. I Fled Three Lives. The smell was making me sick. I ended up smirking.

"Nice guys finish first," Orphan Annie went Charlie Chan, "and want to wash up." Her eyes crinked inside the big red Os. "I know it's nice to have someone to pass the time with and to reassure you of your desirability. But don't fall for the whole romantic scam. Love is nothing but patriarchal propaganda, from the people who brought you slavery, war, and the glamor suicide."

Well! That sure popped the cork on Shelley. Tip him over and pour him out. Lone sands! Nothing remained.

"When you yourself are at a loss, such socially sacrosanct distractions as *luhve* can delude you into glorifying self-sacrifice and emptiness and divert you from the obligatory agonies of discovery. It's *not bad* to keep your distance, a reserve, to be—"

The flush announced my swain's imminent return.

"—solitary. Cool. Critical." Sammy sauntered out, and Elspeth started rattling, "I've been such a lazy shit about painting I decided to blow the whistle on myself. I have to spend an hour every night looking at the prepared surface with paints and tools at hand—"

An accordioned tube of chrome yellow next to the Rose's Lime. The shrouded easel amid rags and cans and cartons like Tut brooding over his stash. Sammy would be having a lot less trouble with this if he'd come out to find me sitting on her face. Or whispering, blushes, tears. He took his seat to decipher our thrumming cool.

"With lazy bastards like me who use their fear of failure to avoid confrontation, this is the only way to force the issue. By substituting torture for real discipline, I hope in time the torture will become the discipline and no longer be torture. Thus, when all was in readiness, and I stood poised to part the impenetrable mists," flourishing a butterknife, "I called you!"

"I wasn't at any creative pinnacle either," I admitted. Sammy winked, which fuddled me a minute. The sandstorms were still swirling through my head. "But you're working, too? You have a job."

"One could shit from grief alone if it wasn't a daily necessity. I illustrate government pamphlets." She hung her head and presented crossed wrists. "I'm the one who draws those cars dutifully pausing at intersections, jovial cops, immigrants in fanciful get-ups in the shadow of the original green goddess. Right now I'm grunting out an update of Little Hot Spot. You remember?"

"Jesus, not—?"

Solemn nod.

"I don't." Sammy decided he wanted to be dealt in. He was a with-it kind a guy.

"He's from Long Island," I explained.

Buffing his leather, "Massapequa."

"I'm so sorry," she commiserated. "Little Hot Spot is the friendly flicker who encourages kids to fink on the household combustibles and to write smug piffle for the city fire-prevention essay contest. My early drafts have been uniformly obscene. Uncle Don, the office pervert, raids my garbage to ogle these clitoral nubs, and my little hot spot is the subject of general smutty speculation. They pass my desk ejaculating their lighters." She clicked her thumb. "Jane, the secretary, takes me to Charcoal Chef, and when the grease catches, she nudges me. Why wasn't I given the sex handbook?" she wailed, clasping Sammy's forearm. "I would not have made the vagina look like Wolfman or the penis like a fireplug!" He patted her hand before she clutched both over her bosom. "If I don't come up with something soon, they might fire me," gazing ceilingward, "and I've got no more pets to eat!"

"That ought to light a fire under you," observed Sam. "You're in the little hot seat."

She rather overdid the delight. He smiled at me—he wanted me to salute his magnanimity—but whatever he saw made him look down at the table, then defiantly flash the toothpaste thirty-two. She sloshed us another round. "The whole thing bores me stiff. I know in my basic genetic fiber I must risk drastic change, but I'm held up by food, clothing, shelter. Is this progress? I thought when I divorced Joe I set the stage for success, but there he is, no internalized conscience, a lush, forsaken by my replacement a year ago and already she's replaced, making fifty thousand smackers a year—and, by the by, the dastardly Paul—"

I blanched. Sammy noticed. Shit. Now he would badger me to come clean about this until I concocted something, flattering himself it was his caring, when it would only be because it made me a better story. I could look forward to days of it, starting as soon as we were alone—the subway home—and I was already tired of it. How to tell him my past was just underfoot, a stench on my sole?

"—dealing deathy drugs and raking in hundreds of thous,

which he invests in legit stuff, rolling in it, no h.s. diploma and ensconced in a fucking duplex in fucking Sutton Place—and here I am, in this firetrap, this prepschool for the Tombs, a total shrink addict, food addict, succumbing to the enticements of exorbitant dating services in search of suitable companionship and offered only dumb lumps, without the solace of a furry friend even, and getting le balls bleu," she blagued, "over the fucking Little Hot Spot to pay for it. I ask you!"

Christ! And I was The Christmas Carol, looking up the skirts of my future. "This Girl is Want, this Boy, Ignorance!" I saw me in my grave, cosy, all tucked up; I wanted to pat the mound. The smell of mildew and rot wadded my head; the muted noise worked my ears like boxing gloves. I could locate my craw. Last Saturday, Sammy took me to a party where friends of his were shooting up. We'd been to the park, collided with a dense mill of nuns, VFW, construction workers, cops, scouts, JROTC, assorted inebriated roughnecks brandishing sharp sticks—the afterbirth of a march in support of the war. The red glare of squadcar gumballs. Bloodvessels bursting in bulbous noses. Trumpets and drums. Racial bellybumping. Fights. The crowd standing, watching a young man endure an epileptic attack, laughing, expressing disgust. Then we had dinner and went on to the party, and people were pulling down their pants and perching on kitchen chairs to plunge needles in their femoral arteries. Sammy smiled, said, "Uh, not right now, thanks, maybe later," checked his watch. Clean cups, clean cups. CLEAN ME. I thought then, and I was thinking now, what am I doing here? How did I get here? How do I get out? "There must be some kind of way out of here—" I wanted out.

"Let's get *down*!" Elspeth fixed me with a pitchman's pointblank. "Let's get depressed!"

"The Hot Spot," Sammy said, "make it look like a joint." He produced one from his workshirt pocket. "They'll love it. Relate to their culture. In basketball sneakers. The ash like an Afro." He put the j in his mouth and wet it down. "You don't mind?"

"Oh, but I do. And I think *they'd* mind very much."

"No, I mean if we smoke." He cracked his smile with the match, tugged, shrugged back his jacket, thumbed the number out at her. He was going native; what the hell? Who'd see him? A happenin' guy. "For dancing. Loosen us up."

"You think I'm an artist, and all artists are heads, but only the former is true." She homed on his eyes. He passed off blindly to me. "When I was in high school my parents handed me over to a quack who submitted me to sensory deprivation as a cure for my crazies. These methods are now commonly used as torture by totalitarian regimes, such as our own. Drugs tend to reproduce the experience in all its horror. But I don't mind," she batted at him, "if you do."

"Wow!" he gasped. The j ticked between us like a metronome. "Amazing. Maybe you were the first. Could you sue?"

I toked, trying to take it in. Drifting in a silent velvet darkness the temperature of blood. Lovely. A siren in the street threaded my head like a needle. I wondered exactly how crazy Elspeth was. Might be. Objectively. I felt chilled brittle.

"Not at all like that." She lowered her eyes to drink. "One of the things about it is you can't know. Even remembering is not it. And there's no telling." Tracking on Sammy. "Yes, there's a light show." Sammy lost his lungful. "Last one I saw reminded me of dilute food coloring dribbling into Saran Wrap, and what do you know? It was! Also strobes to induce convulsions, and black light to make our teeth green and purple. Very groovy. We'll all be shadow puppets."

"You know what you asked before?" Slumped forward,

just recovering his breath—he looked like he'd been chased here. "About the colors? Well, see, it depends. The Chinese—" He sipped some wine, refused the roach. I put it in an orange rind. "—the colors mean something. The color of the face tells the audience if the character is, say, loyal or violent. They can see them on the screen because the light is bright and close and the figures are perforated. The best Chinese puppets are donkey skin, which is very translucent, takes color and lacquer well, and stays flexible. But from the dark colors you describe, I'll bet your puppet was Balinese—"

"Ooh! *Wayang kulit*—"

She'd obviously whanged his dishcover. "Exactly. Probably cowhide. Again, the colors are symbolic. It's so complicated," his long fingers tunneled into his hair, "the meaning changes in relation to what's next to what. You can't see them in the night performance—they use a smoky coconut-oil lamp, the screen's too far away, cowhide is more opaque. But there's a day performance—"

"Aha! Another mystery solved!"

"It's sacred, intended for the gods, so it's almost inaudible, shorter, simpler, and the colors—the colors glow—" He was aglow himself. I got the short course on shadow puppets our first date, but I didn't recall either of us getting so worked up about them. "The colors are everything. They're supposed to have *guna*, a magic power that makes the audience watch—"

"Guna Hayworth. Guna Lollobrigida. Ava Guna."

"The Hot Spot." He slopped back against his chair, smiling like Mme. Récamier.

"You know? You're a genius." Elspeth put her glasses on the table, and her eyes were little hot spots. "He's a lead singer, a child Temptation, spotlighting the hazards at the Little Hot Spot where they're playing." She pulled off the red wig and scruffed up her soft black floss. Instantly small, tender, vulnerable. Gingerbread. "'Too many instruments plugged into that socket, man.' 'Be careful with those cigarettes, sisters!' Satin tux, sequined lapels, grading up from red through orange, yellow, white, to blue face and wisps-of-smoke Afro. Get the writers to jive up his lines, and there you have it. Spot on, Sam! Really, you've saved my bacon. Just when I was at the end of my tether, you tumble from the rafters—the stars—"

"Like Groucho's duck," I muttered.

"Yes!" She blushed like a peach. "The secret woid!" She leaned toward Sammy, swanning her neck, serious, confiding, "The secret word is money. Do you believe in fate?" He pursed his lips, flipped his hair back, intense. She showed me delirious stupefaction. I was sorry to learn I was still here. "So let's celebrate. Trip the light fantastic. No more foolishness, right?"

He closed his eyes over a beaten smile. "No, ma'am."

"We're off to join the circus. Just let me put on my face. Come with me." She lifted his hand off his knee like a hankie. They stood. He arranged his jacket carefully on the chair like a surrogate for a sniper to take a shot at. She splashed more wine in the teacups. I should just twine them in garlands and tiptoe in front of a train. My best friend and my boyfriend and other maudlin country songs. And Christmas!

Except I'd never dared presume her my friend. She was my—idol. That speech about love? I heard it as gospel, as the revealed word. A confidence it cost her dearly to know. It still resonated. How did I really feel? Worthless, unloved. What else was new? Something. Finally undeceived. Resolute. Impatient. Sammy had sleeping pills. He was from Long Island, after all. It was just a matter of getting to them, alone. I didn't think I'd have any trouble pulling it off tonight. Opportunity knocks.

"Else, I don't know." My arms cinched over my stomach. My voice sounded funny even to me—tinny. "I'm not sure I'm in the mood—"

"What *do* you want to do?" I was surprised by the jab. I felt the heat from her eyes. "What do *you* want to do?" It had gotten quiet. Hot. "What do you *want* to do?" She smiled at my snaggle. We were spies, meeting in a crowded station, and I hadn't been briefed. Was she the enemy or my contact? I wished the duck would drop. I couldn't see the pair flying over.

"I could go home," I said.

"Come on, Carrie." Sammy, aggravated. With whom? He avoided eye contact.

"Oh, not you! You go. I mean on my own. I'll be fine."

"Don't be silly." Elspeth took her cup. "Change do you good. A little exercise." She pushed me toward the bedroom.

A pink-shaded lamp nacred the mirrored dresser where she sat. She motioned us to the brass bed that filled the rest of the space, under the soft billows of a tented pink parachute, and I sprawled out on my side. Sammy sat on the edge, at her shoulder, his hands dangling between his knees. It was quiet here. The windows were covered by Indian cloth embroidered with mirrors; the bed, by a batik print. Warm colors—red, pink, brown. The walls were cinnamon, but not much showed for the paintings. I had begun to think she'd eaten them too, but of course they eat her. Sammy stared at one, looked up, stared at another, looked away, another, like someone shaking off a vision. I looked at them with the old awe and a bitter new envy. How crazy did you have to be? I was worried I'd start to cry.

Elspeth pulled back her hair with a white band, pulled the kimono down slightly and puffed her face, her neck, her round white shoulders, and her upper chest with scented white powder. With a fine brush she stroked black, blue, green, gold, purple around her eyes: peacock eyes. Her tongue traced the movement.

"Great room," Sammy said. "Like a yurt. Did Carrie tell you I'm going into the Peace Corps? Maybe Afghanistan." He coughed into his fist. "Or Malaysia."

She lit a cigarette. Secret, forbidden, one a day—I remembered the penciled mustache and the trip to the candy store as if they were the warning symptoms—aura—of recurrent seizures. Somehow Sammy communicated he wanted a smoke because she lit and passed one to him without taking her eyes from her task. "Galvanizing around the world sounds like a gas. Access to bold and wondrous handicrafts—ornate saddlebags, rugs, cloth?" He looked like he was taking this down. "I'll try not to grudge it you. I myself have never been out of the city. I hate sunlight, I *would* mind squatting to piss, inventing Tampax, wearing dripdry, and I think people who don't speak English are stupid. Until I can afford first class, I'll take Manhattan. You do remember the secret word?"

He chuckled, already betraying his calling. The bed jangled. I'd always wondered how it would sound during lovemaking. From my recline his mustache seemed to graze her shoulder. The floating world. My wrist was killing me. I heaved up.

"He thinks I'm kidding. And what about you, shayne madel?" She stopped to look where I must have been in the mirror. "What have you been up to?"

"Nothing." I indulged myself an emphasis.

"Impossible. Try again."

"Nothing. Brooklyn College. Ed major. Then teach."

"Then die. You sound excited. What about art?"

"I'm not good enough."

"You're too young to know. You haven't even tried yet."

"And there's no money in it even for people who are." I thrust my chin at a small oil-on-wood of a seal balancing a red cannonball Edam on a scale in a classic, tiled delicatessen. "You said yourself—"

"So young and so defeated." She sat back in a puff of smoke. She didn't seem to inhale, just to create an atmosphere: Vienna, 1910. I watched her in the mirror. Her eyes were slits. "Are you going to let her get away with this?" she prodded Sammy.

"She's realistic. I really respect that in a woman. She's not," he moistened his mouth with wine, "a lightweight." Peered at his cigarette. "I don't know what she told you about us, our relationship, but it's not, you know, the conventional bourgeois, possessive, dependent, exclusive—"

"I see," she said, "no strings, no demands—"

"Exactly—"

"—no support. All for one and no down payment."

"That's it exactly. I mean, I think she's good—of course, or why would I be with her? But I don't know the commercial potential. She's smart to cover her ass, play it safe." He looked up into the mirror, sad as a lapdog. He hated what he was doing, but adventure called. Anyway, that was the version he was selling himself. He also liked doing something he thought hateful. He confused dark with deep. And I forgave him. In fact, I thought rather better of him. He could see her. Well, almost. A strange smile stitched across my face and seemed to lace me up. All I really liked about him was his liking me. Vanity, vanity, all is vanity. I didn't give a shit about him. I must be heartless.

Elspeth sighted down her shoulder, at him? at me? From my perspective, their lips seemed to meld. "Depends on what you mean by safe." She drew the kimono up to her throat and stabbed out the cigarette. "Tedium is never safe. You know, Cee," our eyes tangled in the mirror again, "the same traits that led Paul to seek you out persist. In the elation of getting free of him, you thought you'd cleared the decks for something great to happen. Instead, you're mired in the bog of daily existence, sending out the same old signals for help, and even tragedy begins to seem like a release. I know because I've been there. Now, understand me, great things do happen, especially to people like us, but the odds against them happening at any given moment are tremendous. You set yourself up for terrible disappointment by demanding the world deliver. The way out of it is in. Get absorbed in something. Go to work. Go for broke. All out. Doing anything well takes so much time. Solitary time. Draw, teach, raise a dog, a baby—these are creative, joyful acts that reward you in the process. To reap, you've got to sow. So let's go."

She removed the hairband, twigged her hair in place, undraped the kimono, and stood. Rolls and rimples, angry red pinches, straining elastic, bagged, faded, tattered lace. The burgeoning black push-up bra bared her taupe nipples like the begging mouths of fish. Her defenseless fat. I ached with tenderness, as though she were showing scars, burn tissue. The quoits in the bed clingled. It was just Sammy getting up to go study BE-4-5789, but I knew it was revelation paging me.

"Lately," she said, looking down at her hands, which she held before her little paunch with the unself-consciousness of a Degas dancer, "I decided to do battle with my most entrenched neurosis. Somewhere, I must have learned I'd better be fat or sick, or ELSE!" She smiled sadly and began picking her way slowly toward the closet. A hole in her poison-green tights bit into the back of her thigh. "So I marched into El Shrinko's office and declared war. Ever since then, every time I deny myself the pleasure of believing myself fatally ill, I have nightmares about death, desertion, dismemberment, disfigurement—arms grow out of my chest instead of breasts, for instance." She slipped on her tap shoes. "I relate a less ghastly one out of kindness." Knelt to tie them. "It's the good fight, I know, but it's tooth and claw." Slid into a bottle green blouse. "I bring this up, not to revolt you, but only to say—"

"Dare to struggle, dare to win," I quoted the politics.

"Yes." Her smile was brilliant, sun on water. She buttoned the blouse, pulled on blue and gold brocade shorts. Her eyes, like hot copper in the peacock feather eyes. She looked beautiful, an aboriginal child in a glade.

"I thought you said the secret word was money." I was sitting against the bedposts with my arms folded and that pained smile.

"So I was wrong. No! Wait!" She raised one finger. "Money buys time." She wiped imaginary sweat from her brow. "I knew I couldn't be wrong."

"If you're so smart, why ain't you rich?"

"Darling, I am. Besides, this," she stirred the air, and the parachute flounced, "is merely a turn on the wheel. I will be rich one fine day, probably postmatrimonial, since we're being such fucking realistic broads, and you will be loaded with self-esteem and lapped in true love. Have you taken the razor from your jugular yet?"

"You know what I really want? I just figured this out. I want the two of you to chip in for cabfare so I can go home."

"Ca-ree!" Sammy couldn't tell if he should be mad, glad, hurt, relieved, cheap, or ante up. The fat kid just jumped off the seesaw. I was about to laugh.

"And paint," Elspeth exulted. "Not draw. Make a big mess. Fuck up, big time, over and over. Hideous things. Nightmares. Total disasters. Real shit!"

"And paint. God, I have so much to learn. I don't know where to start. Except—the sky, this evening, with—"

"Well, not now, you little idiot. Now we go dancing. Shake that thang! We talk art on the way. When we get sleepy, we pack you off in the taxi."

Later, when Sammy was larking about on the dance floor like some cross between a sea anemone and Christopher Robin, his eyes shut so he had no idea he was out there on his own—solipsistic pillow—Elspeth made me lean down to tell me, "I'm only borrowing him. I'll give him right back. Hopefully, improved. Anyway, cleaned. And pressed! You know I can't resist a challenge, especially when there's looks involved."

"Is that why you called me tonight? To seduce my boyfriend? Fine way to save me from the brink," I kidded her. "I still don't know why it worked."

"Save you?" She was sincerely surprised. "Is that what you think? I must be getting devious. Foolish child. Don't you know I called you, as I always do, to save *me* from the brink? It's embarrassing, at my age. How many times has it been? You are the most—" She pondered a minute, while I pulsed in this percolating, phosphorescent undersea cave, pining for northern light, a bare cell, and silence, "forthcoming, understanding, clarifying soul." She held my face between her hands like a booster's letter and radiated at me. "You *see!*" She moved one hand to my forearm, a little starfish. "And you've saved me again. You're a pearl without price. Thank you. I don't know what I would do without you. I just hope I can be there for you if you ever need me."

So now, with Dash bibbling like a poor fish in the swamp of my lap, and Ariel still under anesthetic, if not the actual knife, I'm calling Elspeth for help. My fingers are linked over the cabfare in my bib pocket, and my heart is furiously transmitting an all points on all frequencies. You'd think that brass button would go red hot, smoke. The ice that's been my lenses for so long is melting, trickling down my face into Dash's hair. I don't know where she is, I lost touch with her fifteen years ago, I don't know anybody to ask or any way to track her down, I'm just humming, sparking.

I'm praying.

And the next day, when we know the operation went

well, but it's a question of time, and there's still the withdrawal and the therapy—God, the drinking—and the suffering and the guilt, Karl comes by to get the word and to tell me Elspeth left a message on his answering tape. Do I believe it? She's flying in in two weeks, a Saturday, at two. Can I meet her? I'd better, he laughs; no number, no nothing. Just that wicked laugh. I start laughing. Dash thinks I'm having a breakdown. He tries to contain me in his bony arms, but I guess my jiggling tickles him, because he starts laughing too. Sympathetic vibration, harmonic convergence. We break down and let it all out.

11   We Can Work It Out

$\mathbf{A}$ riel and I are sitting in Gate 48 waiting for Elspeth's plane. No matter how she slumps, Ariel can't elevate her leg in its cement hipwader onto the seat across from us, and it must hurt terribly, especially after The Long Hop here on her crosses—oh, I mean crutches. She declined a wheelchair haughtily—she made her bed, of nails apparently, etc.—as though I was volunteering to haul her tumbrel through hell and high water to Lourdes. Her lips clamp on successive cigarettes, like, well, grim death.

But I couldn't leave her home. You get some idea of her addiction if you know that two weeks out of the hospital, she's still on medication, there's no alcohol in the sty, the nearest store is two miles away, she's physically unable to drive, and I can't trust her. Are there no telephones, no taxis, no compliant young men? Friends? Fawne?

Jesus—the neanderthal.

Look: we traded bedrooms, so now I'm up the ladder in the attic, and tucking her in last night, I was trying to prop some generally favorable dark/dawn ratio on my finally figuring out the arrangement that would have been immediately obvious five years ago to anyone else, and she said, "Hey, yeah, all this and about two thousand cases of Colt

45, and I'm set for life." Gallows humor, man, it sure kicks the nag out from under me. With Betty Bear beside her, the blind stare and stumpy open arms—she tore Betty's tongue off when she was three or four—"*mon semblable,*" I think, "*mon frère.*" My mirror.

The plane is an hour late, and my conversation is limited to magazine, soft drink, snack? She abrasively refuses everything: hellraiser become gouty Salvation Army Sergeant-Major to my airhead hospitality hostess. Two days from the UN deadline for Iraq to get out of Kuwait, I find myself plumping for apocalypse. Get it over with. Save me all this trouble.

The plane puts in, like a whale on toe shoes, activating everyone around us so that I hurl myself to shield the explosive foot, while my eyes gangle at the gangway. Ariel swacks me off, gripping a crutch like an Uzi to sweep her area of some rampageous towheads closing in. Fine—give no quarter. I slink around the pillars, the seats, the counter, into the front of the welcoming committee. I look gingerly, as you would under a Bandaid, wondering what fifty will look like on Elspeth, what these particular last fifteen years will have made of her, and what she will make of me.

When I do recognize her, it's only because she's still short. Otherwise, it comes down to style: it can't be anyone else. Or two on the same plane. Or it's her expression: a beatific mask like a zen mudpack. But these bells start ringing later. First, it's the ripples in the human stream preceding her, the gurgling eddies, the fillip, the spray. She's bald. Her head is shaved shiny as a peeled egg. She's lost the plutonian pallor for a gold-white like stiffened chicken, carrying a mirror-embroidered duffel purse, cloth suitcase, and a lush fur coat, in jeans and t-shirt with, I think, a long-sleeved batik tee underneath, but she's tattooed. Solidly. To the wrist. To the neck. In dark green, cinnabar, ink blue, black. I can't make out individual figures. It's as though she's under a dense, twining canopy or behind an intricate screen; she's her own shade. No glasses. She's thinner than I've ever seen her, muscular; in fact, her breasts are missing. Shit, did the paranoid cancer nightmare come true? After all those extortionate, time-consuming shrink sessions to convince her she's hypochondriac, she gets it? No fair! I must be blazoning my dismay because she has to stop and read it before she opens, warm and wide, to me. In that pause I have time to dismantle and rebuild myself. I fall on her. Her skull feels like a baby's; I kiss it with a mother's immodest abandon. I come to to find eyes stuck on us like grim antibodies. I draw back so as not to drool on her.

"I had plastic surgery," she says; her voice is scratchier, a loofa. "My bazooms are now 32A, upstanding," she salutes smartly from the nipple to a general gasp, "completely optimistic, no more bra, no more aching neck and shoulders. My surgeon was one John Constable, can you stand it?—grandson of *the painter,* and you too can have Blue Cross pay for your titectomy should you want one, so don't put up with pain and bad feelings another second!" Her laugh develops like a breakthrough—Archimedes's laugh. Someone mimics it poorly. She chucks me under the chin, "The years sure have been kind to you, kiddo," and radiates such compassionate knowledge, my automatic objections wipe, my whole life flashes before me, and you know what? The years have been kind. Considering the mistakes I've made.

And they better go right on, considering the ones I'm likely to.

"Gross!" spews a woman dressed like Cowgirl Barbie, yanking in a child in desert camouflage, to a man dressed as a bottle of Jack Daniels with a chaw in his cheek.

We laugh. The mimic ack-acks.

"Come meet Ariel." I touch her elbow. For a moment, I have the illusion we will rise and fly over these hateful

225

groundlings to the spot. I've got such stars in my eyes I've forgotten Ariel may not seem the glorious fulfillment of any woman's dreams right now. She's trying to support herself by one side of the chair, clutch the crutch in the opposite armpit, and pole to a stand with the trembling concentration of a gymnast. The saggy-baggy elephants studying her over their newspapers and *Newsweeks* should hold up scores. I hustle to help, and just as I reach for her, she collapses. The crutch hits the cast. Her face sheers with pain. She's leaching sweat, panting, scowling.

"I see you two have perfected your act," Elspeth observes. "The Freudian Slips."

The elephants huffle their papers, retract their wing-tips.

Ariel fixes on the fur coat. "Butcher!"

"It is real mink." Elspeth sets down the suitcase and duffel and slips it on. It's like a boy's bathrobe, belted in a strip of fur, the dark brown of baker's chocolate. Elspeth looks like an Ewok in a bathing cap. Or a tonsured mole. "I never thought I'd exactly go for a mink, but it doesn't trouble my conscience since the animals are raised like chickens and then painlessly gassed, which is more humane than the way food animals die. I hope it's cold enough to wear it here—"

"Warmest January on record," I tell her. "High fifties."

"Oh, that'll do. I bought it in Boston on my ill-gotten gains as an architect—too friggin' easy to take one's best efforts, or maybe I was not 100 percent obsessed—but we promptly moved to Southern California—more later!—and now I'm en route to Nicaragua, where I dare say I'll have no occasion, but I visited my parents in New York? and they were so cruel about the tattoos, I had to muffle up and wear a wig to get my dinner, like the mitten kittens. But the mink shut them up."

"Slaughter of the innocent," Ariel hisses. "You're wearin' somebody's skin. What makes you think you're so much better'n a mink?"

"The evidence is *in*. Where are their Mastercards?"

"And for what?"

"Glamour, darling. Thrills." Elspeth takes it off and tosses it on my empty seat. "Feel it."

An old lady the one seat over jumps as if it's fondling the knee that lists toward it. Behind glasses, her eyes stretch long fingers.

Ariel glints at the surreptitious staring and indignant rustling of the shrubbery before she deigns to raise her eyes. She takes Elspeth in slowly, and slowly there's a lifting through her, like a beach breeze at sunrise blowing through, and it lifts her features in spite of herself; it lightens her. It's so easy and spontaneous I feel a little chilled, like the faithful diapering drudge when Mummy blows in from Majorca. "Coo-ool," she murmurs, the pigeon. It's just how Fawne reacted to me that first time. Déjà rue. I feel like a cheap knock-off. And an old fool.

"The tattoos! Dare I ask?" I ask. "All over," Elspeth confesses, wafting her eyebrows at Granny, who prims and squares up her purse as though she may be forced to use it. "No room for even one more, so I'm always fully clothed. *A la japonaise*, of course. I'll take you on the deluxe tour when we go bathies. Russ and I almost divorced over them, but we hated our lawyers so much—they kept saying things like, 'We'll take the son of a bitch for everything he's got!' 'We'll hang her out to dry!'—that we decided to stay hitched." Brewing the throaty chuckle is a procedure. It heats up and gives the mob body. "When people ask if they hurt, Russ says, 'Only me.'"

"Awwwww—"

"Yes, it's sickening. But you and Karl—"

"Kaput." I turn up empty palms. "Over five years now."

"Never mind, I'm sure you gave it your best. I'm no great admirer of family monuments."

I can tell her anything. "He installed orange shag wall-to-wall carpeting in my 1890 villa while I was visiting my sick father."

"The fiend!"

"And expected thanks!"

"Da noive uh duh bum." She cackles. Hackles erect. Heckles. People come and go, but the hostility seems to grow. The original mimic has been supplanted. I'm watching my back.

"And he got old," Ariel tags, lighting a cigarette, "fast." Winsome smile of The Bad Seed. "Fast-*er*." She drags.

"Karl," I bristle, "is still a terrific—"

"I forgot. My mother never makes a mistake—"

"—guy, lives in town with new wife, eminently more suitable than I, and their delightful child—"

"Bruiser—"

"—and they provide my ungrateful whelps with—"

"Sta-bil-ity! See-cur-ity! Nor-mal-ity! Ah-ah-ah-men," trolls Smartass. Long, self-satisfied drag, casting lash about at the deadheads. Granny's eyes cross themselves.

"I believe *this* to be a wonderful child," Elspeth pronounces. Ariel would have to agree. "There is yet another?"

"Dash. He's skateboarding at a place called the Vert. He'll be home by the time we get there. He's a peach."

"And what am I? pickled okra? He's a dork," Ariel corrects, the cigarette punctuating like teacher's chalk.

"If nothing else, be glad for the spare parts," Elspeth scolds. "At the rate you're going—" A nod at the leg.

Ariel looks up sharply. Return to your seat, Miss Krasnow. Her leg hurts again. She glares at me.

"Well, your little family makes me all misty-eyed. How's your mother taking it?"

"My father died last month." Is this the first time I've said it? I almost choke. Ariel checks me and quickly looks away. I hurry on. "My mother's on a cruise." I swallow. I can't think what I want to say, but it's pushing hard inside my mouth, a magician's rabbit. Elspeth makes binoculars with her fingers and puts them in front of my eyes. She's all clear face like a full moon or a luminous dial. "I didn't know I'd take it so hard," I stammer. "I feel like such a fake. But everything seems so—pressing," I grab my throat, "so *loud*."

Her hands flare. "It's a telegram from the powers. 'Greetings! You're mortal.'"

"Yes!" The word is a vent. I wonder if anybody sees the light pouring into my head.

"And a stroke, no?" A parting stroke to my jaw. "Not the worst way to go. You'll be revolted to hear that mine just go on and on, the vampires. But Russ, who'd a thunk it? We're happy as pigs in shit, and if you liked him before, honey, you'd lick his dick now."

Even Ariel jounces over this one, and Granny goes on full battle alert. I hear that amplified asthmatic wheezing and the thundering footbeats of the sailors when the Japs are shelling in the submarine movies. Dive!

"He got his head fixed via group therapy and is now the kindest, most loving, demonstrative person imaginable. No longer the fountainhead freak who used to hypnotize the chickens and stack them on the front porch and call his mother out." I giggle; Ariel gapes. "No, he has surpassed my fondest fantasies."

I remember visiting Elspeth, nursing Ariel, and Elspeth blurting, "Look, Russ, the baby's sucking Cee's calories right out of her nipple!" Russ turned on his heel, Karl in pursuit, and four hours later they reappeared, wet, muddy, with beer and Chinese take-out, talking politics.

"And he was always at his best with you, from loving you. He shaves his head now too. I got started because I could not bear to think about hair anymore, and one day he handed me the razor and bowed his head. It feels lovely." She runs my hand from crown to nape and reminds it of caressing dry, warm sand, cradling nursing babies. What do

I look like when the rawk of the crows startles it off? Soft. My daughter looks both mad and mortified. I feel like I'm on a stage, naked, still fat.

"How long are you here for?" I want to set priorities and adjust how fast I talk.

"I have to leave tomorrow night."

"No!" I'm dashed, really, hard against a wall.

"I know—it's too crummy—and I have to see a man about some plants. That's my line; well, one of them—" She scours my wincing eyes. "So let's not waste another second in the nowhere zone."

"Shit!" I accept disappointment with the usual grace. Why did she bother to come? The man with the plants. I'm nothing to her—a place to stay. There go the long breakfasts in bathrobes where we sort my life out and set Ariel straight. I want to put her on the next plane. My heart is an ashtray. Ariel grinds out her cigarette. "Luggage?" I grudge.

She prods the duffel and suitcase. "Just this."

"We're parked right outside. Virtue of Nowheresville. It's so easy. Twenty minutes from everything. What there is of it. Of course you're always twenty minutes from everything—"

"Is that possible? Quick! Call Einstein!"

I don't want to laugh, but it's a joke so familiar—is that possible?—it's part of my repertoire. Ariel double-takes. "Have I heard that before?"

"Call Doppler," says Elspeth.

"You two are so alike—"

"Separated at birth," Else smiles.

"Creepier. Clones." Ariel gathers her crutches. "Only you're the original." (Elspeth.) "You're better." As she struggles up, Elspeth and I both lunge for her elbows. She flats back. "I feel like the last piece of chocolate cake in the school cafeteria."

"What we need here is a sky hook." Elspeth wiggles her

index at a uniform. "Oh sky hook—"

Two pilots break stride, look, mutter, snicker, stride on.

"That's Captain Hook," I tell her.

"Or Sky King," says Elspeth.

"Or King Shit," we say together and curtsy. Ariel slaps us high fives. Else's raspy laugh scrapes the bystanders off the sides of the pot. Even though they change, they're unanimous against us. We cook them up. Taking their heat with her seals in my humorous juices. Mope turns to make-the-most.

"Let's settle for some wheels," Elspeth suggests. "See if you can round up one of those golf cart things—"

Accusing Ariel, "I would, but she won't—"

"Yes, I will." Ariel stops me as if I've been railing for hours. "This fucking leg is killing me. And get me a soda so I can take my drugs."

I appeal for a witness to my earlier slave-girl blandishments.

Ariel appeals to Granny. "I mean, just because I'm a drunk, a drop-out, an arsonist, and a satanist, there's no reason for me to suffer, too, is there?" She shows her teeth.

Granny bolts.

Elspeth buys the soda while I arrange for a cart. Getting Ariel on and off it makes me question its value. Else and I trot alongside, skipping the chitchat as Ariel punts through the crocodiles and leeches, the African Queen. From her elevated post she calls out, "Who asked you? Did I say anything about your cheap K Mart outfit or your chicken-fried hair? Who in her right mind wears pink sweats? Sheesh!" She was born to brandish crutches. Riding shotgun, indeed. The Politeness Police. Behave or die!

By the time she's settled in the front seat, Elspeth nestled in her coat in the back, and I'm behind the wheel, I feel like I've just scythed a path through the vandal hordes. I'm whipped. I sink the key; the engine starts and stops. Again.

Whirring—day of the locust. Reason with it: don't do this to me, motherfucker. Reason works. Ze Lemon jerks awake, brawls defensively, racing, you wanna go? you'll go all right—

"What are you doing with this pretentious old clunker?" Elspeth leans forward to ask.

"Why didn't you speak up at the wedding?"

The chuckle perks. "Thought about buying a new one any time in the last twenty years?"

"It still runs." Barely. I wallow to the left and almost get rammed by a Camaro that was miles in the distance when I started my exit. Ariel and Elspeth are sharing some private joke. "Besides, Ariel has to go to college next year—"

"Hopefully not in this—"

"Not at all," Ariel says. To me: "Get real."

"Summer school," I say determinedly.

"My ass. As in, drunk on—"

"Blackmail! Are you going to pull this on me every time I—"

"You're not one of these people who are afraid to spend money?" Elspeth cuts us off. "When did you get to be such a wimpy little femme? Go into debt, it's the American way. Otherwise, you're a patsy." She chips my shoulder as I'm laboring up the onramp, only to be swiped to the shoulder by two racing semis. I hate this interstate. It's minutes before someone has the intelligence to move over to the left so I can limp into the lane. Ariel is still enjoying "wimpy little femme."

"That's right," she gloats, "you tell her. College, you know? Why not convent? Any institution will do. She's so afraid of everything, always running for cover—"

"And anyway, you know Karl will cover college—he's Jewish. I tell you what, if there's time, I'll have a look under the hood for you. I restore old cars, not only the decorative stuff, but so they run. I specialize in rare prewar Volkswagen trucks. I know it sounds odd, but in California we collect. It's not unheard-of to have as many as six cars."

"Here you have vee-hick-culls. It's not unheard-of to have all of them up on cinderblocks as lawn ornaments."

"I drive a truck," Ariel says, "when I'm not in the hospital or in jail or passed out somewhere." Caustic honesty or bravado, which should I prefer? It just guts me. "How'd you learn to fix 'em?" She turns stiffly from the waist to rivet me. "In *college?*"

"Elspeth went to college." I sound just like somebody's preachy mother. Mine.

"Yeah, and look at her." Ariel can't help it; it's only meant to hurt *me*. Draw a line in the sand, expect to have it kicked in your face. "No offense."

"I have a partner," Elspeth enunciates; she also has feelings, not inured to the scattershot teen tongue. "He's Mexican. I don't know what you've heard about Mexicans, but these are the finest people on earth." Southern attitude check. I don't mind. At some point, I might go blunt and not be able to tell. "Hardworking, generous, sensitive, and patient. He teaches me auto repair, I teach him horticulture—"

"'You can lead a whore to culture,'" I quote Dorothy Parker; somebody's got to expose my child to the classics.

"'But you can't make her think,'" Ariel fills in. "You told me that before. Kinda snotty."

Oh.

"And *she* went to college," Ariel crabs at me.

Let's change the subject. "What I want to know is what happened to painting, dogs—?"

"Ah! My biographer!" Elspeth's confidence fully restored. Or: enough about *you*. I sling her a grin. "Dogs. I couldn't bear Afghans anymore, so I'm raising pit bulls—"

"Extreme!" Ariel laughs until she realizes, "You're serious!" She took in the mink, but I'm not sure she can accommodate this. We hear once a month about some toddler mauled by pit bulls who've been chained and starved by their owners to make them killers in the ring. "Do you fight them?"

I back her up. "Or just feed them helpless infants?"

"I breed and show them." Her tone makes me consult the rearview mirror where some idiot in a Trans-Am charges up my ass, then leaps to the left to pass me in the teeth of an oncoming tractor-trailer. I very sensibly shut my eyes. I'm still able to perceive I've insulted her children. "My dogs are not curs. Defined by an eighteenth-century English rulebook on dog fighting as an animal who will attack smaller, weaker dogs. There's a literature. The one I keep as a pet, Flange, likes to nuzzle. It quite alarms those only familiar with these ugly baby-eating rumors. He elevates himself—" She demonstrates, springing, smooching taut lips. "Once Flange came running along with a cat attached to his nose by its claws like those Garfields on car windows, and his poor muzzle was netted with scratches. I ask you, is this a killer? My ghastly neighbor kept calling me about the dogs, threatening to kill them, and me, to commit unspeakable atrocities in the name of the *dogs'* supposed viciousness, so I went into my kitchen and prayed very, very hard for him to vanish, and guess what? The next day a For Sale sign grew out of his lawn." The curdling cackle.

Ariel and I volley glances. "We've got a neighbor," she angles, eyebrow the hook.

"Do they really fight dogs around here?" Elspeth shrinks back, looking very small in her plush husk, gazing out across the railyard at our pumping smokestack skyline.

I decide to show her the sights and get off at the next exit, which follows within some fifty feet of an entrance. I execute this daring maneuver blind, invoking The Force. The street runs past the bus station, then cuts through the industrial-revolution-brick tobacco factories.

"What is that?" Elspeth sits forward, pointing up at the

"Pride in Tobacco" logo painted on a footbridge that connects two parts of the mill. A fist, thumb up, holding a stylized, three-leaved tobacco stem. "It looks like a guy beating off."

It will never again look like anything else. Ariel convulses, shivered with pain. When I stop laughing and braking over the embedded railroad tracks, I tell her what it's supposed to be. "They recently built the biggest factory of any kind in the world just outside town. I don't know how many million cigarettes a minute. They take the kids on school trips, stop just short of free samples. These old ones are being phased out. I kinda like the decorative gold bricks. Dash and I went to see one imploded, where that parking lot is? Exciting, but not the subsequent duststorm. Spoiled the stockholders' tailgate champagne breakfasts. One crop economy. People wear t-shirts that say, 'Thank you for smoking.'"

"That explains the smell. Do they call this area The Pipe Bowl? Sure awakens the old craving. In LA the self-righteous hound you into the street."

"Ooooh, we could make *jihad!*" I suggest.

"Gee, it's ugly here," Elspeth says, craning to take in the squat twenties buildings with smashed windows, cardboard windows; the dusty, half-empty window of Hong Kong Imports; the naked dummies in Mother and Daughter; the pawnshops and bailbondsmen; the missions; the beauticians; the black men in windbreakers or flannel shirts, their hands in their pockets and cigarettes between crimped lips, walking separately or in twos like the people in train set cities so that even though they're clipping along, they look immobile; the marmoreal post office where a cop is hassling a mop-haired black bag lady with a one-wheeled shopping cart. Dirty Christmas decorations flap in the wind.

"Want me to burn it down for you?" Ariel asks mordantly. "It's my specialty. Did Mom tell you? Put a couple of drinks in me, your decayed little southern town is history."

She thinks she's General Sherman?

"More smoke is not the solution," Elspeth says. "Bad for plants, hole in ozone, stunts growth, cancer. Anyway, I'm opposed to the current infatuation with destruction. Unimaginative. To be fully human is to create. That's our specialty. Everything else just kills time, at best."

"And at worst?" Ariel pulls out a smoke and plugs it in her snide. Strictly against the Closed-Space Pact.

"You know the worst," Elspeth says.

Ariel cricks her neck. "For such a total freak, you sound pretty old."

"Ariel!"

"It's wisdom. Earned through the generations. Not every ape sits on his hands. You don't have to start from scratch. Take it or leave it. Gee," Elspeth pitches toward her window, "that looks familiar—"

"Yes! The Empire State Building on its knees. Built for the tobacco company in 1929 by the same architects."

The lighter pops. Ariel lights up. I slice my disapproval, and she opens the window so we're all freezing, but she's within the law.

Elspeth huddles up happily in her mink. "It's nice. You could have a cute little city here if they let you renovate these pretty things, rather than build any more glass monoliths. Not a bad way to make a living if you don't bog down in the number-crunching nitpickery."

"That's weird," I remark, "because that's what I—"

"And it's great you have the power to choose jobs and your hours and farm out the flunky work. Besides," she insinuates in my ear, "Dominating men in business situations is *fun*."

From my own experience of dominating—the cold blast from the right for example—I have trouble imagining this.

"But I've been thinking of making a really radical change. I did something recently, I'll show you later, that—"

"I can't wait to see it. And speaking of painting, I still do, watercolors mostly, because it's a clean process that can be picked up and put down like knitting, without all the big-deal, get out the materials, move furniture, make a vast, chaotic mess efforts. I also do some interesting things with Polaroids," she raps something hard in the duffel, "all under constraints of time, of which I have none, so I don't know how I do that either."

I don't know, and I don't dare ask. I just drive.

"—and I do performance art with a friend. This came about as we were driving in his Jeep on the freeway, and he was wearing a sort of leather skirt, and these zeros in a passing car tossed an insult at us, and we returned fire, and it seemed to inspire them, buzzing around us, a remark from this side, another from that, refilling their sodden thought balloons from some previously untapped source, and we became The Commandos of Humiliation. It's hard to say exactly what we do, since it evolves from the crowd, and Norm's a whole unknown quantity, but we go as far as we can on the question, 'You wanna make something out of it?' Oh, we're here! Boy, do you need a paint job."

Maybe I slowed down as we turned the corner. I pull in at the curb because Eric's pickup is in the drive. He's done something to my lawn; the mud is covered with hay. I hope he hasn't seeded it; I have elaborate plans of longstanding for that mud. Ze Lemon rattles dead. Maybe Monday I'll start looking for its successor. A Radcliffe, a Yale; alas! Hope dies back, and then the roots rot down through you. Elspeth slides from the backseat in the coat with her case and the duffel over her shoulder—she looks like a Sherpa—while Ariel, spacey—more, I think, lost in thought than from the painkillers, but what do I know? all the time she was drinking, I thought she was just dumb or numb or glum or scum or not getting her vitamins—lets me take her crutches and help her out and onto them. It gives the neanderthal plenty of time to scope us out from his beery, leery tilt at the grill.

"How do, ladies, and, uh, what's that furry little critter y'all got there wicha?" He snorts in a rope of snot, takes a drag of his smoke, and forgets to remove it when he brings the beer to his mouth. "Hold on a second, I'll fetch me mah shotgun."

"This is the growth we were hoping you could remove for us," I tell Else.

"Shee-it! I have seen some sights over't y'alls, but don't that beat all? Cain't even tail if it's a man or a woman."

"What's it to him?" Ariel mutters. "What's he?"

"I'll tell you what I am." How does he hear? He crashes down the front feet of his chair. "I'm the tit inspector. Y'all come on over here and—"

"You go through this every day?" Elspeth asks.

"On our rising up, our going forth, our lying down—"

"Whar's its har?" he blares, tipping back, spreading his thighs, getting comfortable.

"Cancer," Elspeth shouts. "Exposed to Agent Orange in the Nam." Something almost human stays his response until she cackles. Then he erupts, Mt. Filth. "Consider it done," she assures me.

We're at the steps when Dash clobs out, Eric behind him, pink and wet-haired from the shower, pushing up his glasses with a grin, like I've put something over on him. "What did you do to rile Ol' Yeller?" he asks. "Flash some ankle?"

Dash, in a headrag, offers Elspeth his hand. They shake firmly, twice, bobbing and bowing like cranes.

"Cee, he's so much like you when you were that age," she beams at me.

"And I'm like so much nothing." Ariel bunts off my ministrations to scale the ramp alone and unappreciated. "You sound like some old aunt."

"That's what I am. I like to think I'm part of the family." Dash takes Elspeth's case from her, and I feel a ridiculous surge of pride in his doing what I was just about to berate him for not doing. The good child. He must want something. "I like your half-pipe," Elspeth continues. The skate ramp, mysteriously moved to the drive, doubtless by the scheming landscaper. I frown at Ol' Meller, and he acts *blithe*. "Did you make it?"

"Mom did."

"I'll bet putting in those first nails was a killer—"

"I helped—"

"I'd love to see you skate."

"Wanna see me? Put a few drinks in me and step aside." Ariel clears out our hovering to take the porch solo. "I can do it myself, thanks. Where would I be if I couldn't? Flat on my back somewhere and probably a lot happier—and more successful. Rakin' it in and pourin' it down. Oh, Mabel? As long as you're up—?"

She's quoting liquor ads.

"We see a lot of great skating in California. It's like something out of the cartoons, land-surfin': foots on the tires when the car blows up, tea tray on tumblers, and, 'oh no! there goes Rover—'"

Victor rises from the flowerbox, humps out, stumbles the very edge of the porch to twine Elspeth's feet, purring. "Hello, Learned One." She stoops to pet him, and he moans a meow. "He says, 'hello, Grasshopper,'" she smiles up at Dash.

"What's weird is he's blind," Dash says. "Did you know that? Did Mom tell you? Did she say I take karate lessons?"

Victor is grooming her coat. She straightens.

"Jee-zuz, are we going to stand here all day? Doesn't anybody notice I'm on crutches? Doesn't anybody care?"

"I know I don't," Dash says brightly.

Eric holds the door. Ariel drops the rubber tip of her

right crutch to pare Dash's sneaker away from his heel. Her hooting three-legged race and his cursing flap-shoed hop clatter the windows like the state clogging championship. When she's finally camped on the couch with her legs up on pillows, and Elspeth's things are duly disposed to one side—the boys catch their breath when they catch the tattoos—I introduce Eric.

"Mighty pleased to meet you." His cheeks puff up like brioche. "I've heard so much about you."

"I haven't heard a thing about you, which really piques my curiosity." Eric's wattage boosts. They shake. "I know those calluses. You're a plantsman!" Elspeth reads his palm.

"Yeah, and what'd you do to my lawn?" I grum. "Something nice, I bet."

Yellow feathers in his smile, but there's more to it, because suddenly he clouds over. "Tell you later. I made coffee."

"Oh sure, everybody go sit in the kitchen and forget about me," Ariel whines. "Very thoughtful. Have a few drinks while you're at it and whisper and laugh. I'm like some kind of sick relative everybody wants to forget about—"

"Exactly," says Dash. "If only you'd come home in a wheelchair, we'd have a bitch—"

"Watch your mouth, mister," I caution.

"Let's sit by the fire." Elspeth falls into the arms of the chair. "Rustic charm. I love your house."

The sty? I try to see how. Somebody's spruced it up. Dusted, swept. There's a flat of paperwhites scenting the window, forsythia branches forcing in a Ball jar on the coffee table. It's really too warm for a fire, but it makes us glow like a nip of sherry. Snow White, chinking china in the kitchen. The sweetness of it sweats me. What's wrong with him? He pretends to surf in with cups, milk, and sugar aloft on a tray, or he's a carhop on skates. Dash has gotten soda for himself and Ariel and sits cross-legged on the floor, leaning against the couch. I take the rocker; Eric pulls in a kitchen chair and sits it backwards. God, the thighs on him! Nancy hops on Elspeth's lap; Victor mops her feet; Sluggo tries to dislodge them; and the kitten has staked out the mink. Ariel kisses at it to lure it to her; it opens one eye to say, "Are you nuts?" and snuggles in. Now it's official: nobody loves her.

"So tell about what you really do," I ask Elspeth, when the coffee is doctored and distributed. "Plants."

"Plants! Yes. Here's the deal: I found my true calling— I'm a botanist. I got so tired of repressing my scientific self to express art, that one day I knew I'd had enough, I let my scientist out of its box, fed it a few scraps, and lo! it grew healthy, virile, enormous, and I knew I had to serve this master for awhile. I locate seed and custom propagate, selling rare tropical plants as tiny seedlings people can afford. Usually rare plants, if available at all, are bigger sizes and cost an arm and a leg. Some things, I'm the only person in the U.S. who grows them. I work outside or in my greenhouse sixteen hours a day, and there's only joy and beauty, oh, and once a scorpion fell out of a packing crate! I get invited to visit Kuala Lumpur and all sorts of exotic places by my bot penpals. That's what Nicaragua is all about— new bamboo. It uses up my good features: my computer brain, my eye, my gregariousness. And before the afternoon evaporates in a pastel cloud of insipid happiness," she shifts forward, and Nancy shies for the hinterlands, "I have to phone a zoo director interested in palms and find out if I need to race to Ash-something—"

"Asheboro," Eric and I supply.

"That's it. It won't take a minute." She goes to her case and pulls out papers, springing Hugo, and I show her to the phone in Ariel's bedroom. The cats, including poor old Victor, follow.

"Wow!" muffles Dash. "When I saw the fur coat, I thought, gross! you know? and then I got a load of the tattoos— She's from another planet, right? Think she'd like to check out the Vert maybe later?"

"She's only here till tomorrow night."

"Bummer!"

"I could use about a week with her." Eric's eyes flit and lower. "Could I have a moment with you?"

I resist the hiss of jealousy to distinguish myself from the teen. Ariel is asleep. It reminds me of how she looked falling off the breast, that sated, drunken droop of smile, the milky belch; and then I'm tiptoeing in to put the blankets back on her little highland fling, her lips parted to play pipes, "Can I have a drink of water?"; and then I'm pausing at Dash's door, I hear him breathing, hear her jambox drone, ice in a glass, her laugh and "I know!" into the phone, what time is it?; and then I'm in the hospital, the drip into her arm, the mummy's boot, the pinched brow, and her mouth frozen open. My whole past is smashed to slashing edges— "When I look in the mirror, to comb my hair, I see your face just asmilin' there"—my memories dry and shrivel like leaves, like tinder; they burst, oh, they burn. My eyes are burning. Just one look is all it took. How am I going to stand this?

No. How will *she? That's* the question. "Ev'ry step I take, you take with me." My love tethers me. Stand and deliver. Stand and fight. Dash examines the fire and goes for more wood.

Eric and I climb the ladder. The crystals hanging in my window tick spectra across the floor. We sit on the bed knee to knee, and I rub up those firm, thick, smooth cables until my thumbs touch his tender tip. He closes my hands lifting them to his lips, but there's something wrong. I scan his squint behind the glasses. Definitely something eating him. My reservations, my holding out, my flippancy. He feels used, taken. What have I ever given him but the once-over? I've been so scared of his youth, his beauty, my mistakes

with Karl, with men, of getting cornered, or cornering him—
I have a lot of good excuses. "Thanks for making the place
look so nice," I open. "And what *did* you do to my lawn?"

"Simple matter a pride. Thought it looked bad, you
hangin' out with a professional and livin' waist deep in mud.
It bein' so warm, thought I'd get started on your soil, and I
put in a little drip irrigation system while I was at it. In
about a month, whenever it's safe, I'll put in your trees,
pink dogwood, weepin' cherry, crabapple, whatever you'd
like, then maybe some azaleas, some perennials, kinda cot-
tage garden thing, you know, train some wisteria up the
porch pillars or a climbin' rose? moonflowers? so there's
always somethin' bloomin'. Green out the slob next door.
In the fall, you pick up some bulbs. Ought to be right pretty,
and you still won't have to mow. Might want to think about
paintin' though, off your mural money—"

He's been talking down to our hands but now breaks a
smile that bleaches me. I love this guy.

"Eric. This is the most wonderful present anybody— I
can't think of anything that could please me more. Of course
we'll paint the house, that's what Elspeth said too—turquoise,
or rose—I don't know why I don't see these things, but—
look, why don't you move in? Not to paint the house—"
I'm an idiot; he looks embarrassed for me, "What I mean is
I'd like us to live together, give it a shot. I don't know how
the kids will react, it's not going to be easy, things are such
a mess right now," I see the mess lapping below like an oil
spill, and my kids are the struggling, heads-barely-above-
gunk otters, "but I'm willing to—" What a grand offer.

He strokes the hair back from my eyes and rests his elbows on my shoulders. "I'm so glad you said all that, Cee,
but it makes what I gotta tell you harder." He reaches around
to push up his specs, knotting my head in his arms. "I'm
thinkin'—no, babe, it's a done deal—I got a job in California, assistant director of a public garden in Los Angeles.

That's why your friend—anybody else want to call her Telstar? I keep hearin' that organ. But see, I been fuckin' around too damn long, hangin' out with old friends in old places and goin' nowhere. I been exactly nowhere, and I'm thirty years old. Where'd you been when you were thirty? You'd had your kids. I've got to make my move. If somethin's gonna happen musically, well, LA—" His shrug rocks us side to side. "I've been thinkin' about this and puttin' out feelers for about six months, but I didn't say anythin' cause you were goin' through your own shit, and I thought— You know, your life is so full, and when I look at mine—I haven't got one. I thought you'd understand and, I don't know, like me better for it," the smile bobs his glasses, "in retrospect."

I feel like I've got a rag in my windpipe. "I guess risk is what we both need," I say slowly, trying to keep that rag right where it is, "but your risks aren't the same as mine." His arms lock, and I have the impression we're on a raft in the lake or the boathouse at camp, and summer's over. I'm in some pain. "It's great about the job." Do I sound brave or pitiful? I'm looking straight into his affectionate glimmers as if lying my way through a roadblock with a bullet in my chest. "I don't know how to tell you how swell you've been to me."

"You've been tellin' me all along. And I'm not leavin' for a coupla months yet, so you can keep on—" He brings his smile at me so it's a tunnel I coast into in sunglasses on the two-lane blacktop of his tongue. I go under until I hear Dash ragging a sleepy, annoyed Ariel. Elspeth's voice. "She's here such a short time," I try to justify my defection. Thinking, and you're already gone. I peel off a quick one, the last one?—whoa! damp that sucker!—and we descend.

"I can see this guy tomorrow at noon," Elspeth, snapping the papers back in her case, "so this will work out perfectly. I can take the bus or borrow—"

"Don't be ridiculous, I'll drive you." I sit on the couch,

the jar of forsythia in my face. The kiss-off. Too bad I didn't recognize it before making a total fool of myself. I should have known from the hay. And the horse he rode in on. He's riding over me now, perched on the arm of the couch, sidesaddle. Gallant Fox was a horse, right? So was Mr. Ed. Pokey. I should just eat the forsythia. "It's a nice trip. We can go to the zoo while you do business. Ariel loves the zoo."

"And she smells like one too," warbles Dash.

"It's where I belong," Ariel concedes, sitting up to glug Coke like it's hemlock.

"Hey, that's my line," Dash complains. "She's taking all the fun out of it."

"Maybe so," Elspeth agrees with Ariel. "Want me to put in a word with the director?"

She startles. "You mean like a job?" She sits up higher, frowning. This smells suspiciously like hope.

"They must have summer jobs. You can see if you like it—"

The phone rings. Ariel is sure it's someone saying no; I think it's someone saying now or never, and I won't be able to get Ze Lemon started. It's Nate. Something at the club I've got to see with my own eyes. I wonder what it would be like to see with someone else's. Redemption. I ask the others.

"I've never seen your work," Elspeth, "apart from all this," she thumbs up at the homestead, smiling; I think, welcome to Dodge. "That's where I left you, poised with brush on the threshold of greatness. I'm eager."

I'm scared and excited; next comes nauseated. What if she hates it? She could push me over the threshold and into the abyss with a badly timed blink. And what does Nate want me to see? I imagine some tribute from a fan—a candlelit shrine to the King; a big tacky funeral wreath. I can put it over my neck and hoof for the last roundup. Cee

Biscuit.

"I'll go along for the brush with greatness, your greatness." Dash, seeking shoes. "Cee, Part Three: The Threshold." The maniacal laugh sounds like Elspeth's. She chimes in, and he stops dead and listens, then looks at me.

"I'm game," says Eric. He squeezes my shoulder. His every gesture now seems as damning as a consolation prize. "I never got to see it finished."

Ariel looks zonked. She's done her walking for the week today already. "We could have dinner at the barbecue place," I woo her, warily; just watching her wears me out. "It's downstairs from the club," I explain to Elspeth. "My company renovated—"

"Please come," Elspeth asks Ariel.

Ariel nods. Elspeth leaves the mink behind, claiming it's going to rain out of the clear blue sky—I think she's just hot—throws on the duffel. The neanderthal at his hibachi squirts charcoal lighter toward us with a cigarette in his mouth, like the American take on Mannekin Pis. What's there to say? but Eric says it, his pickup is in the line of fire, and the resulting exchange is as ponderous as Ariel's gimp to the car. "They must have a million applicants," she says softly, dropping into the front seat. "And what about my leg?" She spins anguished eyes for the rear, where Elspeth and Eric are discussing running versus clumping bamboos.

"Play it for pity points," Dash coaches her. "Equal opportunity for the handicapped. Sue 'em!"

"They'll never take me—I'm just a falling down drunk."

"Now you're talking. That's just what I mean."

"Why don't you shut up?" Ariel screams between her teeth, bips his nose with a wild fist, he smacks her, and the tears roll. We squeeze one more out of Ze Lemon. I find parking half a block away, and she stumps it like the Bataan death march.

We pause to admire the deco of the façade while Ariel

overtakes us and then up the stairs to Hog Heaven, Ariel finally agreeing to trust the litter Dash and Eric make of their arms, although I can't look. At some point during the mural job, stoned on exhaustion and soul music, I painted the wooden sign hanging over the entry: a perfectly celestial, smiling pink pig, the apotheosis of the lighted pig downstairs, stretched bubble-thin, almost transparent, trotters daintily crossed and eyes subliming, rising above a churning fog into starry blue and vague angels praising Him upon the well-tuned cymbals, rather blasphemous. I bang on the door.

"Some pig," says Dash.

"Radiant," Elspeth nods.

Ariel slumps on her crutches, pale and flaccid. "Everything you paint is like a joke on something. It never comes at you straight."

Now the pig smirks. "We can't see straight. It's too late for straight," I argue, "historically. Too far down the road."

"The pig looks naked. Like it should have on clothes. I mean it's good, and I even like it, but so what?"

"What do you want?" Dash asks her.

She's dug in. "It's like plain pig isn't good enough for her. It's spoiled. It's Disney. Dismal."

"It's a sign for a dance club," Dash, fed-up.

"You wanna keep in touch with these two," Elspeth advises me. "Your bookends."

Nate opens the door. He looks ashy, solemn. Ms. Williams is with him, holding her elbows. The surprise of seeing her, under this spoiled and impious pig, my first thought is, the jig is up. Judgment Day. They're taking my children away. Not Disney enough.

"What did I do?" Dash asks her.

She throws her arms around him, makes warm eyes at Ariel, me. "It's not you, honey. See, I'm a friend of Mr. Transou—Nate—and he—"

Nate is soberly shaking hands with Eric. I introduce Elspeth and even the gleam of her pate, the Ukrainian-easter-egg arm when they shake hands, register only in a bemused, "Nice to meet you." He won't look at me. That frantic ride to the hospital—was I raving? What did I do? He ushers us in, shoots on the lights.

And there's heaven, shattered, smutched, spattered. Under it, the floor, the booths wink with slivers. Spiderwebs whorl where Bessie was. From one side to the other, MURDER in draggling spray and the R slashed through and a D over it. MURDER/MUDDER. Cute. Most of the women and all the blacks have been mutilated. The waitress has a black hole for a head; my father vainly flails the check. Elspeth boils up the mad laugh, and it scalds us.

"Fawne," Ariel says, utterly spent. Eric gets a chair under her. The crutches clash down.

"The viper you nursed in your bosom," says Elspeth. "Fang. Still, you have to love the pop-psych. Not a total wash-out."

"The Doors." Eric leads her eye to where Jim Morrison is noosed in a heart. "Big Doors fan."

"Break on through," says Elspeth.

"She had a key?" I'm trying to put this together.

Nate snuffles a laugh. "Wanted an audience. Hid in the toilet. Timed it so we'd be pullin' in just as she was finishin' up. Big finish—holdin' a piece a glass to her wrist. I called Brenda cause she'd know what we were dealin' with, and she called the parents, heavy confrontation, and you never saw anybody so pleased with herself in your life."

"Well, it makes me so mad." Ms. Williams roosts beside Ariel and drags Nate's table closer to them. "Her fool mother uses this as an excuse to send her back to the no-account dad." She lifts her chin and imitates Lacey Taylor's up-tight Junior League pop-eyed blamelessness. "'I wash my hands of her. I just can't handle her. Maybe her father can. It's

248

what she always wanted. Well, she's *his* now.'" Ms. Williams snorts. "She just wanted that girl gone. And to stick it to the father. Nothing the stepfather or I could say. Some of these kids, you know, they're on their own." She takes Ariel's hand and pats it.

"This is all my fault," Ariel says miserably.

"Your fault?" I want to crack my head between my hands like a walnut. "The fault," I bow to her, "is all mine."

"Everything I touch turns to shit. If I hadn't—"

"Ooh, the pair of youse! What bullshit! What ego!" Elspeth's glee makes me think of Rumpelstiltskin. "Your fault—you wish! Look at you—clueless. You don't know shit from shine." She shrieks and stamps. "And you!" Me. She slaps me lightly upside the head. "Sure, the mother's to blame! God's back in His heaven, and all's right with the lousy world. Female masochism, you self-important simp, ain't it easy? Don't it make sense? Don't it feel *good?*" She razzes. "Give it up. There's no sin that originates with you. Just the famous veil dance of the deadly seven. Stop looking for the grand design, the master plan." She smiles. "And your art will get better."

Everybody's looking at me. I've got Eric bolstering one side and Dash dithering on the other like, I don't know, some servant who trucks the smelling salts around on a cushion. What a ninny they take me for. Do they think I'm going to cry? Run? It's funny: the voice that shouts, "Run!" is barking, "stroke! stroke!" I've never felt so steady. I look at the ruins of the mural and feel nothing. It's absolutely dead to me. There's no music, no movement, what faces are intact have no interior. I try to remember what I thought it looked like. I remember probing Elvis's mouth for his sound, flicking the brush against his upper lip to roll the snarl, but now his mouth is just open. Some paint from the letter D drips into it. I think Fawne did me a favor. Sorry I couldn't do the same for her. But then again, who knows? She got what she wanted.

I want to do it over.

"I don't mean it isn't beautiful, sweetie," El says softly, "but why do they all have to be dead?"

"Heaven." I dislodge Eric's arm and pull up a chair. "I thought that's how you get in." Elspeth and Dash sit; Nate pours drinks, and Eric passes them around.

"Too literal. Take the long view. Putting them all in one room," Elspeth's smile wheels the circle, "that's heaven."

"Plenty more mirror," Nate says.

"Yeah, I could do it again," I'm trying to see exactly how, "but on a much slower schedule—" I look at Ariel to tell her my time is hers. Our eyes lock, and something is spoken—devotion? alliance? we're stuck in this shit together?—I don't know what it is, or if it's enough. She looks like a weary traveler, kept from bed by the prattling maid. "And it'll have to be different."

"Painting is a way to have and to hold and to let go at the same time." Elspeth plies an imaginary brush. "Strokes." Then she rows, "Stroke! Stroke!"

I'm bedazzled.

"Not goin' to pay you again." Nate sits beside Ms. Williams with a beer and some fruit concoction for her. "It's all your fault—you all heard her—"

"Labor of love," I smile, "if you keep feeding me music. But it's gonna take time. I got a lot a responsibilities."

"I've got another project I want you to consider," Ms. Williams steadies at me. "We've got a drab old scabby wall inside the entrance to the school with a twenty-four hour guard to see it stays that way. Now I know there's a little money left over from the PTA azalea sale, and we might be able to pay you something if you don't ask too much." She smiles like a shark. "I want you to paint us a mural. I know it will have real human faces, and they will not all look alike." That canny smile.

And I see it. Dash on his board, total dedication to effortlessness. Ariel resolutely lugging her heavy shackle. Even Fawne's insouciant conceit. The openness of them, their freshness, fluidity, luster. "We could take a photo of them, when they're out in front of the building or at a dance, in class, do it from that. Or we could ask them what they want on it—pass out a form, hold an assembly?"

"Paint everybody in the nude," Dash suggests. "Scandal! School closed!"

"Guidance counselor fired," Ms. Williams cuts him down.

"And listen, I don't have to do it myself. Ask the art majors, anybody who wants to help, I'll show them how to—" I notice Ariel's sarcasm. "After the great success I had with Fawne—"

"I'm so glad Fawne won't be back at school." Ariel looks down, ashamed. Ms. Williams dips to bring her eyes back up and rocks her neck. "Who knows what she'd have told the other kids? I don't know if I could've hacked it—"

"I hope all our problems will just move out of town," I say. Then I think of Eric.

"Let's hear it for Fawne," Dash raises his glass; "she comes through in the end, like a bad stain."

Ms. Williams purses reproof at him. "I can't say I'll miss her, no. But I hate to feel that way about a child. Times I almost felt that way about you, young man." Dash displays sunny astonishment, and she hunfs. "So you'll take the job?" She wants this nailed down.

"Speaking of jobs. Eric, tell." I touch his white, long-underwear waffled forearm.

He pushes up his glasses and hooks his arm over the back of my chair, casual. But his voice is tight; he's beginning to realize he's leaving, he's saying goodbye, he'll have to say it again and again. Elspeth immediately tries to lure him into binding agreements to purchase whole lots exclu-

Julie Edelson

sively from her by proposing to show him more tattoo.

"What about the band?" Nate asks.

"It's generic," Eric allows.

Dash and Ariel are zinging piercing glances like blow darts at me.

"This is like—what do you call it?" Dash ponders. "Divestiture. Or is that something they do to priests?" He leans over to sock Eric. "I never thought you were all that bad, man."

"More of an embarrassment." Ariel twinks me a smile, then her eyes sink. "Well, one less resentment for me to learn to adjust to. Pretty soon I'll have no issues at all. Big flop at meetings."

"You'll still have one," Elspeth says gently. "The same one. The only one." She lifts that "only" to show how light it is.

Ariel nods. "I really hope you like California," she tells Eric. She keeps her eyes down.

He clasps the top of my head. "I'm not gone yet."

"That's what you think," Ariel says.

Am I that transparent? I'm looking at the wreckage of heaven again. "The problem is to keep it moving. You want to freeze the moment but not kill it. You know what I'd really like to paint?" It hits me all at once. "Look." I point to the unpainted mirror on the back wall where a huddle of rather striking individuals sits illuminated in the gloom of an otherwise empty club.

"Is anybody but me starving?" Ariel asks.

We adjourn to the Pork Palace. Elspeth gets her first taste of barbecue, Texas Pete, fried okra, vinegar slaw, and black-bottom pie, and we're dunked in the brine of reaction to her. Afterwards, Nate and Brenda leave to supervise the clean-up upstairs for tonight's exciting double bill, The Fuzztones and Blessed A Monk Swimming. The rest of us pile into Ze Lemon. He trembles, tests the air, shakes no and you can't make me. Ariel sags back against the seat with eyes like the blank bulges in a bust. Elspeth pulls out an emery board, gets out, raises the hood, and sands the spark plugs. Ze Lemon starts.

"She can fix cars too?" Dash sighs.

"What can't she do?" Eric admires.

"Be like everyone else," Ariel says. "Be anybody else." To me, "Doesn't she scare you a little?"

We're almost home, and Ariel is almost asleep, when Elspeth abruptly interrupts an animated discussion with Eric about air layering to order, "Turn here." Ariel groans, and I think of protesting, but I do it. "Turn again and stop."

"What if I can't get Ze Lemon going again?" I argue.

Ariel slews her eyes to the window, wrenches her head up, and twists to look at Elspeth with something like dread. We're at the playground with the fiberglass kangaroo. It's overcast, the clouds a shrimpy pinkish gray saturated with the sweet smell of tobacco. The orange kangaroo, lit from above by a street lamp, seems gigantic, Godzillian, and casts deep shadows like gashes on itself and, across the hard-packed dirt, a jagged fault line.

"I thought we ought to exorcise this mother," Elspeth says.

We all get out. I put up a fuss, but Ariel won't be left behind; she's dragging more than her leg. She hobbles between me and Eric until we're standing in the thick of the shadow, looking up.

"We used to play here." Dash, excited. "I haven't been here in years. There's a slide, right? You go inside, and there's a ladder, and you can climb to the top and slide down the tail, or you can get off in the middle into some kind of pouch deal in the front. I remember it stinks."

"Used to be a little clump a trees here when I was growin' up," Eric tells us. "Run-off from the culvert made a crick, and we'd wade in it and play Rebels and Yankees."

Ariel gapes up, blown wide open. "Just give me a bottle, and I'll go quietly," she says with no hint of comedy. I don't have her memories, but I can see what she feels. My arms ache, remembering trying to pull her out of the pouch, they ache at the armpit where her crutches fit. "Why did we have to come here?" I ask, hostile, protective? No, defensive. Scared.

"You want me to burn it down?" Ariel sounds broken.

"Have you ever smelled burning plastic?" Dash wrinkles his nose.

"No, silly, I want you to look at it," says Elspeth. "Look up at its face."

The kangaroo has a tootsie pop nose, cherry, on a long snoot, and its red tongue slops off to the side. Its eyes are like the test patterns on tv screens, like lit sparklers. It looks deranged with euphoria, and if it made noise, it would be the goosed, shrieking laughter of children in a television audience. Dash tries out a laugh. "I see what you mean."

"No you don't. You don't know what's happened here, you nerd," Ariel snaps at him. "None of you can even imagine." Hugging her suffering to her, her stuffed bear.

"You don't know everything that's happened here either." I'm suddenly furious. "You'd get yourself stuck in that fucking pouch because you thought I paid too much attention to your brother, and you'd whine and fuss and get the other mothers into it, poor you, and meanwhile he'd be ready to jump off the top of the slide because some idiot dared him. Remember the time he knocked himself out? I mean, is that what all this shit is about? Nobody loves you? Because if ever a human being was loved—"

She's crying. "Why'd you have to have him? Why wasn't I enough? You were disappointed with me, and you wanted a do-over. You've always been disappointed with me. You crowded me out, and then you crowded Dad out—"

"Jesus! How can you be so wrong? Karl crowded us all

out—he's a crowd in himself. We had Dash because we thought you needed an ally against us." Our pair of ducks. "We had him because you were so good."

"You're still defending him."

"I'm defending the truth. I can't believe you'd rather cling to this self-pitying bullshit."

She drags her hand over her eyes. "Oh I know it, I *know* it," the hand fists and knocks her skull, "but I *can't feel* it."

I slip my arm around her waist and kiss her ear.

"I'm trying to show you both something," Elspeth says evenly against our heaving breath, Ariel's sniffles. "You get what you put in." She hoists her embroidered duffel back up and folds her arms as though it's time to hit the road. I look up at the kangaroo, unsatisfied. Browbeaten by this grotesque conventional figure of spurious childish hilarity and now called to account for my failure to live up to some conventional standard by the most conventional delusion of childhood. Something wet drops off the kangaroo's tongue, and I think it's spit. It's rain.

"Well, so enough with the soul-searching." Dash, the bones of contention, mashes down his headrag. "I thought we were gonna do something. You know, exorcise it. Don't we have to dance naked or light candles or spin the Airhead or something?"

"Spin the bottle," sobs Ariel.

"I hope you don't expect me to pray," I say.

"I wouldn't mind trashin' it somehow," Eric says, "in the name of tree-huggers everywhere. Must be hotter'n hell here in summer—"

"The slide used to burn us," Dash says to Ariel, grasping his thighs, "remember?"

"—but it'd seem like pullin' a Fawne, you know? They'll just put up another'n and charge us for it. Hey! Maybe overgrow it in kudzu! Shouldn't take but a minute in this rain."

Ariel is tracing the outline of the kangaroo's shadow in

the dirt with the tip of her crutch, then rubbing it out.

"I could draw it," I think out loud, "and then we could burn the drawing?"

Ariel limps forward a few paces, gathers her crutches under her left arm, and puts her hand out to pat the pouch as if she were feeling a sibling kick in her pregnant mother's belly, looking up into the hollow head. She pivots to show us her wet face. "I'm really much too big for this shit." She coughs a short laugh.

I gravitate toward her. Eric is sticking close to me. Dash slots into the space between the paunch and the haunch and after a minute pokes his crazy face out of the pouch, manic smile, flopping tongue, hands waving peace signs—"ROO SPEAKS!" Elspeth whips out a Polaroid, fast on the draw. Red and purple and yellow dots explode in all directions. The rain starts coming down, first in silver chains, then a dense, hissing, drumming torrent. Elspeth shuttles through it, laughing her bone-chilling, burbling laugh, and snapping. Her white head seems to float detached like the moon over a shadowy landscape. The grind and wheeze of the emerging film, a rude tongue. She's everywhere, flashing, lightning. I'm blinded, dizzy, beaten down, drowned. I don't know how many she takes. Thousands. We flee to Ze Lemon, and he peels.

When we get home, drenched, everybody talking and laughing, we change into jammies, build up the fire, make cocoa, and Elspeth spreads the photos out on the floor. We each get as many as we want. She's in a lot of them, like a grin without a cat, but I'm always looking the other way, or my eyes are shut, so I can't say how. But I'm keeping all mine because we look so very happy, and we seem to move so gracefully together from shot to shot regardless of how they're ordered as though we're bound by invisible elastic filaments or very well rehearsed, and what you can see of the kangaroo, it's only a funny place to pose for a picture and to get in out of the rain.

One more thing I want to tell you.

Two weeks later, the neanderthal piles his shit in his truck and drives off. Even the hibachi. For a few days we creep about, watching, waiting, bating breath. Then a For Sale sign appears. Victory dance, including Hoppy. We remember to pause and silently thank Else.

Now we find any reason to go in and out the front door. We circle the house, parade the drive, reveling in his absence. We sit on the porch to read, to eat, just to sit, even when it's wet and chilly, even when it's dark—I put in a new lightbulb. Dash works on his skating technique for hours. Eric plants, starts building a picket fence, hangs a hammock in which Ariel lies doing homework, reading about the care and feeding of ungulates. My mother comes over to berate us for our idleness on her way to bridge tourneys and dance classes and to play bingo on the Cherokee reservation and to let me know the better deal she could have gotten me on my Chevy Thrombos through her ex-car-salesmen friends at Heartwood Acres. I find my old easel from the Spring Street pastel period and begin an oil portrait of the neanderthal, I don't know, maybe because his leaving has been such a gift to us. It's kind of a weird painting for me because I'm doing it from life. I stand out here painting what I see, and I see everything, every least detail, except, of course, him. I don't think I ever really looked at him. Ariel says I'm making him look like King Shit. She says, "I don't mean to insult you, but I like it." She tells me she'd still rather get drunk than do anything, but we go to meetings, and we listen and learn, and so far, so straight. As far as the future is concerned, I mean, what's the rush? It'll get here.

Then one day this gas-guzzler pulls up, and two women get out. The driver is frosted and bouffed, in a puffy dress and heels; the other is a short, pale woman about my age with short, straight black hair cut like a mime's cap, in jeans and a zippered navy sweatshirt and Dr. Scholls. Walking up the path to the door, shadows from my weeping cherry swap over her skin in the breeze. Bouf puts in the key. The short woman looks in, looks in my direction, looks in again, and exclaims, bell-clear, with a ringing drollery, "This is a sty!"

I put down my brush. How am I going to talk her into it?